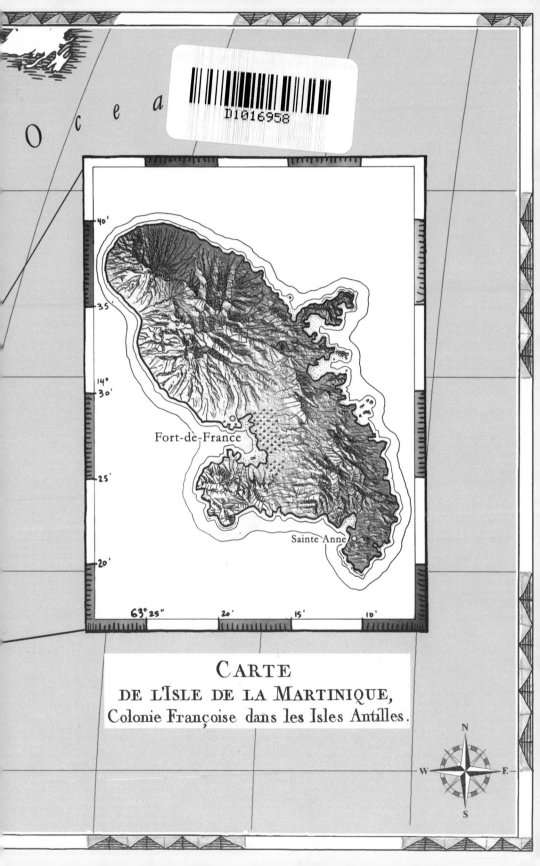

O c e a

40'

35'

14°
30'

Fort-de-France

25'

20'

Sainte Anne

63°25"   20'   15'   10'

CARTE
DE L'ISLE DE LA MARTINIQUE,
Colonie Françoise dans les Isles Antilles.

N
W   E
S

HOUSE OF ROUGEAUX

JENNY JAECKEL

 Raincloud Press

Chico, California

Printed in the United States 2018

All rights reserved. Published in the US and Canada by Raincloud Press and distributed by IPG.

www.raincloudpress.com

Book Design by Raincloud Press
Cover Design by Bookwise Design
Map & Family Tree Design by ZKO Designs

ISBN 978-1-941203-24-8

Library of Congress Control Number: 2017960018

Portions of this manuscript were previously published, in an altered form, in the collection of short stories *For the Love of Meat: Nine Illustrated Stories* by Jenny Jaeckel published in 2016; used by permission.

For my teachers

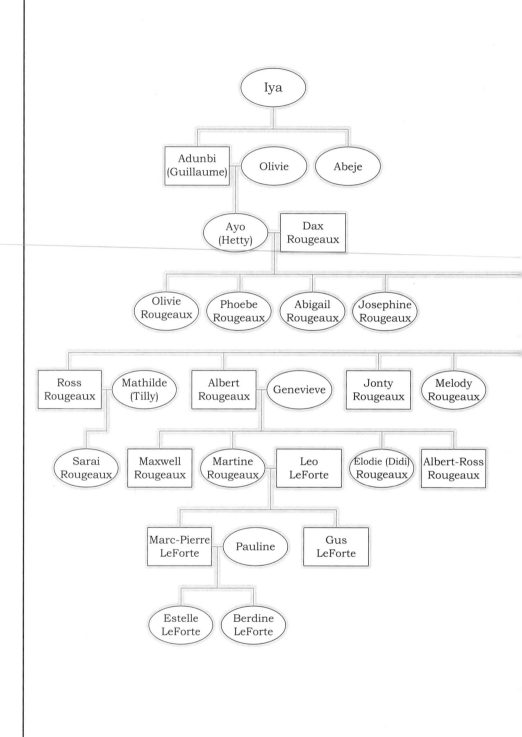

ROUGEAUX FAMILY TREE

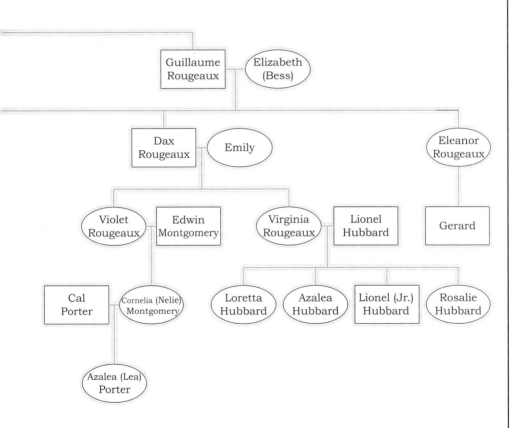

HOUSE OF ROUGEAUX

I

Abeje

French West Indies, Island of
Martinique

1785-1860

Sitting here under this grand old tree, her skirts spread about her in a wheel. The blue cloth carries up the earth in light red dust and so the earth is part of her cloth. The children come. They lay their cheeks against it, now that they've had their midday maize. They cast their eyes up at her, waiting for a story.

A hot breeze stirs the long grasses and the broad leaves that shade them. It makes a whistling noise in the high arc of branches and hushes for a moment the whirring of the insects. She brushes those tender plump cheeks with her rough old fingers. She tells them of the one-eyed dog and the three-legged cat. The gourd that ate a man and kept him prisoner, until it rolled into the ocean and was broken by a sea-goddess. Of the sugar estate that grew people, the cloud boats, the toads that wore clothing, and many other things.

She has more than eighty years, she knows. Among her people few live even half as long as she. These little children are among the first born out of bondage. But as their *mamans* must work the fields, they still need Mémé Abeje, and so she goes on living.

Darkness lay close around the child, save for the light of the cooking fire and the canopy of stars.

"Abeje!" called Iya, stepping out of the hut and closer to the firelight. "Where is your brother?"

The little girl had been charged, for the moment, with looking after the cooking pot, but had become distracted, playing at throwing twigs into the embers. She stood up and pointed at the foliage that edged the Quarters.

"*To-to*, Ma'a," she said. Iya laughed, scooping up the child and setting her on her lap as she sat down at the fire. The boy had gone to pass water.

The boy returned and crouched beside Iya. He smiled up at her, showing the gaps where his milk teeth had newly fallen out.

To Abeje, Iya's face was the most beautiful thing. She and her brother Adunbi hardly saw her in daylight. Iya's arms wound around them and Abeje soaked up the humming her voice made, and her dry-grass smell every night before sleeping. When the fire was out and it was too dark to see, she reached up and touched Iya's face. Her fingers traced the two grooves on her broad cheeks. Each had two shorter grooves springing off to the side, like the sticks for threshing grain. The grooves were smooth, like river water carved into stone. These were the marks of her people.

Iya's voice was high and sweet like a bird. Every night she named the fire, and the children said after her, "Fire!" She named the cooking pot, and they cried, "Pot!" Iya named their feet, the ground, the food, and she named her two children, Adunbi and Abeje.

Adunbi already knew Iya's counting song, the one they sang

with dancing fingers. Abeje followed the movements with her hands, stumbling over the words she longed to master. Each finger had a name in the song. The thumb was a fat man with a big belly. Iya said Adunbi had six threshing seasons and Abeje had four. Then Iya held the children on her lap, as she always did, and sang their other songs, quietly, to make them go to sleep.

This night, after they had eaten, Iya untied a corner of her sash and brought out a handful of colored stones and seashells. She got them while at the bay by the sugar estate when she and other women were helping bring in the shrimp and the conch. It was for Young Monsieur's wedding party, the conches for the feast. It was rare that any hands were spared from the cane fields, and even rarer for Iya to touch the Sea, or have anything pretty to bring them.

Abeje was entranced at once with the treasure hunt, and from then on searched for little stones all across the sugar estate. The older people laughed and said that she scratched and pecked like a hen. Now and then one of them would say, "Come, *ptit*," and slip into her palm a little gem that they themselves had found. Some stones were black, some yellow or white. Once Abeje found a shell in the dust of wagon tracks, far from its salt-bed of the Sea. She rubbed it against her dress, and under the red dust it was pink and smooth, with a blue line that spun a tight spiral on the top. Iya made small holes in the ground by the fire and showed the children a game with the stones, scooping them up and dropping them round and round, one by one like single drops of rain. They dropped Abeje's new shell there. They sang the words that were the names of numbers.

Abeje learned more than numbers. She learned that Iya was

also once a child, and that when she was a girl, they stole her away from the Old Land, a place far away. Iya was carried over the Big Sea all the way to the Island, and so she was called a *saltwater slave*. There were other saltwater slaves on the sugar estate, but none spoke the tongue of Iya, and so she spoke it only to her two children. These were their first words, their language before they learned Creole.

Abeje loved Iya's stories about her village. It was not like the sugar estate. There Iya had her Iya and Baba and brothers and sisters, and though there were chiefs and elders, none were Monsieur nor slave. Abeje understood that in the village there were also a great many animals. There were plants and spirits. The animals spoke as people, and tricked or aided one another. Some were very silly and some very shrewd, some were brave and some too proud. Abeje supposed that it was a pack of wild dogs that had captured Iya near her village, and carried her off to their cruel *béké* King, and took her so far away from her home that she could never go back again.

Adunbi asked Iya one night, "Where is our Baba?"

Abeje stared at him. It had never occurred to her that they had a Baba. The vague form of a tall, broad man took shape in the back of her mind. She looked up at Iya, and then felt terribly afraid, because she saw tears start from her eyes, and spill down her cheeks to meet under her chin. Iya made not a sound, then at last she whispered, "Stolen away." The children did not ask her more.

Abeje's favorite story was about herself and her brother, and she asked Iya to tell it over and over again. In this story, Abeje was a baby and her brother was just weaned. She was playing at the edge of a cane field, when a snake dropped upon her from a clump of shrubs above. Adunbi took up a stick in his small hand and drove it away. Iya heard him shouting and ran to them. She found him shouting at the snake to keep away. He didn't want comfort, but raised the stick and threatened the snake, who was surely far away by then. Adunbi shone with pride when Iya told this story, and Abeje sucked in her breath so with admiration that it flew out again with a great "Pah!" Then they would all laugh.

Iya told Adunbi that Abeje was his to protect. They had no Baba to protect them, feed them, clothe them, teach them. All this Iya had to do by herself, with the crumbs from the Monsieurs' table. Adunbi nodded, his sister was his charge, his face so serious that Iya laughed.

One day an older, light-sknned girl, Lise, took Abeje up to pull weeds in the kitchen garden of the Great House, saying that *Marie* was now old enough to work. But Lise was in a hurry and Abeje had to run to keep up. She kept her eyes on the dusty hem of Lise's skirt, and the feet that flashed out beneath, as they sped up the path.

Adunbi had gone to help two of the big boys with the pigs and the hens. In the garden of the House all who spoke to Abeje called her *Girl* or else they called her *Marie*. Her brother they called *Guillaume*. And so Guillaume and Marie followed orders and worked the long day, and then Adunbi and Abeje went to sleep at night with their Iya.

That first day Abeje felt so alone without her brother. She sat on her little heels in the dust between the rows of green plants, taking out the smaller plants Lise said were weeds. Abeje drove a sharp stick into the earth at the base of the little plants, as Lise had shown her, and pulled with the other hand at the stems. The roots tumbled out with a shower of soil, sending little insects scurrying, and the plants began to wither. She felt them shiver, as if each uttered the tiniest of cries when separated from the earth. She looked at the green strands laid over her palms, and said with a voice from deep inside, "Adu, the weeds are crying." And then, as if he were really there, she heard him answer, *Never mind, Beje.*

The second day Abeje discovered that she could still be with her brother, even when she was somewhere else. She knew it when a horse nipped her brother's finger, and when the groom, who was in charge of the barns and stables, boxed the ears of a boy next to Adunbi, for letting one of the pigs loose. And Adunbi knew things too, about Abeje, such as the fear that filled her when Lise came down the garden path in a blaze to gather broad beans for supper. Lise whispered to Abeje that Young Monsieur was angry again. Young Madame was ill from childbirth, that was the reason. Abeje and Adunbi didn't yet know why they feared Monsieur. Neither of them was ever close enough to him to even see the color of his hair.

Until their last night with Iya.

Abeje woke from sleep when the tread of heavy boots shook the ground. She had been dreaming. Lise was running down the garden path shouting, *Young Monsieur is coming! Young Monsieur is coming!* Now the silhouette of a man crowded the doorway of the hut. A lantern illuminated the strands of his hair. They stuck out from his head like straw.

The others in the hut stirred.

"I want the wenches up," said Young Monsieur.

The girls and women got to their feet, including Iya.

He held the lantern closer to them and then with his free hand pointed at Iya.

"Come out," he said.

Adunbi made to follow Iya but she hissed at the children in their language, "Stay here!" Abeje froze. Adunbi wrapped his arms tight around her, and though they could not see or hear her, they felt their mother. Abeje struggled to breathe, a hand had closed over her face, the sound of a heart beating thundered in her ears, and a monstrous flash of anger tore at her throat. It was Iya, her back arched, the muscles hardening like stone, and with all her strength she pushed away the heavy shoulders that bore down on her.

A brilliant pain.

A crash.

The sound of boots running off.

Abeje began screaming. The others in the hut flew out the doorway and many others ran by. There was fire from where Young Monsieur dropped his lantern, and soon many people rushed there to stamp it out.

"He has killed her!" someone shouted.

"Holy One!" wailed another.

"There is his knife!"

"Bring it to Monsieur, he will know who has done it."

"He will know it by its handle, the ivory."

Adunbi jumped up, pulling Abeje by the hand out of the hut. A cluster of men leaned over something and together picked it up, then hurried away in the direction of the Great House. Adunbi followed, and Abeje ran after him, her feet striking many wet places on the ground.

The crescent moon hung like a white blade in the black sky, cutting the path to the Great House, to the dooryard where clumps of flowers gave out a heavy, sweet smell that turned Abeje's stomach.

She put her hands down on the earth and crouched low. She was conscious of more shouting, and then of large arms gathering her up, carrying her, a heart beating low, and long legs beneath, bearing her back in the direction of the Quarters.

The man who carried her brought her back to the hut and told her to stay there, but she became frantic.

"Ma'a!" she wailed, and wept so piteously that he begged her to quiet, until Adunbi appeared and held her again. The man went away, toward where people were still shouting.

"Shh, Beje," Adunbi said.

Finally when Abeje could speak she asked her brother where their mother was.

"She is sleeping," he said. "I saw them carrying her."

It was a very strange idea, that their mother should be sleeping at such a time, that Abeje nearly laughed. But then, as dread overcame her, she knew that everything was terribly wrong.

Now the people were going toward the Burying Place and Adunbi pulled Abeje's hand so they could follow. Adunbi pointed to a cluster of men laying something down and said, "Iya is there." Several others were busy digging a great hole in the earth.

Someone began singing and other voices joined in.

> *Back to the dust*
> *Coming over the mountains*
> *Like a crawling snake*
> *My heart is in a hurry*
> *My feet don't walk*

Abeje clung to Adunbi, smelling the broken earth. She wanted to tell Adunbi to wake Iya, but she feared to upset him. Abeje stayed quiet, even when they laid Iya down in the deep hole, folded her arms across her breast, and covered her.

The people stood by, some sang, some wept and swayed. An old woman raised her hands up and declared, "Holy One deal with him!"

And all answered, "Hear it now."

The woman's eyes stayed on the sky, the last stars. Tears fell over her cheeks and she said, "Sister gone on, fly away to home." Abeje felt the wind whip her skin. She held tighter to her brother and felt his body shaking.

"Hear it now," said all.

"Mercy on her children…"

"Hear it now."

Old Joseph came carrying a large clay cooking pot. Old Joseph had much grey in his hair, though his shoulders were still broad, and he was lame in one leg. He worked up at the stables grooming the horses, mending harnesses, and fixing carriage wheels. Abeje once heard the older people say that an overseer had made example of him for eating a piece of sugarcane, when he was young. Joseph never walked right after that. He had to swing the whole weight of the lame leg forward to take one step, and then jump forward with the other.

Now he raised the clay pot high into the air, and swiftly brought it down on a stone, where it broke into many pieces. One by one the people placed the shards onto the grave. The dawn came slowly. Abeje heard the tolling of the work bell, ringing as if this day were like any other. Soon she and Adunbi were left alone on the grave mound. They lay so still that vultures circled over. They could not be separated from that place.

By nightfall Abeje's mouth was so dry she couldn't swallow. Adunbi took her hand and they found their way back to the Quarters. As they crouched by a fire someone gave them a gourd of water. Someone else set a bowl of maize porridge before them. They looked up and saw Old Joseph. His mouth was set in a bitter line and the firelight glinted in his eyes.

"*Nyam*," he said, "eat." When they made no move toward the bowl, he said again "Eat!" so fiercely they dared not disobey. From that day on Old Joseph kept them by his side at the cooking fire, feeding them of his own meager rations. Others, when they could, gave them a bit of vegetable, salt-fish or potato.

Despite the care of the old man, in the time after Iya, the children were lost. Abeje waited for Iya to return, to wake at last from her earthen bed, but she didn't come and so the sun no longer rose. Abeje's terror grew and she began to see her brother behave in strange ways. His eyes, before so clear and bright, became clouded. His fresh, alert expression, confused. He sometimes sat in the hut at night, hugging his knees and rocking back and forth, or he wandered in circles around the cooking fire. Old Joseph could make Adunbi eat, but could not otherwise reach him. When Adunbi fluttered around the fire like a moth, Old Joseph would pat the ground beside him and say to Abeje, "Come, *ptit*. Come sit by." Abeje would creep toward him, to lean a little against his heavy side.

One day Lise brought Abeje with her to help carry a set of baskets to one of the barns, where some women were working. A bat came loose from the rafters and tried to attack them. The creature was mad, they knew because it came out in the daylight. It would sicken and kill anyone it chanced to bite. The bat flew frantically to and fro, circling in the rafters, hypnotizing Abeje until Lise dragged her outside by the hand. The bat was like Adunbi when he circled the fire, shaking his hands, not knowing where he went. At last the women beat it from the air with their brooms and buried it in a hole.

When Abeje woke in the night to find her brother sitting up and rocking, she threw her arms around his neck and cried. Slowly he would become still, his arms would unwind from his knees and encircle her instead, and no women came to beat him with brooms.

Now and then when Adunbi was away, and when she was not pulling weeds at the Great House, Abeje still looked for colored stones. She began to venture into a little grove of shrubs and trees near the Quarters, wondering what lay behind that green curtain. It was a different place. The plants were unlike those in the Great House garden, where the green things grew tame and limp, and unlike the cane fields where the cane stalks bent together in the wind. The shrubs and trees and vines of the Grove grew in a great mix-up, threading roots and branches together with leaves that rattled or caught pools of water or pierced other leaves with spines. Birds hopped and called and argued like women. Insects hummed and bore tiny trails.

Abeje liked to sit among the shrubs with the small golden flowers. There was something about them that reminded her of Iya, her dry-grass smell. One day Abeje collected a handful of the tiny flowers. She brought them to her nose and sniffed them, longing for Iya. As the smell faded she began eating them, crushing the golden petals and the green hearts with her teeth, tasting a sourness on her tongue. When the flowers were gone she looked for more, even though they had begun to burn at her throat, pricking like pins in her belly, and making her sleepy. Soon she forgot them and wandered away, toward other flowers.

Someone was singing, but Abeje wasn't sure. A hum, a growl. She felt sick and bent to vomit the bits of chewed flower, which revived her some and she walked on. The singing became louder as she drew near a clump of shrubs, a kind she hadn't noticed before. They had waxy heart-shaped leaves, cool to the touch. She sat down, closed her eyes and listened.

The singing felt like a presence, the voice of the shrub, and it seemed to have a name.

Ah
Nai
Yah
Anaya.

"*Anaya,*" Abeje spoke aloud, and a terrible pain entered her chest, like flesh tearing, and a great darkness opened up.

Abeje couldn't see, but she could feel the waxy heart-shaped leaves in her hands. She heard the song again and it led her beyond the Grove.

From the darkness emerged an Anaya shrub made of lines of stars, like a drawing in the sand made of seashells. It was so large it spread over her like the sky. The song told Abeje that she must look up.

There.

The invisible presence of the Holy One, vast, yet intimate.

Suddenly she was again among the green leaves of the Grove, her feet leading her along back toward the Quarters, one Anaya leaf in her hand. She ran to the hut. It was empty, as it was still daylight, and she laid the leaf under one corner of the sleeping mat she shared with Adunbi. She felt warmth in her heart, where before she felt flesh torn. For the first time in so very long she wasn't afraid.

The next time Abeje went to the Grove she strained her ears to hear the growling song. Instead she heard the cry of two birds as they leapt from tree to tree above her head. She heard insects clicking, and wind rustling the leaves, as she searched for another Anaya, which she soon found. The Anaya had a gentle sway, a soft presence, like feathers. She felt the touch of gentleness steal again into her heart.

For many months when she had the chance Abeje returned. She sat and let the Anaya care for her, and each time she brought home one leaf to place under the sleeping mat. Adunbi began to notice the collection of leaves and assumed it was a game of hers.

One evening as Abeje sat beside the Anaya a strong wind kicked up. Some of the dry leaves floated up into the air, and she chased them. The brown leaves twirled, dancing up, down, and up again. When they fluttered to the ground she saw that she was standing before a short palm tree with great spines on its bark. Twigs covered with globs of red berries grew from its low crown. Abeje knelt before the tree and closed her eyes. Faintly, as if from the back of her head, a spider's thread of song came over her ears. It reminded her of an instrument that a woman in the Quarters sometimes played, made of a gourd and a stick, and a single string played over with another stick. It was the voice of this new plant. The presence of her brother was there, and she knew at once that as Anaya cared for her, this tree cared for Adunbi. She gathered what berries she could hold and ran back to the Quarters where she placed them along the wall of the hut, beside their sleeping mat.

In the next weeks, Abeje saw Adunbi become quiet. He sighed. His eyes cleared. Instead of wandering in circles, he sat beside the fire and helped Old Joseph. She brought more of the berries to the hut, and some of the palm's dry leaves from the ground. Adunbi sometimes picked them up, absently, as he sat up in the night, rubbed them in his fingers, and then sighed and lay down again.

Though they were slowly coming back to life, Abeje and Adunbi did not laugh or even smile for a very long time. But then her brother discovered something new. It began with one of the sow-pigs. One day, she pushed at his ankles with her snout. She had only ever ignored him before. Suddenly he understood the nosing meant the trough was dry and she wanted water. He filled the trough, heard her grunt, and was sure she meant to thank him.

"She is your friend now, so," said Abeje, when Adunbi told her about it that night.

"*Oui*, maybe," he said, "like all of your friends." He gestured to the corners of the hut, where Abeje's leaves were piling up.

Another day Adunbi saw a few geese eating the long grasses. He plucked some green stalks and approached them slowly. The old gander flew at him hissing, and bit his hand with its sharp beak. Adunbi dropped the grass stalks and grasped his hands to his chest, crouching down. The gander strutted around showing the lady geese his mettle. But then the gander cocked his head and Adunbi saw a shadow pass over the yellow eye, and he knew at once the old bird was sorry, though he wouldn't admit it. The gander hissed once more, but without conviction.

Nearly all the estate animals were like this with Adunbi. Barn cats that ran when others came near, rubbed on his legs and purred. Cows too skittish to be milked stood patiently for him, the fowls considered him one of their own number. Even when he led animals to slaughter they showed no fear.

Abeje begged him for stories of the animals.

"What the animals do today, Adu?" she said, each night.

"Eat and sleep, make noises and fight," he always said.

"What they do?"

"Shh, Beje."

"Tell me, Adu!"

Then he shook his head and told her a story, and these were their moments of laughing and smiling.

One morning Adunbi woke before first light and told Abeje he had a dream of Iya. He said she floated into the sky, with her arms raised and a long dress trailing. They went out of the hut to see the sky, now deep blue. Abeje looked east to see the brightest star, the Waking Star.

"That is she," said Adunbi. "Ma'a looking down at us."

A pale line grew from the edge of the earth and as the other stars faded the Waking Star seemed to burn even brighter. The black mountains reached up in the east, the palms waved their arms in the dark west near the Sea, and the air was gentle. The star was just as Abeje had seen it in the Grove. She knew their mother was there.

The groom was a young Irishman in charge of the stables and

barns, the area where Old Joseph labored. One day Joseph brought Adunbi before Groom.

"I need another hand with the buggy today, Boss," said Joseph. "He is Guillaume. Strong, smart boy, if it please."

The Irishman cast his eye down on Adunbi and nodded. "Alright."

After that Adunbi helped Joseph in caring for the horses. Joseph knew so many things about them, and took care to explain it all to Adunbi. Most interesting to Adunbi were the differences among the horses. One was shy about saddling on the right side, another preferred to eat her oats away from the others and nipped at any who tried to nose in. But Joseph pressed other things, how to avoid colic and injury, the right way to accustom a horse to a new bridle. He was a careful teacher, but hard, quick to grow impatient. He cuffed Adunbi on the back of his head if he drove a pick into the wrong part of a horse's hoof, or failed to secure a harness. He shouted at him that New Year's Day was coming and that Adunbi had better learn fast.

They dreaded New Year's Day all the year. It was on this day that the bondspeople were brought to the auction house to be bought and sold. They never knew whom they might lose, where they might go. So Joseph gave all of his knowledge to Adunbi, understanding that this would increase his worth, and lessen his chances of getting the lash, or being carted away.

Three or four New Years' came and went in this way, until one day Adunbi overheard Groom speaking with Old Monsieur about selling off some of the stock. The next New Year's Day was not far off, and from their voices Adunbi knew that by "stock" they were not speaking of the animals.

"Adu, no," said Abeje, when her brother told her what had happened. Adunbi shifted on the mat where he lay and continued. He had been at work pitching hay for the horses when Old Monsieur spied him.

"What about that one?" said Old Monsieur, pointing at the boy.

"He's well with the livery," said the Groom. "Would fetch a good price."

Old Joseph approached them. "Beg pardon," he said, "if it please, I just take Guillaume now to help me with the new horses." He held out his twisted hands. "Fingers getting mighty stiff."

Abeje held her breath. The old people always said one should never show a weakness.

This New Year's Eve was a moonless night. Before banking the cooking fire and leaving to go to sleep, Old Joseph took Adunbi's face, and then Abeje's, into his old hands. He rarely touched them, other than to punish Adunbi, or offer his shoulder to Abeje.

"Holy One be with you," he said to Adunbi. And "Holy One be with you, *p'tit*," to Abeje.

And indeed in the morning, New Year's Day, he went away in the wagon, shackled to four others.

Adunbi and Abeje, tall and thin as reeds now, trailed after the wagon as long as they dared. The work bell was already sounding and they knew Joseph would be angry if they risked a whipping. He faced away and couldn't see them, but they obeyed him as they would a father. At last they understood his great impatience with Adunbi, and his sacrifice.

Abeje and her brother saw the passing of two more years. They were not babies anymore and tended their own cooking fire. Lise still gave Abeje her tasks in the garden, and sometimes errands for the kitchen. One day Lise and Abeje brought up baskets of greens from the garden. Karine, the head cook, told Abeje to wait outside the door while she gathered some metal pots for her to scrub. A half-keg of salt sat by the door where she waited. Karine came out first with the pots, and then a second time with a spoon and a glass of water. Karine scooped a spoonful of salt from the keg into the glass and stirred. The salt vanished!

Karine told Lise to take the saltwater upstairs. Madame had another sore throat. Abeje wondered on this as she rubbed the white stones used for scrubbing against the blackened bottoms of the pots. The salt went in the water, though it seemed to disappear. Sea water and tears tasted of salt. It lay in the water invisible as a spirit in a body. People had called Iya a *saltwater slave*. So perhaps when she died the salt rose back out of her body. Perhaps the stars were nothing more than handfuls of salt, flung from the spirits of people.

With Joseph gone the Groom called Adunbi often to his aid. Groom cast a suspicious eye on the boy and always added to his orders the threat of boxing his ears, or reminding him of the lash. By the time Adunbi was fifteen years old he had grown much, was taller than the Irishman, and quite strong.

"Banan tried to charge Groom today," Adunbi said one night, as he and Abeje tended their supper over the fire.

"The white yearling bull?" asked Abeje. Adunbi had told her how lately the bull, who had been gentle enough as a calf, had been growing wilder.

That morning Adunbi had taken the bull from the barn to

a pen outside, to be fed away from the heifers. Banan went along without trouble and Adunbi left him in the pen to fetch the hay. When he returned Groom was in the pen, tying off the gate on the other side.

"I saw," Adunbi said, "he took it in his mind to charge." Adunbi had shouted a warning to Groom, who just managed to scramble over the fence before the bull smashed into the post closest to him, cracking it nearly in two. Groom was sufficiently rattled, and when he got his breath he reckoned that Adunbi had saved his life, and that somehow he'd known ahead of time what the bull meant to do.

"All day Groom watching me," Adunbi said.

"But not from fright," Abeje said.

"Not at all."

From that day forward Groom changed much toward Adunbi. He gave orders without threatening him. He asked Adunbi what he thought of this or that, regarding the animals, and when he heard the boy's answers, he nodded and said, "That be so."

Not long after her fourteen years, Abeje was set to work the cane fields. One day during the harvest, Abeje toiled with a gang bundling cut canes. The overseer rode around on his horse that morning, wielding his lash and amusing himself by cursing at the people. His voice rang out, in the distance, or close by where Abeje labored, and the sun climbed high in the sky.

On one of his passes by Abeje she felt his eyes on her, and then a chill of fear as his gaze swept over her limbs. She kept her eyes down on her work, but every time he passed her hands shook.

After midday, he made more rounds of the two work gangs, then suddenly dismounted near Abeje's group. His boots struck the ground and he strode straight toward Abeje, at once catching her wrist. The shock of his grip, of seeing his face up close, made her knees buckle. The flat field seemed to wrench itself over and she pitched to one side.

"Ye had better mind!" he barked, and dragged her, stumbling, behind a stand of cane and threw her down. She had no time even to cry out. He was upon her, heavy as a fallen tree, but savage, pinning her to the ground. One hard forearm cut the breath from her throat, while his other hand ripped at her clothing. Just as she thought her head would shatter he released her neck. Then he forced himself between her legs.

At first Abeje thought she was stabbed with a knife, killed, like Iya.

But in the next moment he pushed off of her, stood and staggered back, pushing his sweaty hair from his face. He fumbled to fix up his belt and felt for his pistol. "Get up."

Abeje curled around the pain; it seemed someone was striking her head with a hammer. The fetid smell of his sweat permeated the air, even when he went to mount his horse and resume his rounds.

Once his back was turned, one of the women, Vere, went to Abeje and helped her to stand. "Poor, poor babe," she whispered, brushing at Abeje's clothing and retying her headcloth. "Holy One deal with him." Abeje leaned on her as the field rocked back and forth. "Let's get to work now," Vere said.

Abeje was weak and clumsy. She dropped the canes and her fingers would not tie off the twine. Vere and the others hid her poor efforts from Overseer. At dusk Adunbi came looking for her. Earlier in the day he had suddenly been seized with dread for his sister, but could not get away, as that day he was sent to work in the sugar works. He feared for her life. When he saw her hunched form, and Vere helping her along, he hurried to support her. She hid her face and leaned against him, unable to prevent her sobs.

"Overseer," Vere said in a low voice.

Abeje felt him tremble. She clung to Adunbi as tightly as she could; she was so weak.

"Holy One deal with him," she begged.

That night a fire smoldered and sparked, spreading between her legs and up into her belly. The heat washed up and soon a fever overtook her. Adunbi stayed at her side by the cooking fire, and tried to make her eat, to drink, to lie down. When morning came he took her to the Sick House where she lay for two days, burning with fever. She did not see Adunbi there with her each night. She did not see how he sat with his head in his hands, digging his nails into his scalp so that they came away bloody. Nor did she see the others who also lay sick, or dying, but she did see other things.

She saw Adunbi in a field, raising a machete.

She saw the Sea.

She rose up and saw her feverish body below her.

She rose up over the roof of the Sick House and moved forth over the fields toward a dark sky. The shapes of shrubs and trees crouched in darkness, and the whistling wind became a song. She walked again beneath the great Anaya drawn with stars. The touch of Anaya's leaves grazed her cheek.

Beneath her lay a white path, long and narrow. It was a bridge, the limitless night sky on either side. In her open hand she found a clump of brown fibres. Also a yellow root and a dark green pulp of tiny, bitter leaves. The fibres drew her eyes down, and her hands to a place at her hip where the flesh was torn. The brown fibres knit the ragged edges together. Juice from the yellow root guided the fibres of the first plant and brought out new growth in the flesh. The tiny, bitter leaves removed clots of blood and carried away poisons.

The plants worked together, and Abeje marveled. Anaya was there to soothe the heart. Each plant had a song, its own notes, and they called among themselves as she had heard the birds and insects do. They gave her their names. In her hands they would do their work.

Then from her own belly, her own heart and throat, came her song. It flew high like a bird, and hummed low to the ground in a steady rhythm. It played in the wind, and joined together with the songs of all the plants. Now she lived in their village, and her own song brought forth her strength. She was a rooted tree, a rushing river, and the solid earth. She was the dancing flame, and the wind, the breath of the Holy One itself.

Abeje's feet balanced once again on the narrow bridge. Down below, her brother lay beside her. The bridge stretched out ahead, she who was awake in her dream-body, and her steps were slow. The Holy One breathed above.

Fever burned her insides, leaving a trail of ashes.

She saw Overseer, reduced to his bed with fever himself. She knew that when she rose from her sickness, he would cross his own bridge, and she would not see him again.

In the days that followed Abeje's return from the Sick House, Adunbi didn't want her to go alone to fetch water in the morning. He didn't want her to lift a heavy load of firewood or even go into the Grove. Over what Abeje did during the day's work he had no say, but in the Quarters he watched her every move with piercing attention. One night he shouted at her as she was bent over the cooking fire, saying she was far too close and would fall into it if she became dizzy again.

"Adu," Abeje hissed, "I am not a child." Even as the words escaped her, she felt their falsity, because under Adunbi's gaze she did feel like a child, shameful and unworthy.

She had never spoken in a harsh tone to her brother before and he stepped back in shock, his mouth agape. He turned on his heel and strode toward the empty hut. A loose palm frond from the thatched roof hung over the doorway and he yanked it, tearing it off.

There was fire inside Adunbi. Abeje could see its red halo. The spiky palm tree that guarded Adunbi was ablaze, white and crackling. He screamed, reached up and seized more of the thatch, ripping it off the roof. He tore at it again and again, until blood ran down his arms. No one tried to stop him, not Abeje, nor the others who slept in their hut.

Abeje sank to her heels. Adunbi's fire would consume the Quarters, the whole of the sugar estate. It would consume her, Abeje, the cause of his pain, because somehow she had let Overseer do what he did. She had not been invisible: there in the field, as she should have been, invisible as she had been once, when she was so small. Overseer had seen her female shape, bent over the cut cane, and he had cut her down too.

Abeje scrambled forward, sweeping up the fallen fronds of the thatch and hurling them onto the coals under the cooking pot, where they smoked and sparked. The flames rose high into the sky, a pillar of flame, all the way up to where the starlight Anaya sparkled. For a moment she was alone with Anaya, floating in her peace, and this cooled the flames that attacked her skin. Abeje was just a baby, Anaya seemed to say, this fire did not belong to her. It had not, in fact, burned her.

Now, down on the hard earth, the cooking fire and the palm fronds had spent themselves. Thin trails of ashes lay about Abeje's feet, marking the places where the fire had raged. The hut was half destroyed. Abeje saw Adunbi slumped to the ground, covering his face. She went to him, and he let her tend to his bleeding hands.

They slept that night in view of the stars, thankful there was no rain.

At the end of the next day, when Adunbi returned from the barns, he found that someone had left several bundles of new thatch stacked beside the hut. He did not allow anyone from the Quarters to help him repair the roof, not even Abeje, but he stopped scolding her as she fetched firewood and water for the cooking pot.

Sometimes at night by the cooking fires the people spoke of an Obeah woman, a great healer, who lived on a sugar estate some leagues away. She traveled to tend the sick, and often the sick or injured were brought to her. But travel was quite difficult, especially as bondsmen had little leave for such things.

There was a light-skinned carpenter and his wife, Floria, who had a hut to themselves, a small distance apart from the Quarters. Unlike most of the people, who on Sundays tended to what crops they had and business of their own, the carpenter had Sunday and half of Saturday free as well. He sometimes hired himself out for wages, or was seen mending his roof, or building a pen to keep pigs and the like. His wife took sick when she was heavy with their first child. Louise, who helped many women birth children, went to visit her. The wife had pains and weakness, and bleeding before her time. Louise had strong, clever hands but no knowledge of medicines.

Abeje, now in her fifteenth year, heard Louise tell Vere that the carpenter would not take his wife to the Sick House, saying people went there only to die. So one night the carpenter took a horse from the stable and went to seek the Obeah woman, and the next night she arrived.

She sat erect on the horse, in a long dark dress and a blue cloth wound tightly around her head. Everyone tending their fires watched as the carpenter led the horse to his hut and brought her inside. Several people went to see what the Obeah might need for her work, and to have a look at her. All were curious, and many hoped they might ask for her help as well. They did not see her come out again that night, but early in the morning she appeared in the Quarters. The people bade her to sit down by the largest fire. Word spread around that she wanted coffee to drink, but none was to be had. Someone found some chicory, and another had a bit of blackjack made from burnt sugar, and soon a pot was heating for her.

Though it was Sunday, Adunbi was at the barns feeding and watering the stock. Abeje tended the cooking pot, and kept turning her head to glance at the Obeah woman. She sat tall and straight as a tree, surrounded by people who offered her food and asked of news from elsewhere. Abeje gazed at her blue garments, and her black skin, the colors of night, but when she looked away she saw the Obeah's image, with great fiery waves about her of red and orange, like the blossoms she sometimes saw in the Grove.

Then the next time she glanced at her the woman looked back. Abeje's heart jumped and beat quickly. Never before had she seen the likes of her. When they were children Iya told them of the Great Cat that was yellow like ripe wheat and lived across the Big Sea. The Obeah woman was fierce like the Great Cat must have been, but Abeje could see she was not ruthless. She was a mother who had lost her children, and turned her protection onto all of the people. A great need arose in Abeje to get closer to her. She removed her pot from the fire, stole up and sat on her heels at the edge of the group. Abeje listened, drawing a circle in the dust with a stick, as the Obeah continued conferring with three of the women. Suddenly she spoke.

"What yer name, child?"

The Obeah looked directly at the girl. Abeje did not move at first, but the folks waved her forward.

Abeje stood before the Obeah and her voice came out in a whisper. "*Marie*, Mam," she said, looking down.

The Obeah leapt to her feet, eyes flashing with anger. Her hand shot out and her fingers grasped Abeje's chin, forcing their eyes to meet.

"I said, What yer Name!"

Tears came up and rolled down Abeje's cheeks, and her voice broke from its whisper.

"Abeje!" she cried, "Abeje, Mam!"

"Ah!" The Obeah peered into the girl's face. Her dark eyes grew larger and larger until they blotted out the sky. "Abeje...." Her voice hummed, taking on Anaya's song. Abeje felt the Obeah's rough thumb on her forehead and she spoke again.

"Spirit has marked you, child, I see that well enough." She ordered Abeje to sit at her side, and she resumed her talk with the women. Soon they rose and the Obeah bade Abeje to follow them into one of the huts. She was to watch and listen as the Obeah tended to one of the women, Berthe, who was ailing with swellings under her arms, and in the groin and throat. As the Obeah began her song the lids of Abeje's eyes drew down. She could see much better this way. She found herself joining the song, following until the spirits of four plants appeared. Abeje learned their names and songs, smelled the essence housed in their flesh. One of the plant spirits was called *Queen* of the others, another was very like Berthe herself.

Abeje sat with the Obeah the whole rest of that day, as she tended to others, including the carpenter's wife. Carpenter gave her a strange look when she entered his hut with the Obeah, but no one questioned the healing woman. The Obeah stayed one week in the Quarters. At that time there was a party of guests at the Great House, and Lise and Karine from the kitchen asked Madame for permission to get Abeje's help. Once they put her to work up at the House, she was not so weary each night from the hard labor of the cane fields, and she was able to assist the Obeah in tending folks. In this way the Holy One arranged for her initiation.

One evening while it was still light the Obeah beckoned Abeje to follow her. They walked without speaking into the Grove.

"Show me your own plant," she said. Abeje knew there was an Anaya close by and she led the Obeah there. "*Oui*," said the healing woman, pleased. She caressed a leaf, then quickly plucked a few. She broke one apart and breathed in the scent. Then she asked Abeje, "Do you know a tree with a brown crust growing around the bottom?" She did, and they soon found one. The Obeah brought out her knife, and cut a piece of the crust away from the tree. "Now I will show you something."

39

Back at the Quarters, in a small pot, she brewed a tea from the Anaya leaves and pieces of the brown tree crust. "This drink is for healers only," she said, "to aid in preparing herself for a healing." When it was ready she poured a gourd full for Abeje. The sharp, sweet taste burned over her tongue. She tasted the dark earth, and drained the gourd. The Obeah watched as Abeje began to feel small tremors in her middle.

Soon it was dark and the cooking fires were busy with people. Abeje was unable to move, and sat very still looking into the flames. She heard the healing woman's voice. "Tell me, what do you see?"

"Colors, Mam," she said, in wonder. She saw the colors of fire, of water, of the flowers, of fish and the birds, all dancing.

"Now listen," said the Obeah, "what do you hear?"

When Abeje closed her eyes she saw the colors still, and heard Anaya's song, which became threads of light that laced around her fingers.

"I hear light," Abeje said.

"Good," said the Obeah. "Come along now. Let's see what Spirit brings us to heal tonight."

That night there were four healings, and the Obeah instructed Abeje to put her hands on each person. "Let the right place pull you," she said. The last healing was a final visit with the carpenter's wife. The Obeah asked her to lie back against her husband and waved Abeje forward. Abeje knelt beside Floria and listened again to the light. Her hands moved to the small of the pregnant woman's back, which felt icy cold.

"Oh my," Floria said. "Girl, you are burning me!" But she was smiling.

When it came time for the carpenter to return the healing

woman to her home, she took Abeje's hands and gave her a small bundle of several dried plants. She pressed the girl's fingers over the bundle, looked her in the eye, nodded and smiled.

"Thank you, Mam," said Abeje, her heart so full.

She would never see the Obeah again.

Later Adunbi grinned at her and said, "Now I will call you Big Sister!" Abeje laughed.

The carpenter's wife recovered and went on to bear a healthy child. People began to regard Abeje with new eyes, as one whom spirit had marked, as the Obeah had said. One Sunday, Vere asked Abeje if she might help with her stiff knees. A few weeks later Lise punctured her palm on a nail, came down with a fever and went to find Abeje. Abeje began with the songs, the plants and their spirits, the Anaya, and the threads of light around her fingers. When she touched the ailing flesh she felt its call, and knew how to answer it.

In the months, then years, that followed, more of the people sought out Abeje's help, and every time she learned something new. The people offered food, sometimes a clay pot, a piece of cloth. She and Adunbi suffered less and less from the hunger they had always known.

One night during the rainy season, when Abeje was nearing her twenty years, she felt her brother shaking her arm to wake her. "What is it?"

"Listen," he said. The faint sound of animals lowing and braying came across the distance. "Sure a storm coming," said Adunbi. "Mighty big."

Quickly they roused the others in the hut. Abeje grabbed her two shawls and a few cakes of meal wrapped in a large leaf, then went out to help spread the warning through the Quarters. A great pressure pressed at her ears. The wind struck up leaves from the ground and flung them into the sky. The people began to run in the direction of the barns, which were made of stone, and to the Great House, also of stone, where they might find shelter in the cellars. Adunbi made to follow them, but dread took hold of Abeje. "No, this way."

They ran toward the Grove as dawn broke. The blowing clouds glowed an unnatural green. There was a place Abeje knew from her wanderings, a small cave of limestone hidden in a hillock, covered with shrubs and vines. The wind thrashed the trees now, so violently the two could scarcely move forward. By the time they reached the cave they were drenched from the rain, but they managed to struggle inside before the storm neared its full strength. From the mouth of the cave, a small passage led upward, to where the darkness was almost complete. They crawled along, feeling their way between the walls, and the stones that reached up from the floor and down from the low ceiling. They went as far as they could, then stopped, huddled against the stone. The hurricane roared, far away. Some gusts still reached them, and in places water streamed in. The storm beat hour after hour.

For a long time neither spoke. They listened to the scream of the storm, muffled by the twists and turns of the cave passage. Abeje shivered, and Adunbi drew her close, surprising her by saying, "Beje, do you remember when Ma'a died?"

"*Mais oui.*" Never once had they spoken of that night.

"It felt just like this," he said.

They were quiet some time more, until Abeje said, "Adu, give me your hand." He reached over and she felt his strong fingers.

"Here is Baba," she sang, grasping his forefinger. "And here is Iya," moving to his middle finger. "Here is Adu," and at the littlest, "and here is Abeje."

"Who is the Fat Man, then?"

"Georges."

Adunbi's deep laugh burst against the walls of the cave. Georges was the houseboy that Lise said was always scurrying out of the kitchen, chewing on something.

By the time night fell their clothing had mostly dried. The storm raged on. They feared for the others but didn't speak of it. Here and there water pooled in pockets in the limestone. They drank from these and ate some of the meal cakes Abeje had brought. They sang Iya's songs. Abeje sang the songs of the spirit village and Adunbi listened, and at last the songs bridged into dreams.

The hurricane lasted all of the next day and night as well. At last on the third morning all was quiet. Sunlight danced before the mouth of the cave, sparkling off the green leaves, playing at innocence. Abeje and Adunbi ventured out not knowing what destruction would meet them. The low places of the land were flooded and strewn with the bodies of people and animals. The huts in the Quarters were gone, only pieces of thatch, board and clay lay scattered on the ground or caught up in treetops. Abeje and Adunbi ran up to the barns. The roofing had collapsed and been torn off by the wind, but some people had survived there inside a grain cellar. Adunbi immediately began to round up and secure any living animals and Abeje took her place in aiding the injured people. She felt their turmoil as clearly as if the storm still raged, and this she sought to ease, but she also felt their strength, like iron forged in fire. It was said of the dead, "They are free now."

On the fourth or fifth day after the storm, as Abeje struggled to continue at her work, hardly any strength left in her, Lise appeared saying she was wanted at the Great House. Monsieur's young son was very ill. The *békés* would never accept the aid of one like herself, but because of the Hurricane, and the ruined roads, no regular doctor could be summoned. Lise herself told Madame, "Mam, there is one in the Quarters, called *Marie*, who helps people that are ailing." Monsieur said no colored would feign witchcraft on his boy, but Madame was so desperate she shouted she would go and fetch *Marie* herself if she had to, and that her husband had better not stand in her way.

Abeje had never set foot inside the Great House before. Lise led her through the rooms and she saw all their finery, which was mostly undisturbed by the hurricane, though there were places where water had come in, and shutters covered the broken windows. Lise said part of the roof and one or two upper rooms would have to be rebuilt, but that was all. Abeje followed, climbing a staircase for the first time. Upstairs Lise knocked upon a door, which was opened by a house bondswoman called Zara. Lise ushered Abeje inside but did not follow.

The room was dark save for one lamp lit by the bedstead and a line of light coming from the window where a heavy curtain rested slightly to one side. A man stood there with his back to the room, peering outside. Abeje's legs swayed, and bile burned in her throat.

It was Monsieur, the man who had killed her mother.

He turned around and she immediately fixed her eyes on the floor. She could not bear to look.

A woman's voice spoke weakly, "Come forward." Abeje raised her eyes to the bedstead. Madame sat beside it in a chair, holding the hand of the child who was sunk in a feverish sleep. She approached them and knelt down. A wave of dizziness spun Abeje around. Monsieur and Madame had three nearly-grown daughters and this was their only son, seven or eight years old. She saw his pale, damp hair, greyish skin, the rapid breathing and distended belly, and knew that he would die very soon if she did not do something.

Hatred flooded her. She dared to glance toward him. He again faced away, looking out the window. She saw in the slope of his shoulders that he had been awake the whole night before. She knew without seeing that his eyes were red, and that he feared now more than he had ever feared for anything in his life.

As Abeje struggled, she felt the presence of Anaya. In her mind's eye there appeared several heart-shaped leaves, and she heard the familiar song. She drew a deep breath and steadied herself. She saw better now and looked at the boy. He had drunk some bad water, that was clear enough, and he wanted to live.

There was no time to go to the Grove and search for plants, no time to make tea or paste. She would have to call their spirits only. Abeje leaned forward, laid her hands on the boy's belly, and began to sing quietly, a calling song. The threads of light danced around her fingers.

But the heat that rose from her hands did not penetrate the boy's body easily. A heavy shadow lay between the child and herself. Abeje called on another plant, a vine with tiny thorns that behaved like an axe, severing poisons that stuck to a body. But the shadow resisted, repelling the vine's advances.

Sweat broke over Abeje's brow. She reached for the boy's hand, feeling his limp fingers. Something in him needed waking. She bent to place her ear on his chest. A voice lay over the beating organ, a shrill keen that she recognized as the birth cry of his mother. Something in his birth that had made him weak, something that had not shown itself until now.

Abeje looked up at the woman, Madame, sitting helplessly at the bedside.

"Mam," she said, "if it please, would you hold him?"

Madame assented readily, leaning forward to lift the child to her lap, who whimpered with pain. Monsieur crossed the room to assist his wife. When he withdrew Abeje stepped around the bedstead, lifted by a sudden energy that ignited her tired limbs. She saw clearly now, even with her eyes open, that a little taut string pulled the child's heart on one end and snagged his mother's rib on the other, and Abeje had only to pluck it out. She did this with a small movement so swift it only appeared that she stumbled over the hem of her skirt. She flung the string away and the hanging shadow dissolved.

The child's breathing changed, becoming deep and even. Abeje pressed her ear against his back to hear his heart again; the beats came stronger. She stood and backed up a pace.

"He will be alright now."

Madame gazed at the child in her arms, nodding absently in reply. She didn't know if it were true.

Zara took Abeje back outside.

Walking away from the Great House Abeje took a fresh breath. The sky was clear, with the wind whipping away any traces of clouds. The palm trees bent in relief. If the boy survived, her place on the sugar estate would be all but secured, such as Adunbi's was now.

That evening Lise and Karine came down to the Quarters

carrying a whole sack of meal, a large slab of hard bacon wrapped in a cloth, and a pail of dried peas. They said the boy's fever had broken, that he sat up and took a bowl of soup and asked for his tin soldiers. They said Madame was so overjoyed she bade them to bring the food down to *Marie*.

There was very little to eat in the Quarters still, and though Abeje hungered, her heart was clear. The women took the bacon and peas and divided them among the largest cooking pots, to make a thick soup. Adunbi and the others, even the children, mixed the meal with water and salt, and made cakes to cook in the coals. All ate well that night.

It was another New Year's Day and a prosperous time for Monsieur. The great hurricane was now more than ten years past, and because there was trouble on some of the other islands in the Sea, he got a high price for his sugar. As a child Abeje thought sugar was made by mixing sugar cane with the bodies of the people, because so many died or were maimed in the sugar works. She knew now it was the dead soul of the cane. Just as salt lived in the sea, and could be drawn out, so they drew out sugar from the plants. It was a stolen spirit, and was dear to the people in France, and in other countries where they were in need of souls.

Though the prosperity did not touch the lives of the people directly, it did mean that this New Year's Day none of them left in a wagon bound for the auction house. Instead a wagon arrived that night bringing two men and a young woman. Adunbi greeted the newcomers and brought them to sit at their cooking fire. The newcomers had a bucket of yams from the Great House cellar, as rations would not be distributed for another two or three days.

While the yams roasted, many of the people came to speak to the two men and the girl. Where did they come from? What news, if any, might be known, from other places?

The young woman was called Olivie, and she was eighteen or nineteen years of age. She was a beautiful girl, one could see that even in the dark of the night, though in her large eyes one also saw terror. She relaxed some as the people came by and she saw they meant her no harm. But the fear lay very deeply in her, like the bed of a river beneath the water. Abeje sat beside her, gently took her hand, placed her other hand on top of Olivie's delicate fingers, and silently began a healing. One spirit, the ancient Baobab tree, came forward for Olivie. Abeje was amazed. Baobab was a great matriarch, the Mother of many mothers. She could envelop all of this girl's life, all of her spirit. The presence of the tree spirit flowed through Abeje's hand into the girl's. Olivie leaned against her then, and soon fell asleep.

Olivie was sent up with Karine to work at laundering in the Great House. She slept in a hut with several other women and children, and Abeje and Adunbi invited her to share their cooking fire. She came from another estate across the Island, and before that lived on yet another, which was the place she last saw her mother.

She had a shy but lovely smile, fine limbs and graceful movements. As the weeks and months went by, Abeje noticed a change come over her brother. He gazed at Olivie when she was not looking, and when she caught him looking they both laughed. His voice rose and fell playfully when they spoke, and he asked her questions with tenderness. He sang when going off to his work.

When, after a long day, his heart leapt at the sight of her,

Abeje felt this new joy as well. Now and then Abeje held Olivie's hand at the fire, so that Mother Baobab would come to visit her.

One day Adunbi said to Abeje in confidence, "Sister, I want now to take a wife."

"A wife!" she cried, "*Who*, Adu?"

He smiled and said, "Olivie."

"*Olivie?*" whispered Abeje, pretending great shock. He laughed a big laugh then, because of course she knew, and because he was brimming with new love.

Abeje was very proud of her brother and knew he would make a fine husband, even if all this was a fragile business, since when it came to buying and selling people, Monsieur did not concern himself with questions of marriage. The thing that made Abeje more uneasy was that she felt Olivie's spirit to be light, like a butterfly, even with Mother Baobab, so strong and rooted, as her protector. It helped to see Olivie smile so when she saw Adunbi, and Abeje looked forward to when Adunbi would ask her to be his bride.

Abeje had a length of white cloth from Floria. She and the carpenter had three children now, and Abeje had assisted them all through illnesses. She gave this cloth to Olivie so she could make a dress. Olivie put her arms about Abeje and whispered, "Thank you, Beje." And Abeje said she must now call her *Sister*. Olivie was very happy. She loved Adunbi very much.

Two Sundays hence all the people rose at first light and gathered together around a large cooking fire. First the women began singing, "Guillaume Adunbi, Guillaume Adunbi!"

"Come forward now!" the men sang in answer.

"Guillaume Adunbi, Guillaume Adunbi!"

"Come forward now!"

Adunbi stepped forward, into the center of the circle before the fire.

"Olivie, Olivie!" sang the women.

"Come forward now!" answered the men.

Olivie went forward, in her pure white dress, and stood beside Adunbi. The new sun shone on her lovely face.

Abeje wound a strip of cloth around their joined hands. She kissed them both and stepped away. One by one all the people placed their hands on the cloth. And in this way Adunbi and Olivie were married.

For some time, the hut Abeje and Adunbi shared had been theirs alone. Now Olivie slept with them and kept what belongings she had there. Each night Abeje stayed by the cooking fire after her brother and his wife said good night, so that they might lie down before her and have some time to themselves. The first several months were very happy. Adunbi went singing each day to his work and returned singing. When it was known that Olivie was with child, their happiness increased. She grew round and even more beautiful. Adunbi devised ever more ways to find food and goods to support his wife and soon-to-be-born, and Abeje sat with her while they ate, inviting Mother Baobab to come and nourish mother and child. When Olivie's time grew near Abeje sang much with the spirits, calling for her protection.

The Moon came and went through her phases. One night she rose full on the horizon and Olivie began her labors. Adunbi and Abeje assisted her, and Berthe and Floria came also. The child was born at dawn. A daughter! She announced herself with a lusty cry.

Adunbi and Olivie named her *Ayo*, Iya's word for Joy. Abeje laid Ayo on her mother's breast, and soon both mother and child fell asleep.

Later that night Olivie began to bleed. While Mother Baobab held Olivie in her strong branches, Abeje brought roots, leaves and flowers, and songs of every kind, but still the blood flowed. Adunbi became frantic, he held his new daughter and paced in and out of the hut as she cried. Abeje felt that butterfly spirit grow lighter.

"What shall I do, Beje?" Adunbi asked, struggling to control his voice. He was ready to fly to any place on the estate where help could be gotten. But Abeje had already exhausted herself. She was failing her brother, and this thought nearly cut her in two. She swallowed, feeling as though a lump of hot iron were searing her throat.

"We'll pray now," she said.

Feeling her way in the dark, Abeje knelt at Olivie's feet, holding them firmly to the earth.

"Holy One," she breathed, "don't take her away! Don't take her now." Tears overtook her.

"Stay with me," Adunbi said.

At last all became very quiet. Olivie was breathing, but very shallowly and at long intervals. The baby slept at her side. Adunbi held Olivie's hand. And then Abeje said the words that most pained her to speak.

"We must bring her outside, before it is too late." It was well known that it was better for a soul to rise in sight of the sky.

Adunbi closed his eyes, dropped his chin to his chest. Together with Berthe they carried Olivie out of the hut to where she could see the stars. Adunbi buried his face in her shoulder. Olivie's eyes opened, and she turned her cheek against his head.

Her eyes looked to the stars.

Her teeth bared in something like a smile, and then she was gone.

It hurt Abeje like nothing else to hear her brother weep. Her ears rang with the jagged edges of his pain.

They buried Olivie beside Iya.

Adunbi broke their cooking pot and laid the pieces on the grave while the people sang.

Right away they had to see what could be done for the child. There were only two women in the Quarters who had milk. One had two children already at the breast, and the other had not enough milk for another. They could feed Ayo only for a very short time before all would suffer.

Adunbi went to the Groom, the Irishman, to speak about it. The Irishman was willing to see if there was a woman on another sugar estate who could take the child, and to see if Monsieur would allow him to make some kind of trade. In two days it was arranged. The Irishman told Adunbi to bring him the baby. Abeje went with Adunbi as he carried Ayo to the barns, knowing that sending her away was her only chance at life. They bound the child to the Irishman with cloth torn from Olivie's white dress. Then Groom mounted a swift horse and held out his hand to Adunbi.

"I'm sorry for ye," he said.

Adunbi nodded gravely.

Groom rode away and was quickly gone from sight.

Adunbi stumbled away like a blind man. Abeje let him alone and found that she herself could scarcely move. Their heavy feet carried them, his toward the edge of the Sea, hers back to the Quarters. Already a fever was overtaking her. Abeje made it to the empty hut and lay down on her sleeping mat, and from there she was lost in dreams.

The sound of a heart beating filled her ears. She knew not if it was hers or her brother's. She rose from her feverish form and up into the wide sky. A gull flew toward her, so close she saw its yellow eye, the open beak and pointed tongue as it cried out. The cry rang out across the whole sky. The gull flew past and she chased it to the edge of the Sea, where below a dark figure staggered down a cliff, and then across the sand that glowed blue in the twilight.

He meant to surrender his body to the warm Sea, to follow his wife, and surely his child. The Sea held him in her arms. The water rushed easily over her brother's head.

Three dark shapes emerged from the deep. They circled her brother's body. Round bodies and short, strong limbs. Abeje heard Iya's name for the creatures, it was *awon okun*, sea turtle! The turtles circled Adunbi.

Adunbi lay on the beach, his cheek pressed to the hard wet sand. He coughed and vomited out sea water, spat it out as the warm Sea itself had spit out the man. He lay there a long time, the Waking Star shining alone in the lightening sky.

When Groom came back the next day he brought with him the heifer calf that was traded for Adunbi's child. Groom told Adunbi that Ayo was now at the estate called Auxier, and he named the roads and directions there.

"She'll live, God willing," he said.

The heifer calf bawled nightly for its mother, and it took to following Adunbi during the day. He did not bear a grudge against it, its reason for being there. He patted its head when it nosed his arm, and if the calf complained when he went away from its pen, he let it out, and it trotted along at his heels, trailing as did his thoughts of his wife and child. He had them always in his mind and heart. As he grieved his wife, he also sought a way he could one day go to Auxier.

A new *béké* came to work for Monsieur as a foreman in the sugar works, who was young and skittish, and did not take well to the responsibility. He had a pack of dogs, vicious brutes that obeyed his command. One day he went with his dogs on the path below the barns and one of them spotted the heifer calf trailing after Adunbi. The dog came after it snarling and got it by the leg, and would have killed it if Adunbi had not beaten the dog off with a stick. But then the foreman tore the stick away from him and struck Adunbi across the back.

Abeje insisted he let her look, even though he assured her it was nothing, just bruises.

"Groom stopped him," he said, "told him to keep his filthy dogs away from the barns."

A few days hence Abeje saw Lise near the Quarters.

"Watch out for that new foreman," said Lise. She had heard him speaking with Monsieur and Madame at the supper table in the Great House. Foreman had learned of her aiding the sick, and that she was the sister of the Groom's "boy." The foreman said he didn't wonder if the two of them had the Evil Eye. Madame clucked at him, calling him foolish, at which he glowered and said, "I've seen their kind before." Monsieur asked him where, and the foreman didn't answer.

Abeje and Adunbi kept away from the Foreman, and thankfully their paths did not cross often. Every once in a while though, Abeje felt a chill steal down her spine, and turning her head would see the foreman, at some distance, watching her.

Some months later, Abeje chanced to pass near the sugar works. Suddenly she saw the foreman atop a wagon loaded with hogsheads. He was bent over the ropes, securing the barrels, and his dogs were milling about the wagon on the ground. No one else was in sight. Abeje set her eyes straight on her path, but too late. A hundred needles pricked her scalp. She glanced back, saw him standing straight. Her eyesight was no longer clear enough to see his expression, but it was easy enough to guess.

The dogs tensed, alert as they were to any shift in the mood of their master. Suddenly Abeje saw herself as if from a distance, a woman alone, in open ground, the red dust over her dress, her wrapped head. The foreman gave a yell, commanding his dogs to kill. They lunged forward with a roar, and at once Abeje was back to herself. She could not outrun the dogs. There was no wall or tree she might scramble up to escape. She would not be able to fight them off, even with a stick in hand, they were too many. The clamor flooded her ears.

She had but one choice. She closed her eyes and quietened her breathing, pressing the rise of her fear down into her feet, down deep into the earth. She went as still as a tree, breathing as the trees did, as if there was no time, and no motion, no more than the turning of the whole earth.

When she opened her eyes again, the dogs were staggering around her in aimless circles, perplexed as if their prey had vanished into thin air. They whined and howled, did not see or hear or smell her at all. As fear was not present they had nothing to attack. Abeje then gathered her skirts and hurried on her way. She did not look back at the foreman. She knew he would not try that trick again.

That evening when she was tending her cooking fire Berthe and her grown daughter Lydia approached and stood silently, watching her. Adunbi had not yet returned from the barns.

"What is it?" Abeje asked.

"Is it true," asked Berthe, "that you charmed the foreman's dogs today?"

"He has said so," Lydia said, pointing to another figure standing farther off, the young boy Nathaniel. When Abeje had passed the sugar works that day Nathaniel had been starting down a nearby hillside, carrying a load of kindling sticks. He recognized Abeje by her dress and saw the dogs charge, sure that they would kill her.

Looking from Nathaniel back to Berthe and Lydia, Abeje now saw that a dozen or so others were drawing near the fire, all with a wondering look on their faces.

"Tell what you saw, boy!" said one of the men to Nathaniel, who obliged him, stuttering over his words. When Abeje did not deny it the crowd set to murmuring.

"Praise the Holy One," said a woman.

"Bless me too," said another.

One by one they pressed Abeje's hand. They asked Nathaniel again just what it was he had witnessed. This was a story that would travel far.

A year or so passed before Adunbi got permission to go to Auxier. Monsieur wrote a paper, a pass for him to travel alone, allowing him to be gone on a Sunday. This meant he had to leave on the night before, walk all the night there and then walk all the next night back. He decided to go near the full moon so that he would have light enough to travel by. Groom told him to look for a woman called Phoebe, as the baby was given to her.

A woman in the Quarters named Leola had made a rag doll for her daughter, and he traded her a gourd of molasses for the favor of making another that he could bring to his own child on Auxier. He was very much excited at the idea of seeing his daughter, his Ayo, though beside himself with anxiety that she might not be well or even still living. Adunbi left the next Saturday night when the moon was bright. He set out with a bundle of provisions that Abeje had helped him prepare, the rag doll tucked away inside, his pass and a walking cane. Abeje told him to kiss the child for her.

Abeje slept fitfully, and spent a fretful day wondering what her brother would find at Auxier. She desperately hoped that he would find the baby well and plump, and that he would be able to hold her and look upon her face. But before dawn on Monday she heard him enter the hut, and she knew at once something was not right.

"Adu," she said, "what happened?"

"Not there, Beje. Gone." After a long moment he told her that they sold Phoebe and the child to a slave trader over in Saint-Pierre, last New Year's. There was no way to know where they might be, they could easily have been sold off the Island. Abeje was silent a long time, her heart crushed under a heavy weight. But then, as if from under that weight, a thread of hope gleamed. Mother Baobab and her brother's own spiky palm tree would not let her hope die.

Adunbi and Abeje were past their forty years when Monsieur brought in two new bondsmen, young men meant for the cane fields. They purchased one of these men, called Luc, from the Island of Guadeloupe. Luc was unlike anyone Abeje and Adunbi had ever known. He had many stories to tell, from his time on other islands, and all had but one meaning: freedom.

Young Luc spoke of a great Obeah queen on the Island of Jamaica called Queen Nanny, a saltwater slave from the Old Land, who long ago escaped bondage. She established her own country in the mountains, where the British soldiers could not get her. Her villages grew by hundreds of Maroons. They became warriors and lived in the Old Ways. And not only that. It was true that on the Island of Saint-Domingue the people had risen up, thrown off their chains and banished the soldiers of the French King. Luc told them of two great warriors on the Island of Barbados, when he himself was a child: a saltwater slave called Bussa, and a woman called Nanny Grigg. Luc told them that these two together led a rebellion, with many followers who gave their lives for freedom.

He said there were rebels on their island, Martinique.

Luc said to Adunbi that his good work with the livestock only lined Monsieur's pockets, and that when the Rebellion came they would slaughter the animals and set fire to the fields.

"Is a Healing Woman the same, so?" said Abeje. "Am I the same as my brother, who cares for and heals Monsieur's property?"

"No," said Luc. "You are Obeah, like Queen Nanny. And one day we will not be property anymore."

Luc's words brought Abeje and Adunbi equal parts hope and fear. They had heard already of small rebellions on their Island, and maroons who escaped and were never captured. But Luc envisioned a future there and on all the islands, as on Saint-Domingue, when all of slavery would be brought down, and everyone would be free.

Luc himself, despite much righteous and sometimes angry speech, very much liked Abeje and her brother. At the day's end he asked their permission to sit down with them at their cooking fire, and there he always had many questions for them. He began to call Adunbi *Tonton*, uncle, and herself *Mémé* Abeje, grandmother. Abeje laughed at this, protesting that she was younger than her brother, and didn't even have any children. Luc said she was like a grandmother to the people. The brother and sister were not yet old and bent, but they had much white in their hair and the years had drawn lines on their faces. What Luc said had truth. Like the years, the people had drawn lines on Abeje's heart. It was not long before Luc's name for her became the speech of the others, including those who came from other places for aid.

For several months Abeje and her brother shared many evenings with Luc. Some nights Luc had no taste for stories. He was quiet and said nothing. On these nights Abeje took his hand in hers. She sat by, humming, and let Anaya come to them. Sometimes she saw Luc, the child, holding the hand of his own mother. Even in a young man, so brash and brave, lay a tender heart.

One night early in the month of October, Luc sat very quietly by the fire, his thick brows knit together. He had been more quiet lately, but in a new way. His voice, when he did speak, was tight. In fact, all in the Quarters vibrated with this same tension. People spoke in hushed tones, for some time now, of rebels, leaders and secret movements.

The hour grew late. After Adunbi said goodnight and went into the hut, Luc asked Abeje, "Mémé, is it right or wrong to kill?"

"What do you say?" she said.

"For Justice, for Liberty, yes."

"Then why do you ask me?"

"I don't know."

Abeje took his hand. "I also don't know what is right and what is wrong," she said. "I must look only to my heart and listen for its call. Then I know where to follow."

"That is your guide," he said.

"That is indeed my guide."

Then she told him of the great storm of many years before, the Hurricane, and how she and Adunbi sheltered in the limestone cave. She spoke of the four trees that marked the mouth of the cave. If ever one needed a hiding place, it might serve. As she spoke she undid her shawl and took the hard meal cakes she had made that night and wrapped them in it, making a bundle that she left on the ground. Then she said, "It is late now, my son."

Luc took her elbow and helped her to stand. He raised her palm to his cheek a moment and then bade her good night.

In the morning he was not to be found.

Some dozen of the other young men also disappeared, and Monsieur sent out a party of hired men with guns to search for the runaways.

Two days hence Abeje and Adunbi awoke in the night to the sound of the work bell ringing, clanging on without stopping, the sound of hoofbeats outside the huts, and one of overseers shouting for everyone to run up to the sugar works. An overseer fired a shot into the air with his rifle, spooking his horse and letting the people know that the next bullet would be for anyone who dared to disobey.

Abeje hurried as best she could with the others toward the sugar works, where flames roared and lit the sky. Already every hand was employed bringing buckets of water from the stream that flowed nearby. The overseer was joined by Monsieur and the foreman, also on horseback and carrying guns, shouting directions and threats. Already they could see that the building would be lost and they put the people to work digging trenches and wetting the ground to prevent the fire from spreading.

A low cover of cloud lay overhead, lit red here and there in the distance from other fires. The Rebellion. Staggering with another full bucket Abeje said a prayer for Luc. She threw the water over bare ground where it would protect nothing, only her own life by not disobeying.

Dawn came slowly over the charred remains of the sugar works. There was no more fire on the Estate, but the sky was thick with smoke from elsewhere, and the harsh, sweet smell of burning cane fields. A party of militiamen arrived and left with the two overseers and the foreman toward the south, leaving Groom with Monsieur's two sons-in-law to patrol the estate, until the next day when a squadron of soldiers in blue coats arrived from Saint-Pierre.

Lise spread the word in the Quarters that the captain had met with Monsieur and told him that some forty rebels had been captured, that most were to be executed, and that the soldiers had orders to interrogate anyone who might have known about or aided them. The soldiers stayed three weeks and succeeded only in breaking the arm of a woman who, like the others, had nothing to tell them.

Abeje procured a measure of rum for her from Floria, to dull the woman's pain while she set the bone. But she had little for her own pain, for the waste of young life in a man such as Luc, whom she was certain was now dead, except to think that he had followed the call of his heart. Perhaps that was enough.

Late in the year after the Rebellion there was an outbreak of fever in the parish. A rider came one day to the estate with a paper for Monsieur, asking him to give *the bondswoman Marie* permission to go with him to aid the sick at Mont Belcourt, a sugar estate to the east, and Lise came down to the Quarters with a pass for Abeje.

Abeje studied the fragment of paper marked with looping black lines. She had seen writing but a few times before. Letters were known to possess power, which was why they were forbidden to the bondspeople.

"A fortnight," said Lise, "he says not a day longer."

Abeje went with the rider to the Quarters to prepare a bundle. He was a young man. Not so unlike Luc, thought she. Tears sprang to her eyes for a moment, but she hastened them away.

"Thank you for coming along, Mémé," said the young man, "the people will be happy to see you."

They brought the horse to be watered at the barn, and there Abeje was able to speak to her brother.

It was night when they arrived. Mont Belcourt sugar estate was large, with some eighty or ninety bondsmen. Already a dozen had died and some thirty lay crowded in the Sick House. Two women showed Abeje to a hut where she could lay down her things and sleep for a few hours. In the morning she spent some moments alone, asking the plant spirits to guide her hands. Next she undid her bundle, as she had a great many smaller bundles of dried plants inside. She opened several of the bundles and made a strong tea to bring to the Sick House. The fourth bundle she opened was larger than the others, and full of an aromatic dried leaf. Having unwrapped the cloth she saw another crumpled among the leaves. Something placed there long before, and forgotten. She smoothed it out gently.

The rag doll.

The one Leola had made for her brother to take to his daughter. Years ago she put it with these leaves to keep moths away. Abeje picked it up gingerly, held it to her cheek. She prayed that this was not a sign, there in that place amid so much grief and death and danger, of something connected to Adunbi's lost child. She set the doll down, removed a quantity of the dried herb, and then wrapped the doll back up in the cloth.

A clear stream ran through Mont Belcourt, and there was a small pool near the Quarters where the people drew water and did their washing. After the first day in the Sick House, at twilight, Abeje went to the stream and immersed herself in the pool, clothing and all. She asked the water to carry away all sickness and fear and sorrow, and leave her clean and refreshed. When she returned to the Quarters the women found a dry dress for her and a shawl, and set her before a fire to rest with a dish of salt-fish and yams. The people came to greet her, pronounce their names and squeeze her hand. All the day there were new people, names and faces, yet she felt they were known to her. The first time she had travelled to another place for healing, all the new faces dazzled her eyes. But it was not so now.

Abeje finished eating and a woman took the dish away. A

young girl about ten years old came forth with a steaming cup that smelled of scorched maize meal and molasses. The firelight fell upon her face and Abeje's eyes played tricks.

Olivie.

She blinked and shook her head, but the girl was still there.

Olivie?

But not only Olivie. She saw her brother as a boy.

"Who are you, child?" she asked, scarcely able to breathe.

A woman came forward. "She is called Hetty, Mémé."

Abeje looked at the girl, tilting her head toward the woman. "Your mother?"

"*Oui*, Mémé."

She looked back to the woman, trembling. "And... you?"

"I am Phoebe, Mémé," said the woman.

"An Irishman brought you this child," whispered Abeje.

"*Oui.*"

Abeje fell forward to her knees.

"Bless this day!" she cried, clutching at her heart. "Oh, bless this day!"

The people gathered around, murmuring.

When Abeje spoke again she took Phoebe's and Hetty's hands in hers. The girl looked at her with big, clear eyes.

"Your father," said Abeje, "is my own brother. I am your *Tata*." The girl's eyes flew wide open and she looked up at Phoebe, who drew her arm around her and pulled her close.

"Holy One!" whispered Phoebe. Then she said, "The child knows I am her foster mother. My own baby did not live long." She brought a knuckle to her lips, then lowered it again and looked to Abeje. "Hetty is my joy!"

The two women gazed upon each other's faces, and then Abeje turned her attention to the child, her niece. Abeje told her the names of her parents, and how she came to be with Phoebe. She told the child her own name, given by her parents, in Iya's language, her grandmother's language, and what it meant. They remained there talking together until very late indeed.

The next night Abeje asked Phoebe and the child to sit with her by the fire. Phoebe nodded to the child, reminding her of some instruction.

"May I bring you tea, Mémé?" said the child.

"You must call me *Tata*, and I will call you your father's name for you. Alright?"

A big smile spread over Ayo's sweet face, but first she looked to her mother, who smiled back. "*Oui*, Tata!" said the girl, and scampered off to fetch the tea.

Phoebe told Abeje that Ayo spent her days at the Great House. Monsieur Belcourt had six children with his wife and Ayo was nursery maid to the two youngest, two girls a bit older than Ayo herself. Phoebe said these two girls doted on Ayo and treated her kindly, and, when Ayo was not occupied with chores, they included her in their games. So for now, Ayo was sheltered from harsh work.

Phoebe said that soon after Groom brought Ayo to Auxier they were sold to a slave trader who planned to take them in a ship to Trinidad, with a group of eight or nine others. During the voyage one of the women fell ill with a fever and a rash. The rash inflamed her skin so badly that at port the inspector thought it smallpox and turned the ship away. Having no other choice, they sailed back to Martinique and landed at Sainte-Anne, at the south end of the Island. When the sick woman survived, and no others were infected, it was believed she was only attacked by vermin. The trader had to sell off some of the group quickly just to recover expenses from the extra voyage. And that was how Phoebe and the infant Ayo were brought to Mont Belcourt, not so very far from where they started.

Each evening of that fortnight Abeje sat with little Ayo. She asked the girl to do her a great many favors just for the pleasure of seeing her smile and hearing her say, "Oui, Tata!" But more than that they traded questions. Ayo was a thoughtful child, curious and inquisitive, exactly as Adunbi had been as a boy. She wanted to know about her father and mother, about her grandmother and Abeje herself. During each day she considered all she was told and each night came with a fresh crop of questions ready for her aunt. Phoebe laughed, saying Ayo was always like that. "Like rain on the roof," she said of her daughter's endless questions.

Ayo told her what she liked and what she did not, what she did each day, and so on, but Abeje learned most about her from her questions. The way she asked, the way she frowned and nodded upon hearing answers. When Abeje sat with her the plant spirits also came, Mother Baobab, and her brother's spiky palm. Anaya came, and another, a flowering tree with white and yellow blossoms of five fleshy petals, arranged just so; this was known as *arbre de couleuvre*, the snake tree. Abeje asked them silently for the child's protection, for their strength and guidance.

One night she said to Ayo, "Do you know something, child, I have a gift for you, from your own father."

"A gift?" Her eyes widened again. Abeje brought out the rag

doll and placed it in the girl's hands. Ayo looked upon it in wonder, whispering, "My own father." Then she threw her arms about her aunt and said, "Thank you, Tata, thank you so! Can you tell my father his Ayo says *Thank you?*" Then she gazed at the doll again and frowned. Its eyes made of black thread seemed to look back. "But you did not know before," she said, "that you would meet me." And so Abeje told her perhaps the doll knew, and stowed herself away in the medicines. Abeje told Ayo who made the rag doll, and how Ayo's father had gone to Auxier to see her, all those years ago.

In the morning Ayo hugged the rag doll saying, "I call her *Claudine*. Claudine, Claudine...."

Phoebe smiled. "Claudine is a pretty name."

Though Ayo was cheerful that morning, Abeje noticed her to be sleepy, and, more than that, a certain shadow hung about her. Abeje asked one of the women to bring a cup of the bitter tea that was brewing for the ill. Some of the needed plants were found growing nearby, and so there was yet a good supply. Already some from the Sick House had recovered. Abeje asked Phoebe to fetch her should the child seem poorly, and she did not come all that day while she worked. But then that night Ayo began to cry. She leaned against Phoebe and whined, "So cold, Maman... so cold!"

"Bring her inside," said Abeje. They wrapped her in a long shawl. Abeje heard a voice say *Do not leave her side*. She lay beside the child on the sleeping mat. Fever came upon her, a spell that Abeje herself entered into as well. The hut became a grove where the plant spirits encircled them.

From the dark night rose the two spirits of Abeje and Ayo into a place of gentle sunlight. There they were, walking a road made of two paths, like tracks made by wagon wheels. On either side tall grasses grew, and among the grasses flowers of many colors. The child skipped and laughed, she gathered flowers, and seemed to say, *We will take them to Papa!*

The waves of grass became waves in the sea, tossing a ship. Three young ladies peered into the wind from a round window, two *béké* faces and one dark. Then came other visions that shifted and changed. Abeje saw Ayo's small fingers, playing upon a line of little white plates, that went up and down and gave out music. She saw cold white feathers that fell from the sky. Houses and wagons and roads such as she had never seen before. She saw Ayo much older, and her face much older still, a grandmother who sat beside a candle, with a pair of spectacles on her nose. She held a quill in her hand, and she wrote on a paper....

Abeje then left her niece, pulled away, drawn as a leaf in a current. Below her was the Grove; it breathed. The whole of the Island was breathing, here and there other groves and patches of the old plants, the ones that covered the Island before they were cut away for cane. The sea was swirling around the Island, breathing in its own way. The creatures of the sea were but plants with different structures, able to propel themselves within the body of the sea, to eat and be eaten.

All the next day Abeje was wakeful, but too tired to rise. She lay beside Ayo who slept, still feverish but tranquil now. The women brought water, tea and maize porridge. That evening Abeje went again into the stream to cleanse herself, and slept well that night. Next day, when Abeje returned to the Sick House she sensed the fever among the people had now passed its peak, though it would be some weeks before it was finally spent. She had but a few days left at Mont Belcourt Estate to do what she could, and the people there now knew the plants they could brew for medicine.

Ayo recovered and they had their last evenings by the cooking fire. Abeje taught her Iya's songs and she sang them to her rag doll, Claudine. The other children gathered round and wanted to learn also, and the songs became new when she heard the children sing them together. Abeje closed her eyes to listen. Their voices danced like the sun on the sea. She longed to see her brother. She had so much to tell him.

It was two more years before Adunbi earned permission from Old Monsieur to travel as far as Mont Belcourt to see his daughter, and it took him many Sundays of work to pay for his absence. When he returned her brother was much changed, reminding her of when he fell in love with his wife. He laughed and sighed when he told his sister the story of his visit, and he shook his head in wonder. Ayo, now twelve years old, looked just exactly like her mother, and was so clever. He said he would treasure those days all his life.

But that was not all.

Phoebe told him Madame Belcourt planned to send her two youngest children, Thérèse and Nicola, for schooling in Québec City, in the country of Canada, where Monsieur's son now lived. Madame Belcourt had relations there, and she meant for Ayo to go with the girls as their maid.

Ayo told her father that one day, up at the Great House, she heard the Belcourt girls speak with their mother. Thérèse asked Madame Belcourt, "Maman, why can't coloreds read and write?"

"I guess they are not smart like we are," said Madame.

"Hetty is smart," said Thérèse, meaning Ayo.

"That may be," said Madame crossly, "but God does not want coloreds to learn letters. Their place is for helping their Monsieurs!"

Later when the three girls were alone Thérèse said to Nicola, "Hetty is smart, isn't she?"

Nicola, who was the younger, said, "She surely is."

Thérèse looked at Ayo and whispered, "Would ye like to learn letters, Hetty? If ye could?"

"*Oui*, I would," said Ayo, a thrill of danger running through her.

"Why can't we teach her ourselves?" said Nicola.

"That makes trouble," said Ayo. She did not dare say more.

"When we are away in Québec City, then," said Thérèse.

Adunbi told Abeje how Phoebe held Ayo's small hand in hers, and he said to her, "She is your daughter," by which he meant to ask Phoebe's feelings. Phoebe nodded. Tears started from her eyes and Ayo wrapped her arms around her waist, around the only mother she knew.

"I want her to go," said Phoebe. "Anything the Holy One gives me to bear is worth this chance for her. To be away from here, maybe someplace better." To Ayo she said, "A mother may be away from you, but a mother's love you carry in your heart. Isn't that so?"

"*Oui*, Maman," said the child, hope and sadness both dancing in her large, clear eyes.

Abeje listened closely to everything Adunbi said. She did not like to think of Ayo and Phoebe parting from each other. And still, she remembered the visions of Ayo and her destiny in a faraway place, Québec City, in the Provinces of Canada. Abeje recalled she heard about this land from Luc. He told her of free people, whole villages, that lived among *békés* in parts of America and Canada. There might be bridges for Ayo. This child might yet cross to freedom, while she was still alive on this earth.

Adunbi had more to tell. On his last night at Mont Belcourt, Ayo had asked her father, "Is the Irishman who brought me to my mother still living?"

"Groom, child? *Oui*, he is."

"Can he read and write?"

"I expect so."

"Then when I can write, I will send a letter to him, for you."

"A letter..." Adunbi marveled. "Groom might be willing," he said, "if it be kept secret."

Ayo asked the name of Groom, the names of the sugar estate and the parish.

"I heard him say once," said Adunbi, struck with an idea, "that his wife has relations in America." Groom was married now.

"Then Groom's wife will get a letter," declared Ayo.

"From who, child? Not Miss Hetty Belcourt. That would be dangerous."

"No," said the child, gazing at her rag doll. "A letter will come from Claudine."

In another year, Ayo was gone away with the Belcourt girls. She left behind three old people thinking of her and praying for her every day.

Abeje found she could still call upon the spirits of the plants for her, since spirit-path did not know distance any more than dreams knew the dreamer. And in this same way she called them also for Phoebe, especially Anaya, to soothe the jagged edges of that broken heart.

Now and again the Holy One brought Abeje young people. Brought them as she was brought to the Obeah woman, to learn. They were sometimes with her as little as a day or a week, sometimes for years, it all depended. However long they had, Abeje sought to ignite in them the healing flame. She saw their spark, and the tinder of their nature. Spirit had marked them, sure enough, and it was to them she sang her own song. Abeje taught them to listen to the plants, to feel the messages, to join in their hands the vibrations of plant and person. She sang them her own song to show how one creature joins another. Her way would not be *their* way, no. That could not be taught. But her way opened a door for them.

Abeje's apprentices came to her in their young years, when they were wet clay. Solid enough to take shape, but still new. With her they became vessels of the healing. The girl Addie had quick hands, she set bones like no other. Tau and Pres pulled sickness from bodies like hauling boats onto shore. Camilla, so gentle, brought out new growth with a touch light as a feather. Bayard met Anaya, all on his own.

Eight years passed by after Ayo went to Canada. New faces came and old ones went, seasons turned, Spirit brought Abeje a young apprentice, another, and one more. Her brother and she trod the Earth, slept upon her, ate from her, helped nurture her creatures and helped bury the dead in her bosom.

One night Abeje dreamt of a big ship crossing the Sea.

In the morning Groom's wife appeared at the barns, looking for Adunbi.

She was a kind woman, getting on in years herself, and her

face was flushed from walking quickly. She said she had something for them. Adunbi went to find Abeje and they met her outside Groom's small house. There was a large shade tree with some stumps arranged beneath it and they sat there. Groom's wife drew a kerchief from her bodice, dabbed at her face, and then from the same folds in her dress took a pair of spectacles and a thick folded paper. There was writing on the paper and at once they knew. Adunbi took his sister's hand. They scarcely breathed.

The letter was addressed to Groom and his wife, and came from Canada, from Québec City. She pointed to the place on the paper that bore a piece of writing called the *address*, where a letter might be sent back. Inside, the letter bore the date: November 1st, 1833. Groom's wife read it out slowly. She said she was not so very good at reading, but they heard every word as if it were a song.

This was what it said:

> ...*at long last I am fulfilling my promise to write to you. So long has been its delay. I pray this letter reaches you and that you are still living, and that you can forgive me. Many events and many obstacles stood in my way. I am a grown woman now, as you will guess, and have learned a great many things, including my letters and also to play piano*...

Adunbi asked Groom's wife to read over the first part again, it was so much to take in all at once. She obliged, and then continued as best she could.

...TB and NB have been kind to me, and though life is not always easy I have been very fortunate in many ways. TB and NB returned to the Island two years ago in the company of their cousin and I stayed behind as there wasn't money enough for my passage. TB and NB told me on their return to Québec City that my mother had passed away. Apparently she fell ill, and in just a few days she died. They say she did not suffer much. This news was a bitter pain for me, but I feel she is at peace now, and I am grateful for that.

I also had another solace and that was in the form of a young man, Dax Rougeaux. Dax is a free man, a saddler by trade, who works in a shop not far from where we live. We have been acquainted now for about three years and he has become most dear to me. One year ago he asked for my hand, and then went to speak with TB and NB. They wrote to their father asking permission for me to marry, and also to allow that we make arrangements for Dax

and me to purchase my worth from them.
He did not object and so we have a plan.
Dax works hard, and indeed I am also
earning wages as I am often asked to play
piano music at parties and teach lessons to
children. I am very happy. We think we
may save enough in another two or three
years. TB and NB have gotten used to the
idea of free people. Québec City has been a
new world for them also. There are many
who say that it won't be long before all
people are indeed free.

Here Groom's wife mopped her face again with the kerchief. "I promise ye I won't tell about this," she said, "but ye must burn this letter when we're through." After catching her breath she continued reading. The letter went on to describe many things about life in Québec City, so many events such that Adunbi and Abeje felt transported across the Sea. It was as if they were there with Ayo, all these years gone by. At last she said,

I think often of you and the many things
you taught me long ago. I feel you with me
in my heart always, and I hope you know
I have never forgotten you. One day, God

willing, I will teach your songs to my own children.

Sincerely yours,

Claudine

After Groom's wife finished reading, Adunbi and Abeje were too overcome to speak for a long time. Adunbi took the letter from her saying he would indeed burn it right away, so as not to risk bringing trouble on anyone. They thanked Groom's wife very much for the great favor she had done for them.

All that day passed in wonder. That evening Adunbi sat by the fire holding his daughter's letter.

"I am very tired," he said. "We burn this in the morning. A little while I keep it with me."

He went to lie down in the hut and Abeje brought his supper in to him. She placed it beside the sleeping mat. "I am happy, Beje," he said, closing his eyes.

In the night Abeje dreamt she and her brother were once again little children, sitting on their mother's lap, chattering and singing and laughing together. Their little hands were soft, and Iya planted kisses on them. As young and small as her brother was, he was still big and strong to Abeje, her wise and clever protector. Funny that his hair was black. For some reason she thought she remembered it being white.

"Don't ever go away from me, Adu!" she cried, in her little girl's voice.

"I won't, Beje!" laughed he.

Iya held them and held them, and the stars sparkled above.

When Abeje woke in the morning, she saw her brother had not moved at all in the night. The letter lay on his chest, with his hand over it. His supper was untouched. And his body was cold.

That night they laid him in the ground beside Iya and Olivie. Groom came down to help dig the grave and also brought the hide of a goat. Abeje preserved a scrap of the letter where the address in Québec City was written, and the rest she left with her brother. The letter lay on his chest with his hand over it, as it had all night. They laid the goat hide over him and with it prayers that his animals would always keep him joyful company. Abeje broke their cooking pot and all placed shards on the grave.

The people brought her shawls and food and tea, and she kept vigil on the grave for a long time. She saw the Waking Star rise and set. The dream of them with Iya seemed to continue on. She watered the fresh earth with her tears. She had never known life without her Adu, but in truth she would never have to know. As long as she looked in her heart, her brother would always be there.

One or two months later Abeje awoke one morning with a feeling of great anticipation. She had no reason for this feeling, yet it flowed in all her movements. When she poured water for cooking she was suddenly reminded of the limestone cave in the Grove, and a place within where water formed a pool from a spring. After rains the spring gushed up with a force that made little flowing hillocks of water above the surface of the pool. Abeje could go now to the Grove most any time she needed to collect plants, as she had leave from the Monsieurs to do so. After all, she helped to protect their property.

So she went to the Grove, while it was still early, and set out toward the cave. As she approached she stumbled slightly and then felt her foot turn on some root or stone. She reached out, caught the smooth trunk of a small tree and fell toward it. She hugged herself to it. She breathed against it, feeling the life inside the tree.

Something inside her fell away.

She understood that the life of the tree was no different from her own. Opening her eyes she saw some ants treading over the bark.

These too were no different from herself. If they were not different, then what was *she?*

She was but salt in the water of the world. All of her elements were dissolved and were no longer separate from that which was *not she.*

She and *not she* were one thing.

Abeje felt no pain, but thought that surely this was death. That the moment had come. She thought of her brother, tall and strong like an old tree. He was also she, and she was he.

Abeje, the old woman, sat beside the tree, having sunk to the ground, for one moment or for all of eternity, she didn't know. The sun traveled a long way across the sky, shining through the leaves of the tall trees, changing shadows all the while. Her body became thirsty, and thirst moved her, as it once had moved her and her brother from the grave of their mother. She made her way to the cave and drank from a stream that ran down from the spring. Abeje seemed not to be dying or dead, but very much alive indeed. In fact she would always be, had never been born and would never die. A great peace overtook her. She became the very heart of peace.

After this did life go on as before? It was the same and also changed. Everywhere she went she met herself. Everywhere she found peace.

It lay behind all things, even sorrow and pain and fear. When she was not at work aiding sick and injured she looked after the little children, those who were weaned and not old enough for work. They followed Mémé Abeje around like little chicks. She taught them Iya's songs, as she had with the children at Mont Belcourt. And she told them stories, which were their great delight.

By and by, Groom's wife helped Abeje to write a letter to Ayo, another great miracle, so that words could journey back across the Sea and reach the child, now a grown woman, in the country of Canada.

> *Dear Claudine,*
>
> *The Holy One carried your letter to us. Now may this paper be carried and placed into your own hands. We had such joy to hear about you...*

Abeje told Ayo of her father's last years, such as she could recall. She told her how he chased off the snake that fell upon her when they were little babes. She told her how he spoke to his wife so gently, and how wild songbirds landed on his fingers. Lastly:

> *I am sorry to tell you now that your father died the same night after we received your letter. But he went on very happy, and he is with your mother, Olivie, now. Bless you*

Ayo. Bless your freedom and new family,
as both will surely come to you.

Love from Tata

Great changes would occur on their Island in the next years. In the year 1848 slavery was abolished at last. The people paraded in the streets of all the towns, singing, dancing, cheering, weeping, embracing....

Now many children went to school houses and learned letters. And sometimes, those who could not go to school had a chance to learn anyway. Such as at the estate where Abeje still lived. Many mornings she sat with the children on a rise that overlooked the Sea. Young Miss came walking up the hill with books and a slate and pieces of chalk. She was the granddaughter of the Monsieur's son, the one Abeje had helped to heal after the hurricane.

Young Miss taught the children; she sang songs about letters. Each letter was a friend who danced. They captured the letters on the slate with chalk, and they made them into words, and these words spelled out their future.

Freedom meant old Mémé could come and go as she pleased. She often went down to the bay, with her slow step and her walking cane. She went in the cool of evening, to sing and rest. One night she dreamt of her brother as a boy, a boy just becoming a man, with clear skin and hard white teeth and eyes black as wet stones. Her heart marveled at his beauty, and the sharpness of his mind. His young face floated before her, as he talked on all about the animals. The calves that followed him, and how he would not be outsmarted by that mean old nanny goat. He smiled and rolled his eyes at the admiration of the old woman, always his little sister, little Abeje.

Just a few days later the Holy One brought a new boy to her, one marked by Spirit, sure enough. He arrived alone and asked to see her. She was outside her hut with a basin of water, washing roots dug from the Grove. He stood before her, small but robust, shirtless and barefoot, wearing torn sackcloth trousers.

"I have a toothache," he said. Abeje saw no swelling, nor any crick in his form that would belie pain. When she didn't answer he tried again. "Well," he said, "it's my ankle. I turned it very badly." He made a show of limping in a small circle.

Abeje dried her hands on her skirt.

"Tell me why you are really here," she said.

He shrugged, then pursed his lips to keep from smiling. "I just am," he said.

His name was Silas, but she called him *Awon Okun*, Iya's name for sea turtle, because in his eyes she saw the tranquil Sea. He slept on a mat in her hut, ate from her cooking pot and learned very quickly. In time he was no longer a boy, but a man. A healing man, who didn't need Mémé to teach him anymore. His song was strong and bright. And he was a kind man, just as her brother was, and helped old Mémé in most everything she did. When he learned from her she sang her song for him, her last apprentice. Then she gave him her story.

Now, on the rise overlooking the Sea, sits old Mémé Abeje, under the great tree, her skirts spread about her in a wheel. Her Awon Okun will be down below at his hut, taking care of ailing people, and Abeje can be at ease. She is the tree who spreads the canopy, and she is the one who sits beneath, as if she were her own mother, and her own child. And she just wonders.

Children gather around her in a loose ring. Some lie with eyes closed, but she knows they are awake, ready to hear a story. The hot breeze carries the Sea, the scattered shadows of the leaves moving over their quiet forms.

"There now, children," she says, "let us take our rest." Abeje breathes, her eyes travel to the horizon, to the beginning and end of the world, and then back to the children.

"Now I will tell you the story of how my mother became a star. How she rose up on her wings into the Heavens.

"Most stars rise and set together in pictures, you see—the Hunter, the Serpent, the Lion, and so on. But this star follows her own path. She is the one that we see sometimes in the evening and sometimes meeting the dawn. She is the brightest. The Waking Star, mother of us all."

II

Nelie and Azzie

Philadelphia

1949

One o'clock on a sunny Sunday afternoon finds Cornelia Montgomery and Azalea Hubbard on their knees, bent over an early flower that has pushed its way up through a crack in the sidewalk. The clack of heels on the pavement and laughing voices surround them. Folks are still trickling out of church, shaking hands and paying respects, after the post-service social hour.

It's a tiny thing with velvety red petals and an interesting yellow sprout in the middle, made all the more curious that, despite the sun, it is not yet spring. But here comes an adult voice, Cornelia's mother to be exact, saying *Get on up*, because they aren't little girls anymore, and their mothers (who are sisters) didn't wear out their fingers stitching those Sunday coats and dresses so they could ruin them playing on the ground.

Between them Nelie and Azzie have a passel of brothers and sisters, but none are as close as they. Now they stand brushing off their hands on their skirts, one pink and one mint green, smiling slyly at each other and saying, *Yes ma'am.*

Azzie's little brother Junior sidles up to them, holding a piece of cake in a napkin. It's his curse to need eyeglasses, in thick black frames, frequently askew as they are now, having been knocked to the side by a squeezed-past elbow or handbag. The girls reach out as one to straighten them.

Nelie and Azzie skip to school each morning with their arms linked. They trade dolls and candy and hair ribbons. They whisper secrets, make up rhymes, find the same things funny and suffer the other's indignities as their own. Azzie is a little bolder, Nelie's singing voice is a little better and her coloring is lighter and decorated with a few of her father's freckles. But not much disturbs their harmony. It is said that, like twins, the two share a soul.

After supper Edwin Montgomery relaxes into the brown brocade sofa, his well-muscled arm on the rest, sipping a cup of his evening coffee with chicory. His stomach bulges a little now with age, starting to go soft in the middle. The four children sit scattered to his left, glued to the radio set, Nelie with her eyes fixed on the dark sky beyond the street light out the window.

He rests his eyes on her, this daughter he sometimes thinks is both closest to his heart and most out of his reach. *Come on back from the moon now, Baby,* he says to her as he often does. And she turns to him with that pressed-lip smile, the same as his wife's, that says, *it's you that's being foolish.*

Violet Montgomery is finishing up her work in the kitchen, putting leftover potatoes and the remains of her famous roast chicken with rosemary away into the icebox. There is a sudden knock and a voice calling her name. She pulls the latch and opens the door to see her brother-in-law, his face a knot of anxiety, in the dim yellow light of the hall. It's Azzie, she's taken sick, fainted right at the supper table and he's got to run around to the drug store to ring Dr. Leventhal, and please come quick.

Violet grabs her coat and calls out to her family, who have already collected behind her. She steadies her voice, giving instructions to the wide-eyed children, there's school tomorrow. She locks eyes for a moment with her husband, before running out into the cold night; she already knows it's bad.

Dr. Leventhal is a white man, but a kind one, not heartless, like some others, as the adults are heard to say. He came to Nelie's house once when her mother was ill after her youngest sister was born. He'd removed his hat and spoken in low tones, always careful to say mister and missus.

Nelie imagines a heart like a little valentine, pinned to the inside of his lapel, red paper with white lace edges, hidden so that he looks like other white men on the outside. Like the owner of the Five-and-Dime, for instance, whose icy blue eyes make the back of her neck prickle. Mr. Ainsworth is one of those who hasn't got a heart, but rather something like a lump of coal rattling around inside an old coffee can. Nelie and Azzie refer to him in this way, Old Coffee Can.

It is a penchant of Nelie's, this seeing into the interiors of people. These perceptions she whispers to Azzie, who, without a second thought, takes them on as her own. It's not just Old Coffee Can who has a secret nickname, but a whole community of neighbors and schoolmates whom Nelie has at one time or another observed. There is Mrs. Snowflake, called for the thing inside her that is like the snowfall inside a globe, ever since her husband passed on, and her grown children moved far away.

There's a boy in Azzie's class whom all the girls adore, with a ringing laugh and a flashing smile. He has a sun inside, young and strong like himself. Also in the neighborhood live a shy mouse and a sticky box of half-melted candy, a book with hard edges, a razor-strop, a barrel of lemons, the curlicue beside a line of notes on sheet music, a sad hat, a bloody nose, a green forest, a chessboard knight, lost money, lost time.

Sometimes the things are fearful and Nelie would prefer not to see. Azzie will grab her by the hand and they'll get going a game of fast hopscotch, or skip rope and sing all the songs they know, or make some kind of race or contest until they are out of breath and laughing.

One day they spent all afternoon making a picture with their Crayolas and shiny paper saved from last Christmas, of two magical birds perched on the branch of a cherry tree, whose elegant necks bent together and whose black eyes sparkled. They wrote their names at the bottom in their child's cursive and decided at last to hang it on the wall above Nelie's bed.

That night Nelie floats in a yawning darkness greater than the night itself. She is deaf to her father's assurances that whatever it is their cousin has, Azzie will be just fine. His steady hands on their shoulders as he shepherds them off to bed, his efforts to smile and joke placate the others, but not Nelie. A fear has struck her like nothing she's ever known.

Azzie is no longer safe at home, in her own bed, as she is, but in another place. By morning, Nelie half asleep under the crocheted coverlet and their two magical birds, sees the strange, high white walls, and something tiny and sinister up inside Azzie's throat, a scattering of yellow pin-points bubbling up, like the thick, wet yolks of raw eggs.

Her mother is home again. Nelie is the first up and finds her at the kitchen table still in yesterday's clothes, eyes red, she hasn't slept. Violet Montgomery enfolds her daughter in her arms and explains that Azzie has been taken to the hospital. She pronounces the name of a disease, and the names of the good doctors and nurses who are caring for her. Aunt Virginia is there, and they can maybe go visit in a few days when Azzie is settled.

Settled.

Nelie feels a battle underway in her cousin. It has to do with those minuscule, evil, yellow yolks. Nausea claims her insides. But she nods to her mother, keeping her mouth shut, and everything to herself.

An ache sits with Nelie at her school desk, the shadows of the day are the most noticeable things. Beneath a windowsill, behind a door, thin lines where wall and ceiling meet, the black spaces seep together like ink. Miss Carmine knows her as a dreamy child, but today catches something in her eye that has her let Nelie alone. She will know what that something is presently, since by noon all the teachers will have been notified, that one of the Hubbard girls is gravely ill, and all should be aware, it is after all contagious, and they must keep a close eye on their pupils.

The day is interminable, or so it seems. After the final bell has rung, the shadows follow Nelie along the bricks and pavements home. Her mother has her watch some of the younger children, and Nelie sits hugging her knees on the stoop until it's time to come in.

In the Montgomery apartment, a card table has been added to the usual supper table to accommodate the Hubbard children.

When supper is served Edwin says grace and Violet adds a prayer for Azzie, that God help her to get better quick and come home, and Rosalie, the baby, bursts into tears. She carries on so that Violet takes her into the next room and rocks her little niece until she is calm enough to eat. What would normally be a boisterous meal is naturally subdued.

The next afternoon Nelie's mother has devised to keep her busy with errands. Nelie has spent the day again with the shadows. The ticking of the clock has taunted her, the round face an adversary lording over her with a threatening hand.

Nelie presses her mother's list into the pocket of her dress and buttons her coat. A box of soda is needed, a quart of dry beans, some green thread from the Five-and-Dime, a bread pudding is to be delivered to Mrs. Snowflake who is having difficulty with her rheumatism.

Nelie shifts the warm parcel in its wax paper into the crook of her elbow and knocks on the heavy, brown-painted door. The aged woman has been resting on the sofa by the window in the front room. The apartment has a similar plan to Nelie's home, but differs in most every other way. She feels suddenly suffocated by the smell of mothballs.

Mrs. Snowflake has heard about Azalea, what her poor mother must be going through. Have mercy. She tugs at an earlobe, an ancient habit that reaches as far back as her own girlhood, way back to a sunny meadow when a boy cousin had tickled her with a feather.

Something has stolen her gaze now outside the window, the few stark trees and the white sky. Nelie perceives anew the snowfall, somewhere behind the milky eyes, or at the glass that divides the sitting room and the street outside, somewhere between now and a long time ago.

Wednesday afternoon: Nelie rides the streetcar with her mother, on their way to the hospital with several shopping bags for Aunt Ginny. Nelie is carefully transporting a large, rolled-up piece of paper tied with a string, the picture of the magical birds that she has just before unpinned from the wall above her bed.

Azzie's room is at the far end of a soap-green corridor. A starched nurse leads them there and Nelie is not permitted inside. She sits on a small bench opposite the door after her mother disappears into the room with the nurse and the shopping bags and the rolled-up picture.

The door opens again a few minutes later when the nurse comes out, and just before it closes Nelie glimpses something she wishes she hadn't. It's only Azzie's arm, just from the elbow down, visible from behind the half-drawn curtain and lying atop the white sheet. But the color is wrong, ashen where it is usually rich and warm, and worse, as Nelie's mother and aunt are just moving her upward in the bed, the arm slightly jiggles, as if there is no resistance, no life in it at all.

Nelie stifles a scream with both hands, and keeps it down during this one time that she will sit on this bench, in this green corridor, as far away from Azzie as she has ever been. She keeps it in all the way home, until she can't hold on anymore. Her mother gets her up off the floor and onto her lap, big as she is, sobbing like little Rosalie, but more terribly, because she is too old to be that innocent.

For a time. For a time.

Finally, Nelie is lulled by the faint smell of lavender, her mother's cheek against her braids. Her mother says, *Remember that day at the shore?*

Nelie recalls the long, hot train ride two summers ago, the children bouncing on the seats between the adults and the picnic baskets, clear down to Atlantic City. The ocean was a marvel of sand and shells and darting fish, and way out beyond, of fishing boats and soaring gulls. She and Azzie had waded out along a sandbar, so far it seemed they might cross the whole Atlantic. Most marvelous was the refraction of the sun on the water, on the small waves and in the air as the children splashed and screamed. Azzie was a laughing silhouette amid all that glitter.

Let's remember that day, says her mother, *it was an especially happy day. There's going to be a lot more. Don't forget.*

Thursday morning Nelie awakens from a dream of refracted light. A glint of sun pierces the edge of the curtain, ringing from the windowsill. This is the change Nelie notices all day, a light coming in and sucking the ink from the dark places. All day at school she floats, subsumed in a dry bubble that muffles the raucous voices around her to a distant murmur. What is loud is the light. She almost can't tell the time above the classroom door, the numbers are so faded from a glare over the clock face. It is neither cold nor warm, but expectant, so that she has begun to jump at small movements, turning quickly to see what has flickered at the corner of her eye.

By Friday the gleam has grown in intensity and spread. White surfaces seem powdered with glitter dust, a passing automobile burns hot, even though the white sky is still clouded over. There is a bare branch that scrapes an insistent finger against a classroom windowpane.

Nelie sits still at her desk, gripping the metal ring on the end of her pencil. One might think her tense attention is for the arithmetic lesson, intent on the blackboard floating before her in its white ether, but it is not. She is waiting.

It comes.

A movement outside the window. She whips her head around, her heart pounds. It was there, she is sure, the flash of an iridescent wing, silver, blue and purple feathers. She doesn't know if it is joy or terror she feels.

Nelie runs toward home, walks, circles, with her book bag hitting at her ankles, through the streets searching every tree and rooftop, every light pole, fence post and patch of sky. She might see a squirrel, a brown or black bird, an alley cat. These are no more than loose leaves or gravel. Her ears hear nothing. She finds nothing.

Friday changes to Saturday. Someone has filled Nelie's ears with cotton wool. The shadows and even the light have somehow given over to it, the muffled sounds become an almost soundless world.

Sunday. One week is all since the last one, it can't be. The whole Atlantic has been crossed since then. The cotton wool is a filter, or perhaps it is changing, giving over again to something new. Nelie, the whistle of the tea kettle, a low gust of wind through a pipe, a bicycle bell, the church bells. The ring of a coin dropped on the stone stair. Everyone has gone inside the church now.

Nelie has one hand on the iron rail. A wind, her handkerchief, she turns to catch it, it eludes her. Something shimmers up ahead in a tree.

The highest branch, bare and black, perched there, the golden claws clutch. Silver, blue and purple feathers ripple like water, the arched neck reaches up, and the flashing eye meets Nelie's own. It opens wide its wings, spreads its tail like a Chinese fan and leaps.

The high white walls, and the white sky. And the iridescent bird flies higher.

Nelie's soles ring out against the brick. Faster now. Because maybe, just maybe, she can catch up.

Rosalie

Philadelphia

1964

It's the last day of February, and Rosalie Hubbard, a junior at William Penn High School in North Philadephia, is scratching out a few notes for her next article for the school paper. Cassius Clay has just won the heavyweight boxing championship and there's been dancing in the streets. Rosalie is covering current events, and so much is happening. President Johnson has launched his War on Poverty, boys are getting sent over to Vietnam, only to come back dead or crippled or stuck on dope. Civil Rights workers are murdered in their beds. There is tragedy left, right and center, but there's a lot of hope too.

Rosalie's notes are a mess, since she's riding a bus, up Broad Street, to her evening course at Temple Secretarial. The course is alright, especially since a school friend of hers is taking it with her, and the two girls share a desk. It takes the edge off the tedium of the typing and shorthand drills. Rosalie likes journalism, and photography too, but doesn't dream of such a career for herself, not yet anyway. She does have her eye on a secretarial future though, at least as something to fall back on. Not many kids she knows go on to college, especially girls.

Stuffing her notes into her school bag, Rosalie gets off early, and so she has time to stop into her favorite record shop. She buys that Coltrane album, the one with Johnny Hartman she's been hearing so much about, with money earned from babysitting. She holds it gingerly as she rides the bus up Broad Street, thinking how pleased and impressed her older brother, Junior, will be with the record.

A few months later, Junior goes to see *Goldfinger* at the Boyd Theater with his friend George Stewart, whom they always tease for having a first name for a last name. George has a high, barking laugh, loud and unstoppable, and five minutes after the blonde in charge identifies herself to Bond as "Pussy Galore" the usher comes over with his flashlight and makes them leave. Out on the street George keeps on laughing, and the next week Junior takes Rosalie to the show instead. He owes her one, especially since he appropriated the Coltrane album for himself, and then went and loaned it to George.

Rosalie is the youngest of the three, once four, Hubbard children. She dearly loves her parents and siblings, her Aunt and Uncle and cousins, and earns excellent grades in school, though she does not stand out socially. She is pretty in a quiet way, her mother says, and that little bit of acne will no doubt fade with time.

Rosalie likes to read, likes to dance, she likes to run up and down the stone stairs when she goes to the library, with her heels clickety-clacking and her book bag swinging from her shoulder. She likes Coca-Cola with ice cream in it, her mother's yams and roast, and is awed by the young people who march and protest and fight against Jim Crow.

Goldfinger is pretty good, though Rosalie likes it less than Junior, who digs it for the gadgetry and the you-know-what. But even Sean Connery doesn't hold a candle to Sidney Poitier, if the truth be told. Mr. Poitier has just won an Oscar for Best Actor, the first black man to win it, and Rosalie got to write it up for the school paper. All the girls at school are in love with him, and Cassius too, of course.

At the Boyd, Rosalie sinks into her plush seat. She glances over at Junior. He's slouched down, leaning on an elbow, and flashes of color make the lenses of his glasses appear opaque. His long legs are folded up so his knees almost block his view of the screen. Junior never did so well in school but he does have a knack for mechanical things. Momma said once that Junior could already read at the start of first grade, but after Azzie died that changed.

For Junior it was like the letters got all shaken up inside his mind, and didn't line up into words as they did before. His teachers started to say he was slow, though he surely never was. He can fix a radio or a blender or just about anything you want. Many nights he lays a towel over the kitchen table and covers it with neat rows of tools and the parts of whatever he's working on. Silent and concentrating, with his clever hands moving like big brown spiders. He graduated high school last year and one of these days he'll start at the technical school, but for now he's still a delivery boy for Freihofers Bakery. Junior likes being out on his delivery routes, no one telling him what to do, swinging around the neighborhoods in the bread truck and running up to stoops and porches. He looks good in his uniform too. Cap and bowtie.

The day after the movie, Sunday, Rosalie drops in on her cousin Nelie after church. Nelie is twenty-five and married, with a baby daughter, Lea. Rosalie has a shopping bag with some things for the baby that her mother gave her to *bring up to Cornelia*. Momma and Aunt Violet are the only ones that call Nelie by her full name.

Nelie and Cal have a little one-bedroom apartment on the second floor of a row house about ten blocks from the Hubbards. It is tidy and comfortable with wonderful light in the front room from the south-facing windows. It's late May and warm, so these windows are open. Rosalie, like most of Nelie's visitors, doesn't bother with the bell.

"Hey, Nelie!"

Her cousin sticks her head out. "Hey, Baby, come on up."

Rosalie climbs the stairs and finds Nelie in the kitchen, in a cute little sleeveless dress and apron, fixing up a pan of potatoes for supper. The baby is lying on a blanket on the front room floor, trying to get herself up to crawling position. Rosalie sits down on the floor.

"Lea-Lea," she coos, to the baby's instant delight. No one can pass those fat little cheeks without putting at least thirty kisses on them. "Where's Cal?"

"Up at Marty's," says Nelie. That's Cal's best friend. He and another friend of theirs go up there most Sunday afternoons. *Roosting with the roosters*, Nelie calls it. She's not a big talker though, preferring to save her words for when they are most needed. Some people talk a lot without saying much, Rosalie has noticed, and some people say a lot with just a little. Her cousin Nelie definitely belongs to the second group, which is a lot more rare than the first.

Soon Rosalie hears voices from down on the street, two or three women, and then, "Nelie Porter!" called out from below. Porter is Nelie's married name. It's a friend of hers from the neighborhood along with a sister and a girlfriend, they want to come up

102

and talk to Nelie about something important, if she has a minute. The three women don't bother to wait for the answer though, and a moment later burst into the living room. Nelie asks Rosalie to mind Lea and takes the young women back to the bedroom. Nelie has visitors like these on a regular basis, women mostly. They need her advice on matters of the heart, and sometimes other business, money, health, the things that matter most to folks. Sometimes it's playing the numbers, but Nelie doesn't do that. Maybe she could, but that's a dangerous territory, and a slippery slope, as they say in church.

Rosalie picks up a storybook that's lying on the sofa and reads it to the baby. It's not much of a story actually, just a dog and a ball and running and jumping, but Lea is enthralled. Her big brown eyes soak up everything and her babble makes Rosalie laugh, which makes the baby laugh, and they laugh together. Then Lea falls to one side, bopping her head, and starts to cry, until Rosalie plays Five Little Piggies with her and she smiles again. About a quarter of an hour later the bedroom door opens and the women emerge. The girlfriend is weeping into a handkerchief and the two others hustle her out the door clutching her arms on either side, calling back *thank you!* to Nelie, who sees them out.

"Her man's running around like she thought," says Nelie with a sigh, as she drops down onto the sofa. "She'll be alright though, long as she don't marry him."

There's some clatter on the stairs and Cal comes in, which makes the baby shriek with excitement. She knows her daddy's footsteps. Cal is tall and thin like Junior, but broader in the shoulders. He kisses Nelie on the neck and hands her a brown paper bag with a few groceries. "Hey Little Momma," he says to Rosalie, and scoops up Lea. "What's shaking at high school?"

"Readin', writin' and 'rithmatic," says Rosalie.

"Okay, okay, what else?" Cal tries to steal a look at her between swats at his eyes from the baby.

"Got a newspaper article I'm working on about the new chess club at school."

"Good game," Cal grins, nodding his approval.

"We better get going," says Nelie, "I want to bake these potatoes over at Aunt Virginia's." They head out together into the hall, Rosalie with the baking pan, Nelie with Lea, and Cal bumping the baby carriage around.

Out on the sidewalk, it's a fine afternoon to be out walking. The flowers on Nelie's dress catch the sunshine, and Rosalie thinks she may need one just like it. When they get to her house she'll have to show Nelie what she's done, with Momma's help, with one of her sister's cast-offs.

Sunday dinners at the Hubbard home are regular and lively occasions, rivalled only by the Sundays at the Montgomerys when Aunt Violet, Nelie's mother, is hostess. In either case the participants are the same, the growing clan that centers around the two sisters, Virginia and Violet, and now includes the spouses, children, and sometimes friends. Not everyone makes it to every single dinner, but the seats around the table are always full, the conversation bubbling, and the grace always includes the line, *May our cup continue to runneth over.*

Most Sundays Rosalie's big sister Loretta is there, making sure, together with Aunt Violet, that their mother doesn't work too hard. Loretta has an apartment by herself, living the glamorous life of a switchboard operator at Bell Telephone. Her apartment is decorated in the latest style, with drapes and throw pillows in garish colors that Rosalie thinks are the ultimate, but that give the older generation a headache. The thing about Loretta is that she's twenty-eight and unmarried, a fact that bothers exactly two people, her mother and her beau. Nearly every Sunday night, cleaning up after dinner Aunt Violet says, just to tease, "Ain't Charlie proposed yet?" And Momma sighs, "Only about seven times. That girl is too independent for her own good."

Not long ago, over at Loretta's apartment painting their nails the sassiest shade of pink, Rosalie asked her sister if she planned on marrying Charlie.

"Yeah, I will," Loretta said, smiling slyly, "soon as I'm ready."

The old radio set in the Hubbard parlor is draped in a white linen runner with lace edges tatted by Rosalie's Grandnan Hubbard on her father's side, who came up from the South with her family, as did her mother's mother around the time of the First Great War. Most everyone Rosalie knows has people in the southern states, though she, like many of her peers, has never been to visit. Upon the linen runner are arranged numerous framed photographs of the Hubbards and the Montgomerys, Aunt Violet's family. And above these on the wall hang the older generations. Among them are Rosalie's maternal grandparents, Papa Dax and Grandnan Emily Rougeaux, on their wedding day. Rosalie never knew Papa Dax, the one exception to the family's Southern origins. He came down alone from French Canada, as a young man. All those pictured on the wall are now gone, while those on the radio set still dance with the music of life. All but one.

Rosalie was only three when Azalea, nearly twelve and second to oldest, was snatched away from them by a case of diphtheria. So Rosalie's memories of her sister are scant. She remembers her laugh, like a handful of jingle bells, and how once they danced at a birthday party, the song was "The Gypsy." In fact they danced to that song every time it came on the radio, during the After Supper Music Hour. Rosalie remembers how Azzie shook her finger, mouthing the spoken line in the song.

She looked at my hand and told me
my baby would always be true,
and yet, in my heart I knew, dear
that somebody else
was kissing you…

Last year Rosalie found a copy of *The Best of the Ink Spots* at the record shop on Broad Street. That day when she arrived home the house was empty. She unwrapped the record, laid it on the family hi-fi and played "The Gypsy" over and over again for an hour. Why was that song so terribly sad? Well, because the man knew he couldn't keep his baby, even though he loved her so, and that the other part of his heart still held on to the dream. Rosalie drenched herself with tears.

Nelie named her baby daughter after her, which is one way her name carries on. Well before the baby was born Nelie knew she'd be a girl, and that her name would be that most beloved one,

Azalea. They call the child Lea, she isn't Azzie after all, and needs the name to be her own too.

Rosalie also remembers the funeral. Or rather she remembers a lot of black clothes, and the awful sound of adults weeping. And she remembers Aunt Violet's lavender smell, as she carried her down a hallway, saying they were all of them in God's hands.

There weren't words to describe the axe-blow Rosalie's mother Virginia experienced when her daughter died. The blow that never ended, and stretched out into the most unbearable future. In those first terrible days and weeks the grandmothers of the community took over, directing prayer meetings and casseroles in a steady stream. They bore up Virginia and her family as they themselves had needed it in the past, and would likely one day need it again, asking God collectively for His grace. May He lighten the burdens He allowed them to carry. May He teach them to accept even His reasons, however unknown to them, for calling little children Home.

When the initial storm cleared and life presented itself as needing to go on, Virginia was blessed to be supported, especially by her sister Violet and her oldest child, Loretta. Loretta was fourteen and steadfast, and would have rushed to her mother's side had she not already been there. She saw the care of her parents as her first duty, while her aunt stepped in to help with the younger children. With time, Virginia and Lionel Senior righted themselves again, though Lionel lost that easy merriness he'd always had, and Virginia remained just slightly bent forward, as if walking perpetually into a strong wind.

The other person perhaps most deeply affected by Azzie's

death was Nelie, so much so that the family feared they might lose her too. "Two peas in a pod" didn't describe what Azzie and her cousin had been, because they were far closer than that, and far less alike. Cornelia, who was shy and dreamy by nature, was like a balloon held to earth by Azalea. Azzie protected her fiercely and never gave a second thought to the ways Nelie was different, nor to the unearthly things Nelie seemed to know sometimes.

Indeed that balloon hovered indecisive for a time. When Nelie fell ill and lay abed with her eyelids fluttering, they feared the diphtheria had returned. But Dr. Leventhal, who came to the house straight away and examined her with the utmost concern, assured them it had not. This was a case of shock, he said, packing up his black satchel. He prescribed a regimen of broths and rest and massages to the feet. Harold Leventhal had learned the scientific care of the body in medical school, but his own grandmother had taught him a thing or two about the care of the soul.

When Nelie recovered she said that Azzie had visited her in her sleep, and that Azzie had shown her Heaven. She said Azzie was happy and had asked them all to please not be sad. Azzie was with God, and God looked a lot like the Goodyear blimp, but much shinier.

Virginia held the hand of her niece and said, "You say Azzie is happy, Honey? And that she's with God?" And Nelie said *Yes'm* all over again.

Virginia looked at the ceiling a long time.

"Okay," she said at last. She touched her heart, and said again, "Okay."

A year or two later Virginia began to notice pains in her knuckles.

Now and then she had to put down her cooking or her sewing, or whatever she was doing, to rub on some ointment. Then she began to feel it in her knees. Lionel rang Dr. Leventhal who stopped in the next evening when he was in the neighborhood seeing another patient. The doctor lived with his family up at Oxford Circle and this was back when he still made house calls. He asked her to come into his office just as soon as she could so he could examine her more thoroughly.

Loretta insisted on going along to the appointment. She sat in the waiting area when her mother went in, flipping nervously through copies of *National Geographic*. The doctor had his white coat on at the office, unlike the regular suit he wore on house calls, and a red and brown checkered tie. Had Mrs. Hubbard been more tired than usual? Dr. Leventhal wanted to know. Yes, come to think of it she had. Any skin rashes? Fevers? Yes, that too. Had she perhaps noticed any hair loss? At this Virginia lost a little of her balance. The brown and red checkers of the doctor's tie suddenly loomed forward, and it was harder to make sense of what he was saying. But she caught the word *Lupus*, and the recommendations for extra rest, and to take care not to get too much sun. He said it looked like a mild case, a blood test would be needed, and asked her to come back in a month. She did, and continued to see the doctor every few or several months when the symptoms flared. This was a malady without cure, and was commonly crippling and even fatal.

Blessedly, up to now, Virginia's illness has progressed only very slowly. Her mother's "spells" always hold a special dread for Rosalie, a little line of terror that seems to drop from the top of her head down into the pit of her stomach, every time she comes home from school and finds her mother in bed. Like after last

Thanksgiving. Rosalie had found her mother in bed with a fever and dialed up Loretta, who came as soon as she was able, bringing with her a small package from the drugstore. Rosalie wanted to stay home from school the next days but her parents wouldn't allow it, reassuring her that this was nothing serious or new, and that Aunt Violet would be coming over. Still, each time her mother falls ill, Rosalie harbors the secret fear that her mother, in her absence, will somehow slip away.

Rosalie's junior year in high school winds up filled with parties and dances and awards for outstanding achievement. She receives a special certificate for her work on the school paper, and even wins a prize at a dance for her rendition of the Nitty Gritty. Anyone can do the twist, you know, but not everyone can pull off the Nitty Gritty. There's a girl's prize and a boy's prize, and Rosalie takes home a smart, pink, faux leather handbag. The boy's prize goes to Chester Washington, a graduating senior, who receives a shiny brown wallet on a chain. Ches dances the next song swinging his new wallet around like a cowboy, making the boys laugh and the girls swoon, just like he always does.

The last day of classes is a Wednesday and, as her mother has a doctor's appointment the next day, Rosalie goes along. Rosalie has the new handbag with her, which is already accumulating the essentials: coin purse, compact, a little jar of Vaseline and a miniature package of Kleenex, comb, hairpins, chewing gum, nail file, nail varnish, bus schedule and transfer, subway tokens, address book, two ballpoint pens. She is just locating her nail file when she overhears Dr. Leventhal's red-headed secretary, Miss Carey, on the phone talking about the girl who comes in to help in the office twice a week. "Had to leave without notice," she says, "in case you know of anyone." Miss Carey has had to come in today, instead of visiting her mother out in Cherry Hill as she usually does.

Rosalie completed her secretarial course a few weeks ago and has a perfect "To Whom it May Concern" letter of introduction on her bureau at home. The next day, without telling anybody, Rosalie takes the bus back up Broad Street to the doctor's office. She has the letter folded in an envelope in her handbag, and has on her best skirt and jacket set. Miss Carey is there in the office as before, and looks up at her when she comes in and walks up to the front desk.

Rosalie breaks out in that prickly sweat under her brassiere that always comes over her in debate club matches, or if she needs help from a white salesclerk.

"Ma'am, I'd like to help out in the office," she says, "just until you can find someone else." She hands Miss Carey the letter. The chilly silence that follows is broken by the appearance of the doctor, exiting the examination room behind an elderly patient. He looks curiously at Rosalie.

"Hello Miss Hubbard," he says. Sometimes being formal is his way of being friendly. "Your mother is alright, isn't she?"

Rosalie says, "Yes sir," and explains why she's come today, that she's done a secretarial course and has brought her letter of introduction that describes all of her skills, and her high marks besides.

Miss Carey turns her bewildered and mascaraed blue eyes on the doctor and says, "Oh I don't think…." But he plucks the letter from her hands and looks it over.

"Well this is splendid," he says, "this will be just fine!"

Rosalie can't quite believe her ears and breathlessly answers

111

"Yes sir," again when he asks if she has time to stay for an hour or two right now.

He says Miss Carey can show her how they run things and she can start tomorrow morning. "I know you are anxious to see your mother," he says, smiling at Miss Carey. Rosalie is elated. She has landed her first job.

By early July, Rosalie has been on the job three weeks, Thursdays and Fridays. The other days she babysits, helps her mother, sees friends, and shuttles large bags of books to and from the library. One afternoon she comes up the street to her door just as the postman is hopping down off the stoop. She lets herself in and bends to pick up the letters and circulars, calling out to her mother in the kitchen. Virginia is sorting the laundry she has just pulled in off the line. Rosalie sees there's a letter from her mother's cousin Martine on top of the stack. Momma will be happy about that.

Martine is Virginia's older cousin, on her father's side, who lives up in Montreal. In Canada. Martine and Virginia struck up a correspondence some years before Rosalie was born, after Papa Dax passed on and Virginia wrote to notify the family. Martine's reply, expressing condolences and describing her childhood memories of Dax as a young man, touched Virginia with its tenderness and eloquence. Much later, when Virginia's letter carried the awful news about Azalea, Martine wrote back entreating her to "write her heart" any time she was able, because Martine herself had lost a child, her boy Gus when he was only seven, and she knew. It helped Virginia to have someone outside the immediate family to confide in, still does. Some worries or pains are just too close.

Rosalie leaves the mail and her bag on the table and takes

the milk bottle from the Frigidaire. She's getting a glass from the cupboard when she hears her mother say, "Oh, Lord." Virginia is standing at the table looking at an envelope with her reading glasses on. She wears them on a chain like a librarian so they are always handy. Her hands are shaking. It's from the Draft Board, addressed to Lionel Hubbard, Junior. Rosalie feels the blood drain from her head.

"What's it say?"

They sit down at the table. Virginia tears open the envelope and reads the letter over. There's not much to it. Junior is to report to the Draft Board office for a medical examination on August first. Failing to do so is punishable by law. Rosalie's mind races. Hasn't she heard that sometimes boys are found unfit for the army because they limp, or because they have a bad ear or something? What about Junior's eyes? He can see things just fine up close, but without his glasses anything past an arm's length is a complete blur. Surely a pair of glasses would be the easiest thing to lose in a jungle war zone; they can't have soldiers running around blind as bats. This is the topic of the evening, of course, once the men return home from work. Junior tries to make light of it. "They can't take me," he says, giving Momma a squeeze. "I'm Mr. Magoo!" But late in the night, stumbling to the bathroom after a few fitful hours of sleep, Rosalie passes by Junior's room and sees the glow under the door that means his reading lamp is still on. She thinks about knocking, but doesn't.

"How are you this morning, Rosalie?" asks Dr. Leventhal, looking over the roster of today's patients.

"My brother is being drafted," says Rosalie, without preamble. She can't help it.

The doctor looks up from the roster and stares at her a long moment.

"Has he been for the physical yet?"

"No sir, not yet."

"Doesn't he wear glasses?"

"Yes sir, he does," she says, a spark of hope rising in her chest. "We're thinking maybe they won't take him on account of that."

"Why don't you bring him in, and I'll see what I can do."

Junior comes in at the end of that same day. After the examination the doctor has Rosalie take a letter, which she then types up on the office stationery that the doctor signs with his gold-tipped fountain pen.

It would not behoove the Armed Forces to induct this young man... the letter reads.

Behoove, thinks Rosalie on the bus home with Junior. She has a habit of collecting words and this one's a keeper.

But the letter from Dr. Leventhal doesn't work. Junior tells it all later on.

The white officer in charge scoffs at Dr. Leventhal's letter, when Junior hands it to him.

"This isn't grammar school," he says, "this is the United States Army." He looks down at the form Junior has filled out, and the line where it states his occupation.

"Delivery boy," says the officer. "Drive a truck, do you?" Junior says yes. "Then you can see just fine."

He checks the final box on the physical record where it says

"Fit for Service" and stamps it with an induction date. September 19th. Less than two months away.

Virginia's next letter to her cousin Martine has a desperate tone. She's praying to God every day and doesn't know what to do. Two weeks later on a Tuesday night the telephone rings, an international call from Montreal. This is the first time Virginia has heard her cousin's voice, unfamiliar over the crackling line, in nearly forty years.

It says, "Bring him here."

The next Sunday, after dinner, a family discussion ensues.

Lionel Senior still respects the late President Kennedy and remembers his famous "Ask Not" speech. He has questions about loyalty and duty, service and sacrifice, though not for a second does he take lightly the fate of his own son. Uncle Edwin, Aunt Violet's husband, weighs in, citing the Second World War, and the Black battalions that served with honor against Hitler.

"That may be so," allows Charlie, Loretta's beau, "but this is different. This is the white man's war. There ain't no Hitler over there. The Black man is the white man's cannon fodder." Dr. King has spoken out against the war in Asia, and Brother Malcolm too. Charlie has never followed the Nation of Islam, but he still refers to the now ex-minister in this way. Indeed, Black boys are being drafted at twice the rate of whites, and are suffering double the casualties of white soldiers. That's cannon fodder, if ever there was such a thing.

The women are less concerned with the politics. "If he goes up to Canada," says Aunt Violet, "he may never be able to come back."

Everyone stays quiet after that. The meeting, for tonight at least, is adjourned.

The last Friday in August, Rosalie finishes up at the doctor's office and decides to drop by her sister's apartment before going home. It's five o'clock and Loretta will be back from the switchboard at the Bell Telephone building. Fridays she starts early, seven a.m. When Rosalie arrives Loretta is out of her work clothes and in her slip and dressing gown, the Japanese silk one printed with purple grape leaves. Her long, hot-combed hair is up in a French twist, and she is ironing a shiny silver party dress.

It's obvious, notes Rosalie with a measure of envy, that Loretta has inherited the elegance of their mother and their aunt. In their youth Virginia and Violet Rougeaux were both beautiful, and also gifted in the art of enhancing that beauty. *What is it about those two?* folks used to say. Edwin Montgomery and Lionel Hubbard had come out on top of a large pile of eager suitors, winning their engagements each in his own way. In Edwin's case with gentle kisses, and in Lionel's, a pair of sizzling eyes.

"Where's Charlie taking you tonight?" says Rosalie from the sofa.

"Up to the City," says Loretta, turning the dress over to iron the other side. By "City" she means New York City, which means Harlem. She doesn't mind shaking it once in a while at a nice nightclub.

The heat of the afternoon, the smell of Loretta's perfume, the hiss of the iron and the end of the activity of a busy week soon conspire to make Rosalie's eyelids droop. Before she knows it she's waking up to the sound of the telephone ringing, and the sun is slanting in at a much lower angle. She hears Loretta answer in the next room.

"Momma, Momma, she's right here. She's with me, she's fine. Came right after work."

Rosalie staggers up and over toward the bedroom where Loretta has the phone in one hand and the receiver to her ear. She glances at Rosalie and gives a gesture with her free fingers meaning not to worry. "Okay," she says, "okay, we will. Charlie's coming any minute now. We'll see you soon."

"All hell's breaking loose up on Columbia Avenue," she says. Just last month race riots raged over Harlem and Rochester, and everyone knew it could happen in North Philadelphia too. Rosalie had read a recent newspaper editorial that called North Philadelphia a "tinderbox," describing the heavily grieved black community as at a near breaking point with the white police force.

"Is it a riot?" whispers Rosalie.

"Maybe," says Loretta. "As soon as Charlie gets here we're taking you home. Momma was scared to death you were still up at Dr. Leventhal's." The Broad Street office is only a few blocks from the Columbia intersection.

They haven't even knocked before Virginia flings open the door and drags them all inside. She bolts the door behind them and embraces them savagely. Loretta sees their father coming up behind them from the kitchen.

"Where's Junior?" she says.

"On his way," says Lionel Senior, doing his best to calm the situation with his steady voice. "He just called over here from Freihofers."

"You all heard anything else?" says Charlie. Lionel gestures for him to follow, he's got the transistor radio on in the kitchen and wants to leave the women alone for a spell. Loretta leads her mother to the sofa and sits her down. Virginia is trembling. Something wild has sprung up in her eyes.

"I'm taking Junior up to Montreal," she says, "soon as I can." Lord knows she can't afford to lose another child.

Unhinged. That is the way the world feels to Rosalie during the days of rioting. In fact, ever since the draft letter she has felt this way. Now smoke spills over the sky and turns the sun a bloody red. Church leaders, her father among them, remain in close conference and go out in teams trying to quell the chaos. Her mother forbids the children from going out at all, except to Aunt Violet's, which is only four doors down. Nelie is there with the baby as their apartment is nearer to the fray. Nelie, who wraps an arm around Rosalie's shoulders, reassures her they'll get through.

By Monday it's all over. On Wednesday evening Rosalie calls Dr. Leventhal on the telephone to ask if the office is open that week. It is, but the doctor certainly understands if she would rather not come in. The shopfront windows downstairs are broken, but nothing was disturbed in the offices upstairs. Rosalie has her parents' permission to go, as they feel sure the fury has been spent. Folks need to see the doctor and it's time to pick up the pieces. This will be her last two days at the office. School starts up again next week and Rosalie will be a senior. All of it is hard to believe.

What she isn't telling anyone outside the family is that she is about to accompany her mother and brother on a journey to Canada, just after classes begin. It won't do for Momma, what with her pains, to travel back alone. Loretta will look after Daddy, just to put their mother at ease. He could survive if he had to though, on steak sandwiches and coffee and the *Philadelphia Tribune*.

Last Friday night when they were all assembled at the table Momma declared her intentions. Daddy, as a formality, reminded them of the other considerations, and everyone else stayed quiet, including Junior. Finally Lionel Senior turned toward Junior, and said, "What do you have to say, Son?" This was his life after all, and he was a man now.

Junior looked around the table, then down at his hands, and said with soft-spoken finality: "I don't want to kill nobody."

Rosalie hovers anxiously at her bureau, opening one drawer and then another, not knowing what to pack. Half an hour goes by and all she has in her suitcase is a nightgown and a hairbrush. If anyone on the train asks, they are headed to Montreal for a cousin's wedding. Junior will bring only a few items of clothing, a photograph of the family, his father's silver wrist watch, and what cash they can get together. The train fare is terribly expensive. Rosalie can get what school assignments she's missed upon her return, as she'll be out of school a week or so. No one is too worried about that for a change.

It's four a.m. when they board the train at Pennsylvania Station on 30th Street, and they catch the sunrise over New York City. Rosalie and her mother do, anyway. Junior is asleep. Up through the Hudson River Valley, they spend the long hours playing pinochle, napping, walking up and down the aisles, gazing at the passing landscape and cracking sunflower seeds. Momma busies herself with her knitting bag, making a muffler and stocking cap for Junior out of balls of soft, gray wool. The Montreal winters are so bitter. Rosalie reads the new Steinbeck memoir, recommended by her English teacher. Junior has a copy of *You Only Live Twice*. George Stewart gave it to him the night before they left, and has written on the inside cover:

> *Junior, you candyass. As soon as my number comes up I'm heading up there too. I'm going to steal your girlfriend, so make sure she's pretty. I'll miss you a lot. GS.*

A few times Rosalie takes out the French textbook she was just issued at school. French class suddenly seems a lot more relevant, in light of recent events. Her mother has explained that their family in Montreal belongs to a largely English-speaking community, but that the city and province speak mostly French. She tries out a number of phrases, tries to interest Junior. He humors her with a few *bonjours* and *mercis*, but then drifts purposefully away.

Later on they put in another chapter of their long-standing critique of the songs of the day. For Junior, musicians and their music fall generally into three categories: *cool, Mack Daddy,* and *fruity*. Little Richard, The Beatles, and The Kinks are cool. The Four Seasons and The Beach Boys are fruity. Coltrane is Mack Daddy. Rosalie agrees on what's cool, and gets Junior to admit he likes "Dancing in the Street." That Martha can sing. Junior calls her *choice*, as he does all three Ronettes and all four Crystals, which pretty much means he'd marry them all. If they'd have him.

Rosalie likes those syrupy love songs like "Walking in the

Rain" and "Cry Baby," that Junior doesn't go in for. She harbors a sensible but romantic heart. She has never been on a date, but there have been three or four boys from school or the neighborhood who have caught her attention, and starred in more than a few soft-focus daydreams.

They glimpse the Catskills and the Adirondacks, and the lush pastures and changing forest along Lake Champlain, with its wide expanses of water and snowy peaks that sometimes appear in the distance. Virginia has packed far more lunch than they need, and three tired-looking men traveling to Utica gratefully relieve them of some of the extra hard boiled eggs, pickles, bread rolls with cheese, and green apples. One of the three men lets out a whistle. "Holy Jesus, potato chips too."

Late in the day, at a place called Plattsburgh, the conductor comes through the car joined by a uniformed officer with a cap bearing a crest and "Canada Customs" in gold letters. Virginia grows more and more nervous as he comes closer, checking tickets and asking passengers if they are carrying fresh fruit. Rosalie looks over at Junior, who puts his finger to his lips.

"American citizens?" asks the officer.

"Yes sir!" Virginia blurts out. "We're going to Montreal to my baby cousin's wedding." She hands them their tickets. "It's going to be beautiful, you know, she has the dress all picked out and everything!"

The officer nods, and moves on.

"My, oh my..." breathes Virginia, sliding down in her seat. Junior mouths, "smooth" and Rosalie giggles with relief.

Not two hours later they arrive at Windsor Station, grand stone archways and all, in the heart of their destination, the city of

Montreal. Cousin Martine's son Marc-Pierre, forty-five years old and balding, but otherwise the picture of his mother, picks them easily out of the crowd. He shakes hands warmly with everyone and directs them outside to his blue and white Edsel, where he hefts their three suitcases into the trunk. A short drive later they arrive at a block of familiar-looking brick row houses. Flower boxes overflowing with pink and purple blooms perch on the stoop of number six. Dusk is taking over and the buildings and walkways stand in shadow. A few moments after ringing the bell, Martine is waving them inside, exclaiming "It's them!" to the other sister, making her way heavily up the hall. Cousin Martine, in a neat green dress and grey hair held back with combs, looks them over between embraces and further exclamations. Cousin Elodie, or Didi, is decidedly older and stouter, and dressed in navy. What's left of her white hair clings to her scalp in thin plaits, but this does nothing to diminish the air of authority about her that is immediately evident. The children will call them *Auntie*. Marc-Pierre apologizes for having to leave right away, but says he'll see them again soon.

Auntie Didi pats down Junior's arms and murmurs something to Martine.

"She says you're sweet," Martine says in her lovely, lightly accented English.

Didi next stands before Rosalie, taking her face between her leathery old hands. Her milky eyes bore into Rosalie's with an unexpected intensity. Rosalie would be unnerved if she did not perceive them emanating kindness. "She has the Rougeaux eyes, that's for sure," pronounces Auntie Didi. "And she is made of fine cloth." When Rosalie looks puzzled Martine explains that means a person listens and speaks with a special sensitivity. Rosalie isn't sure what to make of this but feels flattered just the same. She looks over at Junior, who just shrugs and smiles.

In front of Virginia, Elodie frowns. She takes the younger woman's hands, squeezes them, and then exchanges a look with Martine. "My dear, you are not well at all," Didi says.

They are all a bit unnerved, but Martine smoothes things over. "We'll speak of that later," she says. "Right now let's get you settled in."

Rosalie and her mother will stay in Martine's room. Martine will bunk with her sister and Junior will sleep on a pallet in the parlor, as the sofa is too short. They eat an early supper of pea soup with bacon, stewed greens and a baguette that Martine slices into chunks on the table. The Aunties inquire about Rosalie's schooling, and cluck their approval over her summer job in the doctor's office. They want to know if Junior works hard and if he attends church regularly with the family.

The hours of the evening merge with the rivers of bygone days, aided by two heavy black-paper photograph albums. The sisters point out who is who and who did what. Here is a picture of their own father, Dax's oldest brother. Do they know why Papa Dax left Montreal? Virginia knows it had to do with seeking a job, but it wasn't something her father ever spoke too much about. And did they know he was named for his grandfather, a free man here in Montreal, who married a girl who was born into slavery on an island in the Caribbean? And that one of her forbears was known to be a great healer? That sort of thing runs in the family, don't you know, and the second sight too. *Nelie*, thinks Rosalie. The second sight. She never thought of it that way before, but it makes sense now. All those visitors asking her advice all the time. The Aunties seem very matter-of-fact on these last points. Their words carry no greater embellishment than they do when remarking on who was a farmer and who worked in what industry.

As for Virginia's father, Papa Dax, what happened was he got into some trouble when he was a very young man, working with the railroad unions for labor reform. There was a situation one night when a gang of company men came in to break up a union meeting. One thing led to another, one of the company gang ended up dead and three union boys were indicted for murder. Dax was one of those boys. The family knew Dax didn't stand a chance against the company lawyers and so under the cover of night they sent him packing. He was just about Junior's age, says Martine. By the time the constables came to arrest him he was gone. He went to New York first, where he had a sister.

"Your Great-Aunt Eleanor Higgins," Virginia told the children.

"The musician?" asks Junior.

"That's right."

Papa Dax then continued on to Philadelphia to work in the shipyards. A few years later he became a union steward, a position he maintained all his working life. Rosalie is entranced, but ever so tired. Auntie Didi smiles at her, as she tries to stifle a yawn, and orders everyone to bed.

In the morning, the Aunties are in a hurry to discuss some business with Virginia. Martine gives Rosalie and Junior a few heavy Canadian coins and a hand-drawn map of their district, Little Burgundy, showing the Rue St. Antoine and the Rue St. James, and the Canal-de-Lachine. They shoo the children out the door, telling them to go look around. The day is crisp and brilliant. Being

124

a weekday the streets are quiet at this hour. Rosalie is enchanted with the French street and shop names. They find the Canal and walk over a bridge of old industrial steel. A lonely freighter laden with lumber chugs along at a distance. They stop into a diner and eat some kind of mess called *poutine*, that is not wholly unlike certain dishes fixed by ladies from church back home.

Hours later they return to the Aunties' house where Martine and Didi are in the kitchen making sandwiches. Junior is always ready to eat again, but Rosalie isn't hungry. She leaves Junior in the kitchen and goes to find her mother in the bedroom.

Rosalie is met with a pungent smell when she opens the door, and the sight of her mother lying in the bed, covered up with a heap of blankets.

"What's going on?" Rosalie asks, confused. Momma seemed just fine this morning. "You ain't sick, are you?"

"Oh, Honey, this is some voo-doo or other," says her mother drowsily. " Auntie has me wrapped up under here with oil and leaves and God knows what all. I couldn't say no."

"Yeah, okay," says Rosalie, not knowing what else. Spotting something that draws her in, she steps over to the chest of drawers. A small framed photograph of her sister Azalea sits there, together with a flickering candle inside a white votive. Her mother opens her eyes just barely.

"I sent that picture to Auntie Martine after Azzie was sick," she says. "Auntie Didi brought it in *for my dreams*. I do believe I've been seeing my little girl..." she trails off, but then says to Rosalie, "I'll just be a little while, you go on. The truth is all this is making me kind of sleepy." Two or three seconds later Virginia is snoring to beat the band. In fact she sleeps the rest of the afternoon, rises briefly to take a little supper, and goes off to bed again.

The next day is similar, with the Aunties eager to get Rosalie and Junior out of the house. Marc-Pierre has taken an hour or two off work to show them the sights. Rolling along in the Edsel, he gestures generously in all directions, pointing out all sorts of historical landmarks: the Basilique Notre-Dame, the Musée des Beaux-Arts, the Oratoire St-Joseph, the Place d'Armes. They take a short walk through the Jardin Botanique, vibrant with autumn colors. He leaves them back at the house with a wave. "You will feel at home here soon," he says to Junior. "I promise."

The afternoon is spent at the house. The Aunties get Junior to try fixing the kitchen clock, which is inconveniently slow, and Rosalie spends a couple of hours studying French and reading in the parlor. Their mother, it seems, is back in the bedroom full of strong-smelling vapors, fast asleep somewhere under all the blankets. When she finally wakes that evening she shuffles back to the kitchen for some of Martine's chicken soup with chives and dumplings. "I don't believe I have ever slept this much in my life," she says, declaring the obvious. Rosalie and Junior exchange a look, but Auntie Elodie brushes off her hands like everything is in order, ushering Virginia back to bed.

The next morning is notably cooler, what with the changing of the seasons. Rosalie is awake first, and gazes at the lace curtains and the pale blue sky as her dreams recede. She rises quietly, dresses and sets about combing and pinning her hair into her usual 'do. Leaning forward toward the small mirror atop the chest of drawers, she catches her mother's image stirring into wakefulness.

Virginia yawns and sits up. She stretches. Rotates her wrists and flexes her fingers.

"I don't know what's come over me," she says in wonder, really awake now for the first time in three days. "I feel miraculous."

This is Friday and the Aunties' marketing day. They load up Junior with packages from the butcher, the fishmonger, the fruit-seller, the grocery. Virginia has more energy than the children have ever seen in her. Her usually wind-bent frame has sprung up straight like a sapling. She wants to go in every shop and exclaims over every curiosity. Auntie Didi smiles with particular satisfaction, while Martine shows her the specialties of each locale. Rosalie and Junior look on as if their mother had suddenly sprouted a pair of wings.

Later on at home Virginia chatters up a storm with the old ladies. She wants to know the secret behind the broth from last night's soup, and she'd like to make a special preserves pie for after supper. While they eat, every funny story in their family history occurs to her, and she laughs louder than anyone. She looks repeatedly at the kitchen clock, now running perfectly thanks to Junior, and exclaims every few minutes, "Still right on time!" By nightfall she quiets down and begins to yawn again, though still radiant with this new energy.

That night after the Aunties retire, Virginia unrolls Junior's pallet and plumps his pillow. She kisses her son and tells him not to stay up too late. After tomorrow night he'll have the bedroom, she reminds him, and a proper bed. The train will be waiting to take her and Rosalie back to Philadelphia on Sunday, so soon. Their mother goes off to take her time in the bath and Junior couldn't care less about the bed.

He stretches out on the pallet, still dressed, and folds his arms behind his head. Rosalie lies back on the sofa and the two of them stare at the shapes in the whorls of plaster on the ceiling. "See anything?" asks Rosalie.

Junior is quiet, but then says, "You going to write to me?"

"You know I will," says Rosalie. "You going to write me back?"

"You know I will."

An hour later Rosalie and her mother are in their night clothes and have settled into their reading. There's a soft knock at the bedroom door. It's Junior, edged in the dim lamplight from the parlor. He steps into the room with a grave face.

"Momma," he says.

Virginia opens her arms and he collapses into them, his muffled sobs filling the room. Rosalie sits down on the bed on his other side and wraps her arms around them both. Her tears go down the back of Junior's collar.

Soon enough Junior is quiet and Virginia strokes his cheek. "You've got your whole life now," she says. "Things happen that we don't expect. And that's what we *can* expect."

There is such tranquility in her voice that it takes over the room. It ripples across her children and soothes them like her lullabies when they were little.

Junior sits up and wipes at the back of his neck. "Girl, you made a mess on me!" Rosalie apologizes. She's still the sloppy baby, always was.

It's Saturday, the last full day for Rosalie and her mother. Didi has declared she will be doctoring Virginia one more time. "What

128

more could she do to me?" Virginia says as she walks the children to the door, eyeing the forty-pound sack of salt a young man delivered during breakfast. Rosalie and Junior step back out into the neighborhood, to roam around again and see what they can see. Junior says he wouldn't mind getting some more of that poutine. Rosalie wants to go to the dime store on Rue Notre-Dame and buy some stamps and postcards to send to folks at home. Maybe a little something for Baby Lea. Marc-Pierre will be coming by that afternoon, with his wife Pauline, to talk about what Junior might do for work. Until then, the bright morning spreads out before Junior and Rosalie. They still have plenty of time.

At supper Martine tells them they are expecting some special visitors afterward. Rosalie supposes there will be some more relatives, maybe from Auntie Didi's late husband's side, or maybe elders from their church. Martine goes to answer when the bell rings. Rosalie and Junior are helping to clear the table, while Didi is at the sink and Virginia makes coffee. But it isn't any church elder who enters the room following Martine, as Rosalie is startled to see. It's two girls in stylish dresses and a tall boy in a suit with a skinny tie. More relatives, yes, on that point she was right. Estelle and Berdine are Marc-Pierre's daughters, Martine's granddaughters, and Jean-Louis, who reminds Rosalie of Nelie's husband Cal, is a cousin on their mother's side. "We thought you young people might like to go out for the evening," says Martine with a knowing smile.

Virginia glances anxiously at Rosalie, but Junior, who has perked up considerably, says, "I'll look after her for you, Momma." And Didi adds that these are good children, *Very good children.*

The new cousins say a respectful goodnight to their elders

and whisk Rosalie and Junior down the stairs, and out into the night. Berdine clutches Rosalie's arm. She's an inch or two shorter, but she's twenty-one and miles more sophisticated. "We're going to show you the real Montreal," she says, and the three of them break into sparkling laughter.

"Here's our taxi," says Jean-Louis at the curb, opening the doors of Marc-Pierre's blue and white Edsel. "Girls in the back!" He shoves Junior into the front seat and jumps behind the wheel.

"Café Villenueve, first," says Estelle. "It's still early."

"Our cousins are American," cries Berdine. "We've got to start them off slowly." Which causes everyone to giggle and guffaw all over again. Jean-Louis flips the car into gear and pulls away more than a little too fast. *If this is slowly*, thinks Rosalie, squeezed between Berdine and Estelle, *I can't wait to see what's next!*

The place is alive with soft jazz and conversation, tinkling glasses, cigarette smoke, and all the glamour of a Harlem nightclub. Rosalie notices, as she will the whole night, faces of many colors mixed in together. Even the band, with its beautiful lead singer, has a white drummer. Berdine leads the way to a table where they'll sit and get acquainted.

A waiter with a little round tray approaches the table, and the cousins order drinks in French. When the waiter looks to him, Junior, who has never ordered a drink in his life, clears his throat and says, Bond style, "A martini, shaken not stirred." He winks at Rosalie, who smiles and then blushes, suddenly aware of five pairs of eyes intently upon her.

"Coca-Cola, *s'il vous plait*," she squeaks and everyone bursts out laughing again. Jean-Louis and Junior are soon engaged in a conversation about automobiles. Estelle and Berdine want to know everything about life in Philadelphia, though they turn out to be extremely well-informed. Friends of theirs pass by to say hello, whom they greet easily in English or French, always introducing Rosalie and Lionel, their American cousins. The band plays a captivating version in French of that popular new song, "The Girl from Ipanema."

Before long they're off in the Edsel to another club, a bigger one, close enough to the first place that it hardly seems worth it to drive. This is the place for dancing. The hour grows later and the crowd denser. The music swirls around them, intoxicating. A young man asks Estelle to dance and they take the floor, followed by Berdine with Junior and Jean-Louis with Rosalie. The young man Estelle is dancing with leans over to say something close to her ear. Estelle smiles and shakes her head. He says something else and she laughs. Rosalie wouldn't mind if Jean-Louis paid her that kind of attention, or if somebody else nice did, but that familiar pang of disappointment is soon washed away by the thrill of the music.

"Look at Little Sister!" shouts Estelle, noticing Rosalie's moves. Berdine claps and Jean-Louis shouts out *"Ouais!"* Rosalie feels as though she could go on dancing forever. If only tomorrow didn't ever have to come.

Somewhere around midnight they hit another venue, the smaller downstairs of Rockhead's Paradise, where the music is decidedly Bluesier, and later still, finally end up at a diner, where they order ham sandwiches, famished from all that dancing.

At last, they pull back up to the curb in front of the Aunties' home. Jean-Louis turns off the motor and no one speaks for a minute.

"Little Sister," says Estelle, "you need to save your money and come back next summer." Rosalie thinks that is a marvelous idea. Maybe she and Loretta could come. Maybe even drive up with her beau. Charlie likes to drive and would do anything Loretta asked him to.

"What are you doing next weekend?" Jean-Louis says to Junior.

"No plans," he says. He has never had fewer plans.

"Alright," says Berdine. "We'll take care of that, don't you worry."

Too soon it's morning, time to get ready, time to go.

Rosalie opens her eyes after just a few hours of sleep. The colors of dawn steal in through the lace curtains. Turning over she sees the other bed empty, the blankets folded and the stripped sheets in a little bundle next to them.

She tiptoes past the parlor where Junior is still fast asleep and over to the kitchen where she hesitates on the threshold. Momma and Auntie Martine are there at the table, warming their hands around their coffee cups and speaking in low voices. For all Rosalie knows they have been up most of the night as well.

The two women smile up at her, and her mother waves her over to join them.

"Here's my baby," says Momma.

A framed photograph lies on the table, of a much younger Martine with her late husband and their two little boys. The older one must be Gus, thinks Rosalie, the one she lost. Auntie Martine stirs her coffee thoughtfully. Rosalie takes in the delicate way she holds her spoon, the fine lines etched around her eyes. If hardship is part of the necessary clay of life, grace is the hand that has shaped it. Rosalie swallows at the sudden lump in her throat.

Marc-Pierre and Pauline come to take them to the station. Pauline has a small gift for Rosalie wrapped in tissue paper. It's a diary, bound in thin powder-blue leather, with the words *mon journal* embossed on the front cover in tiny gold script.

On the platform the tears are inevitable, and there isn't a whole lot more to say. *Take care*, and *Be good*, and *Write*, and *Don't worry*, and that most inadequate of phrases, *Love you*.

Rosalie and her mother board the train, take their seats and wave out the window. Marc-Pierre has an arm around Junior's shoulders and Pauline stands at his other side, her hands occupied with her purse and handkerchief.

Momma takes Rosalie's hand in hers as the train pulls away and gains speed, huffing and screeching, whipping through the city. They cross the St. Lawrence River, and head south toward home.

Sometime later Virginia gets out her knitting bag. Junior's going to need another muffler. A spare. Rosalie takes out a ball point pen from her handbag, and her new powder-blue diary, which she opens to the first page. She watches out the window, at the trees, rivers and buildings speeding past. The train rumbles across a trestle over an arm of Lake Champlain, and then enters an area of dense forest. Rosalie is just imagining someday writing an article on rail travel when the train emerges from the trees and shoots out straight over the open water.

The arc of tracks follows a curving line of land scarcely wider than the train itself, with the blue expanse of water on both sides extending almost as far as the eye can see. In that second there seems to be hardly any motion at all, just an unbroken sky, and some distant mountains, and everything invisible on the other side.

Martine

Montreal

1925

At twenty years old, Martine Rougeaux lived with her parents and her younger brother Maxwell on the Rue Normand, in the district of St. Antoine. Her sister Elodie, the oldest, lived several blocks away with her husband and three children, and her brother Albert-Ross was just married and living just a little further over in Saint-Henri. With the two oldest married, and Martine working steadily as a domestic, Papa and Momma laid their focus on Maxwell, seeing to it that he finish school and maybe even go on to college. Martine stayed out of the tussle. Maxwell didn't exactly adhere to his parents' ambitions, even when Momma enlisted Martine to help him with his studies. Her brother's lack of interest baffled her. Martine had had to leave school five years earlier and missed it dearly.

Often enough she sat with Maxwell in the evening, his history or English book open on her lap, while he leaned back in his chair, tipping it back on two legs, and walking his own feet up the wall.

"The War of 1812," she'd say.

"Barneymug that shit," he'd say, smirking as Martine would hurriedly reach to close the bedroom door. Momma did not abide foul language.

"Have you heard that new song?" he'd say next. "That one

that goes, *Saint Louis woman with her diamond rings, pulls that man round by her apron strings....*"

He had a good voice, she had to admit, but she'd say instead, "What is wrong with you?"

And he'd say, "Aw, you sound just like Momma. Why don't you come help me figure it out?" They both played the piano, Papa had left them no choice on that, and she would relent, leaving the War of 1812 for some other time.

Like the majority of the men in the community, Papa was for years a sleeping car porter with the Canadian National Railway, spending the better part of every month away on a train and working twenty-hour days for twenty-one days straight. When he was at home he slept most of the time. And he sat by the fire with his pipe and listened to his children play the piano. Momma was the one who kept the order, made sure the wheels of the household kept rolling, with chores and school work, and all manner of community commitments. The study of music was obligatory in the family, with lessons paid for with hard-won funds for the older children, who then had to turn around and instruct the younger siblings.

Papa's grandmother, Hetty Rougeaux, had taught him to play as a child. When Martine was small he came across the remains of a spinet piano, half burned up in a saloon fire and ready to be carted away by the garbage man. He hauled it home in a wagon and set it up in the tiny family parlor, where he and his youngest brother, Martine's Uncle Dax, worked on their days off to replace the damaged parts. Papa bartered with the piano tuner, when the time came, who left with a keg of Papa's home-brewed beer. That was the beginning of all the music. The Rougeaux children were to have a skill that paid. If they enjoyed the music that was a bonus, but it was certainly not a requirement.

The Rougeaux boys might find work in the cabarets, hotels and nightclubs, and the girls might teach lessons, or accompany singers at private celebrations, since the nightclubs were no place for them. If the boys played the clubs they were not to take up with any dancers, as they were considered one step up from prostitutes, if that. The pillars of their community did not embrace the girls who went around *in their drawers*, such as did Martine's childhood friend Lucille Travis.

All the children turned out to be fine players, if not legendary, and inevitably some enjoyed it more than others. Martine was one who found the music to be a living thing in and of itself. When she put her hands out to play it was as if the keys stretched up to meet her fingers. The music was eager to live, and the piano itself was there to do its part to let it be born. Saturday afternoons she taught lessons to a handful of children whose families could spare the ten cents she charged per lesson. And she sometimes warmed up playing with melodies her father made while working.

Papa didn't play himself anymore. Years of unending labor had stiffened his fingers so, but time had refined his ear. "See if you can do something with this," he'd say, and sing a few notes in his rough bass. If he liked the results she'd hear the tenderest words he would allow: "That's nice." And he might give her a little pat on the shoulder.

Papa didn't work for the railroad now, since with the help of his family he had expanded his beer brewing into a successful small business. He had painstakingly invested in bottles and equipment, during his years as a porter, that eventually filled the tiny basement of their row house from floor to ceiling. Albert-Ross, Martine's older brother, drew out the lettering for the red and white label, including the beer's slogan—*Enjoy a Rougeaux Today*—and many a customer did just that. Prohibition brought Americans in droves to Montreal's saloons and nightclubs. When Papa turned forty he was able to retire from the railroad and run his business full-time. Martine was still a child and spent many evenings with her siblings cutting the sheets of labels with scissors as they came from the printers, and sticking them on the filled bottles with rollers and pots of glue. Later these bottles would be collected and boiled and refilled again.

Momma divided her time between her paid domestic work, helping Papa, and, as usual, commanding her household. She still managed to devote considerable energy to the betterment of the community through the church and the Colored Women's Club, which among many other projects sponsored the lending library. With God's grace the Rougeauxes now paid a mortgage, rather than rent, a source of great pride, and had their eyes on furthering the education of Maxwell, the youngest child.

Martine worked in service to a well-to-do family over in the Westmount district. The Braddocks had two children away at boarding school, a gardener who came twice a week and a full-time cook, the short, plump Caroline Tulane, from Martine's own neighborhood, who played the organ at church on Sundays. Martine kept the house. It was her third position since leaving school, and she'd been there since March. It was June now.

The previous position, one she'd had for three years, was easier. She took care of Madame Lambert, a decrepit old thing who slept most of the time; she needed bathing and spoon-feeding, and sometimes reading to. Aside from these things her duties were light, which allowed her the time to sneak into the library, which was vast. If any of the other servants found her there she had the ready excuse of looking for a book for Madame.

Besides playing the piano Martine loved to read. Indeed, there was nothing she treasured so much as books, and these, for a girl in her station, were hard to come by. In school she read everything she could. Time and again she visited the school library to ask permission to borrow nearly every book they had. There was also a small lending library, housed at their church, Union Congregational, and in the years since finishing school, Martine read every publication there several times over, excepting the mechanics manuals and navigational texts. Martine herself owned no books, save for a small Bible given to her on her eighteenth birthday, that she knew pretty much by heart and used to press flowers. Books were alive as music was, if not more so, and what she loved most was poetry. She'd had one teacher in school, a Mrs. Ives, who made them learn and recite the English poets, with a special emphasis on Shakespeare, Keats, Byron and Blake.

Martine read Madame Lambert's books with a desperate haste, well aware the job could come to an end at any moment. Her favorite titles she noted down on the endpapers of her Bible. If one day she could acquire them for herself she would do so. She dreamt of having her own library, however small.

The day dawned clear and gentle. Martine woke at Momma's knock and her voice passing in the hall calling out, "Rouse yourself, Sister." She washed her face at the basin on the table in the corner of her small bedroom, put up her hair with combs in the postcard-sized mirror and slipped on her uniform. Her friends often complimented Martine on her good hair, which was soft and pliable, and grew long enough so that her plaits reached her shoulders, not that she bothered to do anything special with it on a workday.

Down in the kitchen she got the coffee on for Momma, who was upstairs still and engaged in the daily struggle to get Maxwell out of bed. Martine served herself a bowl of porridge from the stovetop and checked the oven. Momma's bread rolls were almost done baking.

When Martine stepped out onto the street, handbag hooked over her elbow and still buttoning her coat, the world smelled of green and flowery things. Spring had come late this year, but now every tree and courtyard bloomed. On her way to catch the streetcar she passed several neighbors. Mr. Anson, sweeping out in front of his grocery, waved and smiled.

"Lovely morning," he said. It surely was.

Martine arrived at the Braddocks at eight o'clock, as usual, and let herself in the back door. The Braddocks were finishing their breakfast in the dining room and Caroline was cleaning up in the kitchen.

"Morning, Miss Caroline," Martine said, hanging her coat by the door and taking an apron down off another peg.

"Honey, see to those dishes, would you?" Caroline said, clattering pot lids. "I'm about to overcook these greens."

Martine tied the back of her apron standing at the sink, looking out the window at the wide back garden. It was a pity to have to be inside.

Caroline stepped over to the kitchen door and cocked her ear toward it, wiping her hands on a tea towel. "I think they're done." She nodded at Martine by way of asking her to go out to the dining room to finish clearing the table.

Mrs. Braddock was on her way upstairs for her bath, and Mr. Braddock was in the front hall putting on his hat. He caught sight of Martine in the dining room and touched the brim with two fingers. He was the kind of employer who was congenial with the help, more so than his wife, but Martine didn't like how his lips looked, wet under the sandy moustache, and always felt much more comfortable at work when the Braddocks weren't at home.

An hour or so later Mrs. Braddock was on her way out too, to the hairdresser or dressmaker no doubt. She left the house reminding Caroline that her Horticulture Club was coming at tea time, which set Caroline to muttering to herself as she peeled the onions for that night's supper. No one tried Caroline's patience so much as the ladies of the Horticulture Club.

Martine knew better than to interrupt, but when Caroline had finally vented, Martine asked her how her little niece was getting along. The child had been ill that winter with whooping cough.

"Oh she's right as rain now," said Caroline, pleased to be on the subject closest to her heart. "I made her the prettiest little dress. You should see it. The collar and trim are real velvet." Martine smiled as Caroline went on about the dress; she wondered which Caroline liked more, her niece, or the fun of dressing her up.

Midmorning Martine was busy brushing the furniture in the parlor. Caroline went out to do the marketing. She left some chops for Martine to prepare for braising. "Mind you," she said, just before stepping out the door, "I just sharpened that knife."

A quarter of an hour or so later she heard the heavy click of the front door latch. Caroline must have forgotten her grocery list again. There was movement in the foyer and then Martine heard footsteps behind her. It wasn't Caroline, it was Mr. Braddock.

"Hello Martine," he said, "has Caroline gone out?" Martine didn't have time to answer. "I have some briefs to pick up I suppose I left them in my study."

"Yes sir," she answered, turning back to her work.

A few moments later she heard his footsteps again, this time from the dining room, the light slap of something hitting the table and the scrape of chair legs on the floor.

"Oh, Martine," Mr. Braddock called out, "why don't you bring me a cup of tea, eh? I'm just going to look these over while I'm here."

"Yes sir," she said again, a little uneasy. She had never been alone with him in the house before. On numerous occasions she had served tea to Mrs. Braddock and her guests, but guessed now that Mr. Braddock would like something quicker and would not need all the usual accoutrements.

"Good girl," Braddock said when she came in. He smiled at her again. "Why don't you have a seat with me." He pushed his papers to the side, clearing a space in front of the chair next to him. Not daring to disobey, Martine lowered herself slowly down and perched on the edge of the chair. She stared at the silver tea service where she saw her reflection, bright and small in a strange fishbowled room.

"Ah, this is nice," said Braddock. "A little break. The office can be monstrous busy, you know. Clients on my back all the time, the partners shouting, letters piling up...."

Martine hadn't the least clue how to respond, and desperately hoped this little interlude would end quickly. She peeked up at him, just at his mustache, which was working from side to side. He pursed his wet lips and took a drink of the tea.

"Well," he continued, "then I come home, and my wife–" he paused to plop a lump of sugar in his cup, stir it and tap off the spoon. "It's just she doesn't understand me."

Martine looked back to the tea service.

"You seem like a sympathetic person, Martine," he said next. "Are you? A sympathetic person?"

All at once he reached over and gripped her hand. His shadowed gray eyes seemed to bore into hers.

"A man needs a woman who understands him."

A heavy thud was heard from the direction of the back stairs.

Martine shot up. "That must be Caroline," she stammered, leaping at the door. She rushed to the kitchen window and spotted a pair of flour sacks on the back porch and the retreating figure of a delivery man. She thought of running after him, but then behind her, several rooms away, she heard the heavy slam of the front door. Mr. Braddock had left.

Nothing bad had happened, so why was she shaking? It might be hours before Caroline returned, and for all Martine knew Braddock could come back.

Get your things, she told herself. She found her coat, her handbag.

Now get out of here.

She let herself out the back door and came around to the street.

Don't run.

Walk.

She cut a wide circle through the neighborhood and then pointed herself in the direction of home.

Crossing the Rue Notre Dame, Martine arrived back in her own district but kept walking. She heard the noon whistle from the railroad, and still she went on. She walked until every tremor left her body and relief took their place. Then she retraced her steps up to a little green park and drank at the water fountain. She couldn't go home just yet, and was suddenly so tired. She sat down on a bench. A deep feeling of revulsion clouded her senses. Had she done something to give the wrong impression to Mr. Braddock? If she had she couldn't think of it.

A situation like this had happened to her sister Elodie once. An employer like Braddock. Elodie had fled too, but without being able to call upon recent references she was never able to find another position. It was lucky for her that she was already engaged to be married at the time, and was soon able to fall back on her husband's income. Martine had no such prospects. She couldn't just run out on a job. The Rougeauxes were not desperate, but the family depended on Martine's contribution, especially where Maxwell's future education was concerned.

Tears rolled down her cheeks and she rummaged in her pockets for a handkerchief, thankful that at least for the moment there was no one else around. At last she blew her nose and felt a measure calmer. Then that same voice of self-preservation spoke again. This time it said: *Eat your lunch.*

From her handbag Martine drew out the sandwich wrapped in a cloth napkin that her mother had prepared for her early that morning, half a baguette stuffed with cold cuts, pickles and Momma's homemade mustard. A man's kind of lunch. It was cut in half again so two twin sandwiches lay there on the napkin on her knees. She ate one, diligently chewing every bite. There were crows in the trees, and there was a man in worn-out clothes poking around in a rubbish bin.

Now quit feeling sorry for yourself, and go see Didi. That was the order that punctuated the end of her shock. She got up and with some effort she caught the eye of the man by the bin. She lifted up the second sandwich in the napkin so he could see it and laid it down on the bench. Then she hightailed it to her sister's.

At this hour the older children would be at school; Didi would be home with the youngest and the two little ones she minded for a neighbor. She came to the door with a finger to her lips. The children were napping.

Elodie, ten years Martine's senior, had always seemed to her like a grown woman. She had much of their parents' solidity, and could be every bit as practical and stern, but she also knew things no one else did, and didn't waste time pushing against something that wasn't going to budge.

Once, a year ago, Martine had spent much of the day so engrossed in Madame Lambert's copy of *Lord Jim* that she felt as if she were living in two worlds at the same time. When Didi came to see the family that evening she took one look at her sister, who was kneeling on the floor with the three children around her neck, and said, "Well, look at you, surrounded on all sides by the open sea." And not long after that, Heathcliff from *Wuthering Heights* secretly made Martine's heart flutter, and he lived in her mind as she went about her work. On an afternoon when the two sisters were helping Momma prepare a crate of pears for canning, Didi pronounced, "He's no good."

"Who's not?" asked Martine.

"Your new beau," Didi said, and winked before Martine could object.

But Elodie had much to say on important matters too, and after Martine had related the story of that morning at the Braddocks', her sister stayed quiet a good while.

"You can't go back there," Didi said at last. "Won't be nothing but a tangled mess." She rose and went to the sideboard where she had some potatoes soaking in a basin.

Martine bit her lip. "What am I going to do then?"

"Find something else."

"Damn."

Didi turned back toward her. "You swearing now?"

"Only on special occasions."

Didi laughed. "Well this one is worth it. No doubt about that." She gazed out the little window over the kitchen sink. "Listen," she said, "why don't you go down to the placement office? It's not even noon yet. Get a jump on things."

Half an hour later Martine was climbing the stairs to the downtown office of the placement agency, a dimly lit set of rooms on the second floor of a brick building off St. Laurent Boulevard. The waiting area was packed; Martine certainly wasn't alone in seeking work. When it was her turn, the clerk behind the front desk handed her a form and a pencil. Martine filled out her name, age and qualifications, but stopped cold at the place for references. She couldn't use the Braddocks, obviously. Madame Lambert was dead, and her employer from before that was almost four years ago. How would she explain that kind of gap? She slowly laid down the pencil and said she'd have to come back the next day with the form. Her deft hands were suddenly clumsy, folding the paper and putting it away in her handbag. What little hope she'd had crumpled into her throat and threatened to force its way out in tears. Damn it if she hadn't already cried enough for one day. She headed for the stairs. Outside the sunlight hit her eyes and she was momentarily blinded, and in that second of blindness she heard her name.

"Martine Rougeaux, is that you?"

Blinking furiously, she quickly recognized the approaching figure. It was Lucille Travis, her old school friend.

"It *is* you," cried Lucille, seizing Martine's hands. "My, it's been so long!"

"Lucille," said Martine. The nightclub dancer who had quit church two or three years ago. The *wayward* one, the older people called her. Lucille's older brother had died a soldier in the Great War, and her father had passed on right after she left school. Martine had heard lately that her mother was ailing, and that her youngest brother Tony was struggling to stay in school. People shook their heads over that.

Martine had imagined that Lucille went off to cheapen herself in those clubs, and as her parents discouraged the friendship she had let it drift. She remembered with a sudden shame how she had quit going by Lucille's house, had once even pretended not to be home when Lucille had come by.

But Lucille didn't look like a lost woman now, standing there right before her on the sidewalk. Her face looked healthy and open, if a little tired, and happy to see her old friend, as if Martine had never done her any wrong. Martine took in the stylish hat with a dark red ribbon that matched her dress and handbag, but it was the smile that outshone everything else.

"I can't believe it," said Martine. "How are you?"

"I'm fine, just fine," said Lucille, "but I'm late. Can you walk with me a minute?"

They turned the corner onto St. Laurent. Lucille asked Martine what she was doing downtown and how were all her family, and Martine asked her the same. A moment later they stood before the Club Marcel, an upscale place with a couple of side doors down a little alleyway.

"Rehearsal," Lucille said, with a note of apology. She was not unaware of the attitudes that surrounded what she did.

Just then one of the side doors flung open and another young woman appeared.

"There you are," she said, heading for Lucille. "Mr. Alain is having a conniption. The piano player showed up drunk, and he threw him out on his ear!"

"Hey, Donnae, this is my old friend Martine," said Lucille.

The young woman nodded at Martine over her shoulder and turned back to Lucille. "You better come in, we'll have to do what we can without him."

Lucille looked at Martine. "Are you busy right now? You want to fill in for an hour? I know you play. Mr. Alain will give you five bucks." Lucille's eager tone pulled on Martine's heart, as if they were still children and her friend wanted her to visit.

Martine sucked in her breath. "I don't know," she hesitated, "I don't have to be anywhere, but…." What would her parents think? Not only socializing there on the street with Lucille, but walking straight into a nightclub? On the other hand, it was daytime, just a rehearsal, just an hour, and maybe they need never know….

"Come on," said Donnae, catching one of Martine's arms. And with that she was inside Club Marcel.

The three women hustled down a corridor and up some stairs, pushing through a door that opened into a large hall with a stage, a long bar to one side, and an open floor full of tables and chairs. Five or six other women in partial costume milled around or practiced steps. Lucille and Donnae took Martine over to one end of the bar where a tall white man with slicked-back hair shouted in French into a telephone. Donnae interrupted him.

"Mr. Alain, we've got a piano player," she said, loud enough for him to hear.

He turned around, looked Martine up and down rapidly, said something curt into the telephone and hung up.

The next thing Martine knew she was seated on the lacquered bench of a massive grand piano, looking over the sheet music. She spent a few minutes warming up, getting it right. Mr. Alain leaned down and snapped his fingers, telling her to up the tempo. Martine had never touched a grand piano before. She played the spinet at home, of course, and the old upright belonging to the church, but never had music come to life under her fingers in such large and sonorous tones as these. The sound filled the hall around her, and seemed to fill every hall that echoed inside of her too.

Every now and then she looked up at the dancers, who flowed and hopped and turned with the music. They *were* dancing in their drawers, but not any kind of drawers Martine had ever seen. None of the women in her family had undergarments studded with rhinestones, that was one thing she could be sure of. Lucille was the most luminous of all. For every resonant tone of the piano, Lucille responded in the suppleness of her movements. Nothing lewd in it at all. If anything it was grace Martine saw, and *fun*.

Before she knew it, it was over.

The dancers dabbed at themselves with towels and Lucille took Martine's arm and led her over to the bar. "Well done!" she told her several times, "you played that thing right out!"

Mr. Alain was leaning on the polished surface of the bar smoking a cigarette. He reached into his coat and pulled out a billfold, from which he withdrew a five-dollar bill and held it out to Martine with two fingers. This was more than she made in a week working at the Braddocks'. Taking the money, she spotted a row of beer bottles just behind him on a shelf, bearing the familiar Rougeaux label. She sent them a silent message: *Don't tell Papa.*

Lucille put a coat on over her dancing costume and walked Martine outside. It was quiet in the little alleyway outside the door, removed now from the music in the hall and the traffic from the boulevard.

"It sure is good to see you, Martine," said Lucille. "You were always kind to me." Martine shook her head, actually she was not and she hadn't been. But Lucille didn't seem to notice the gesture. "Folks used to look at me like I was some kind of wild animal," she went on. It appeared being spurned by people in the neighborhood still hurt. Martine's shame returned and her cheeks flushed. No wonder Lucille had quit church.

"I suppose I seem a little wild to you," said Lucille, her eyes on the ground. "I know what folks said about me. I try not to think about it too much. Somebody's got to pay the bills, take care of my momma, keep my brother in school." Lucille looked up at her. "Do you think I'm a bad person? Aw, you probably wouldn't tell me even if you did. You must think I'm crazy, going on like this."

Martine was duly overwhelmed. "No, surely I don't," she said. "I admire you."

Lucille met her eyes in a grateful look.

"You should be proud," continued Martine, "taking care of your family all alone. Why is it anyone else's business how you get your money? I saw you in that dance hall. I can see you work hard. And you're good at it too. You dance like an angel. You're beautiful!"

At that Lucille covered her whole face with her hands and hunched forward. Her shoulders shook. Martine wiped at her own eyes.

"Listen, I'll tell you something," Martine said, hurrying to give Lucille her last clean handkerchief. "I'm out of a job because the man of the house tried to get too friendly today. Scared the living life out of me."

Lucille dabbed at her face with Martine's handkerchief and blew her nose.

"That dirty dog," she whispered. "Believe me, I know the kind."

The two girls were quiet a minute. Lucille twisted the handkerchief.

"Martine," she said, "I could use some help at my house. My momma is getting weaker and I need someone to help look after her and Tony while I'm working. Someone who could stay over the night a few times a week. I can pay."

"You all need someone to help?" said Martine, suddenly feeling as if she were floating.

Martine walked away in a daze. Why was it the Rougeaux household could contribute music and alcohol to places like night-clubs but drew the moral line at associating with dancing girls? If she was going to work for Lucille she was going to have to get her parents' permission. To convince Papa, she'd have to get Momma on her side first, and for that she'd need Didi again.

But she didn't go straight to her sister's house this time. It was the money, Mr. Alain's five-dollar bill tucked away in her handbag. It became another live thing, like the grand piano, chirping with a song only she could hear. This money was of a different kind than the money she knew; gained so easily and illicitly, it seemed both sin and windfall. She should donate it to the church, that's what she should do. And that's what she resolved to do, even as she realized she stood before the ornate, polished doorway of the Blanc et Levesque Bookshop.

She could see stacks of books, visible through the gilded letters on the shop windows, great shelves of books that disappeared into the shadowy ceiling. Something beautiful in there could be hers.

When she emerged again she carried a thick volume of the great English poets, bound in sturdy, charcoal-colored cloth. Her cheeks burned. She had the book, wrapped in paper and now squeezed into her handbag, and she had two dollars and thirty-five cents left over. That she would give to God.

Martine's feet flew. In under twenty minutes she rounded the corner onto Rue Delisle, where the stately grey stone of the Union

Congregational Church came into view. A man was busy with a broom, sweeping the sidewalk around the two linden trees that flanked the arched entryway. Martine hopped up the three stairs to the door and skipped inside.

The collection box was kept in the church office on weekdays. Martine heard the voice of the new young minister, the Reverend Charles Este, finishing up a conversation with his secretary and two women from the community, about plans for renovating the basement. The Reverend had only been instated that month, but already initiatives were afoot for numerous new projects. He was a person who inspired tremendous confidence in those around him, and he did so with great warmth.

Martine hesitated in the foyer, outside the half-open office door. Reverend Este caught sight of her as he followed the ladies to the door.

"Miss Rougeaux," he said, treating her to his wide smile. He already knew most of the congregation by name. "What brings you here on a weekday?"

"Just a donation," she said. The Rougeauxes gave to the collection plate each Sunday, so it was unusual to be bringing money now. "I have something extra, Reverend," she tried again, "I wanted to bring it in before I was tempted to spend it." She dug in her pocket for the two dollars and change, and then held it out to him.

"Very thoughtful of you," Reverend Este said, taking the money to the collection box and waving her inside the office toward a chair, "to give us your extra." He took his seat behind the desk. "Have you something on your mind, Miss Rougeaux?"

His look was so kind, that despite herself she sat down and told him she'd run into an old friend, and that her friend just sort of worked at a nightclub, and that she was kind of thinking about helping her out at home.

"That sounds like a very beneficial kind of arrangement," he said, smiling again.

"Yes," said Martine, "especially since this morning I lost my job."

"Is that so?" he leaned forward and rested his broad chin on his clasped hands.

"And Lucille, my friend, said I was always so nice to her..." surely she was taking up the Reverend's time now, but she couldn't seem to help it. "It's not true though, not true at all. My parents don't approve of dancing, of girls going into clubs, and they didn't want us to stay friends. And I don't suppose they'll let me work for her."

"So there's the rub," said the Reverend.

"But I really think I could. Help them. They say her little brother Tony is doing bad in school. I was good at school, I could help him too, not just keep the house." She saw Tony in the street sometimes, running around with the other boys. He was ten and always outgrowing his britches. Last summer she'd seen Mrs. Travis, walking slowly with a cane and carrying groceries. Martine hadn't seen her since then, maybe she was too ill to go shopping now, and she thought with another pang that she hadn't offered any help to Mrs. Travis with that heavy bag. She'd turned her back on her because she hadn't wanted to risk seeing Lucille, and Mrs. Travis had always been kind to her. Martine bit her thumbnail.

"But your parents may object," said the Reverend.

"I suppose they want to protect me," said Martine, though this had not before occurred to her.

Reverend Este nodded sympathetically. "I say," he said, "does your friend Lucille ever come to church?"

"No sir," she said, "they used to. I mean her family, the Travises, before her papa died."

"Well," he said, "I hope she might come again one day. All God's creation is welcome here."

"Yes sir." Martine stood. "Thank you." She turned to go.

"Oh Miss Rougeaux," he said, "you say you are good at school? Good with children? We have a new tutoring program starting up in the fall. Might you have time in your week to volunteer? We certainly could use someone like you."

Heading back outside and down the stairs, lost in the events of the day, Martine nearly ran smack into Leo LeForte. He was a friend of her brother Albert-Ross, but it had been quite a long time since she'd seen him.

"Oh, hey," he said, "I thought I might see a Rougeaux today."

"Have you been away?" she asked. She thought she'd heard from Albert-Ross that Leo was working with the railroad now.

"Yeah, but I'm here for a few days. Ma's already got me working." He held up a shopping bag, full of something to deliver to the church. "I've been staying in Toronto, with my brother's family." He rubbed at the back of his head and smiled, showing the points of his canine teeth. "I guess it's funny being back." He pushed the brim of his cap up to his hairline.

"Why is that?" Martine brought a hand up to pat her hair, suddenly thinking she must look a fright from running around all day in her maid's uniform, probably smelled like cigarettes from the Club too.

"Well, you know, everything is the same, so much the same it's strange somehow."

Martine had never been outside the city, but after everything today she knew something about strange.

"Maybe it's you that's changed," she said, and he laughed.

"Maybe we all changed."

"Did you like Toronto a lot?" Martine asked. Leo's big smile was contagious and she was smiling like a fool.

"I like it fine. Did you ever go there?"

She shook her head. For a moment neither knew what to say. The sun was low in the sky now and their shadows stretched out long and blue over the pavement.

Leo looked regretfully at his shopping bag. "I better take this in," he said. "Hey, where are you headed?"

"To my sister's."

"Are you in a hurry? Could I walk with you?"

That evening after supper Elodie came to help Martine talk with Momma before Papa arrived home. They sent the children to play outside and sat in the kitchen. Momma received the news about Mr. Braddock in silence and then stood with her hands clasped to look out the window, facing this new adversity with her customary grave composure.

"First we are going to praise God that he didn't harm you," she said, sitting down again at the table. "A woman's got to always be on her guard." She rubbed her eyes with one hand and then looked at Martine with tired eyes. "Especially you young ones. Maybe it shouldn't be so, but by God it is." She took Martine's hand, something she rarely did. Martine felt her strength and it fortified her. "You did right today. You did everything right. I'm proud of you, and your family will stand by you. There are risks we just won't take."

"Thank you, Momma," said Martine, reaching over to hug her.

Momma patted her on the back with one hand and laid out the next steps. Martine would have to send word to Mrs. Braddock through Caroline, with some excuse; she would have to forfeit her pay for that week, and they would just have to hope that Mrs. Braddock wouldn't say anything against her among the ladies in her community. Reputation was everything. In any case, Martine would have to find another job, a position with another white family, if that was still possible.

Didi looked over at Martine and raised a finger. "Momma," she said, "wouldn't you know it, but Martine has already been offered another job."

Martine bit her lip. This one might shock Momma even more than the Braddocks.

Martine stood in her bedroom, washing her face at the basin with fresh, cool water. The sky out the window was dark, and her image in the little mirror was lit from the lamp beside her bed. That morning seemed like such a distant memory it couldn't have been the same day. Downstairs Papa and Momma were talking things over. Momma hadn't said yes or no, but with Papa, Martine knew it was a long shot. The thought of working for Lucille filled her with hope, and the energy that comes with the opportunity for a wrong to be made right. She pressed the towel to her face and prayed for the chance.

Martine changed into her nightdress and got into bed. She

picked up the package from her bedside table and tore off the paper, admiring anew the beautiful book of poetry that was now her own. She opened the book and gingerly turned the crisp pages to the William Blake section. There was one she was looking for, the one about the tiger. She read it over a few times, lingering on the last stanzas.

> *When the stars threw down their spears*
> *And water'd heaven with their tears:*
> *Did he smile his work to see?*
> *Did he who made the Lamb make thee?*
>
> *Tyger Tyger burning bright,*
> *In the forests of the night:*
> *What immortal hand or eye,*
> *Dare frame thy fearful symmetry?*

Reverend Este's phrase, *All God's creation is welcome here,* echoed in Martine's mind. What if *here* wasn't just church, but everywhere? What if *here* was the human heart?

In the drawer of the bedside table, together with the little Bible secreted with pressed flowers, a few ribbons she'd won in school, and a drawing of a cat Maxwell had once made for her, Martine kept a fountain pen. At some point she had borrowed it from her father's desk and had neglected to return it. She took it now from the drawer and turned to the back end of the book where there were a few blank pages. In the top corner of one she wrote out two lines from the poem.

Did he smile his work to see?
Did he who made the Lamb make thee?

And then, of her own idea, she wrote,

Did he smile his work to see?
Did he who made the Lamb make me?

Martine closed the book, placed it and the fountain pen gently in the drawer, and blew out the lamp. She lay back on the bed and drew up the covers. Tomorrow would be tomorrow. For now it was still night.

Hetty

Montreal

1853

Margaret held Josie on her lap, the girl's long legs draping over onto the ground where they sat. Their bare feet were muddy from the chase, and Margaret's fair hair spilled over her shoulders in soft waves, having lost all its pins, which would now be scattered in the grass, to be found later by crows. Tiny beads of sweat shone on Josie's forehead and Margaret smoothed them away, singing softly.

Hetty watched, stretched out next to the baby, Joah, who slept on his carrying cloth. Margaret and Josie could almost be mother and child, Hetty thought, if it weren't for the fact that in color and features they were near perfect opposites. Hetty allowed her eyes to close, listening to Margaret's song, to the breeze that swept the embankment and the blackberry bushes where they had filled their pails, and to the sounds from the river beyond.

Of all Hetty Rougeaux's children it was Josephine that most reminded her of a certain part of herself, of faraway places, the ones she had known as a child. Because unlike the others, who took for granted roots that bore straight into the earth, Josie never quite seemed of this world. By 1853 Hetty had spent most of her life in Montreal, having arrived in the Province from the Caribbean a girl of thirteen years, the company and property of two sugar estate heiresses scarcely older than herself. She remembered much from her girlhood on the Island, but when she sifted among these memories, looking for the thing that was like her daughter, it always eluded her.

Once when Josie was very small, three or four years old, she pointed to a man who had come to do business in her father's saddlery. She declared there were two owls flying about his head.

Another day, upon waking she told her mother that she had floated up out of her bed, up through the ceiling and all the way up to the sky to visit the stars.

"What a lovely dream," said Hetty, petting the child's round forehead.

"But I saw Papa too, Maman," Josie said. "He met an old wolf in a house and didn't want to buy his leather." Indeed, Hetty's husband was away that night, meeting with a trader about a shipment of goods for his saddlery shop. He returned later that same day with an empty wagon, saying the leather he meant to buy was of such poor quality that he refused it. Hetty looked at Josephine, playing in the corner with her rag doll, and suddenly remembered a place she had never been.

Thérèse and Nicola Belcourt began their education in Québec City. They attended a school for young ladies where they learned dancing, pouring tea, piano, poetry, proper French, and other charms. In the evenings they taught Hetty to read and write, to read music and play piano, and because Hetty was curious, how to figure numbers. These were lessons carried out in secret, minutes stolen here and there out of sight of the elder Belcourts. Learning piano was permissible, but not letters and numbers. Hetty collected candle stubs, hiding them in interior pockets, with which to illuminate the books the Belcourt girls gave her for her nightly reading practice.

Though the clandestine tutoring afforded Hetty no small nourishment, the four years after landing in Québec City were the loneliest of her life. She was parted from everyone who loved her, from the only mother she had ever known, and whom, she feared, rightly, she would never see again. Thérèse and Nicola were both kind and familiar, and Hetty was obliged to them, but they existed in another world. They brought her stories of their days the way they had brought her tidbits from their dinner table back when they all lived on the Mont Belcourt Estate. The stories were colorful, full of gossip about other young ladies and their overly proper instructors. Nicola was a great mimic and they did laugh.

But while the Belcourt girls were at school, or parties, or outings, as they often were, Hetty was alone in the house scrubbing the coal bin, ironing shirts, peeling vegetables. The best she could hope for was a trip to the market for groceries. Even if the Belcourt girls had once in a while thought to ask Hetty about her day, she would have had no amusing tales to tell them.

There was one treasure that Hetty had brought with her from Martinique, a threadbare rag doll given to her by her father, that she had named Claudine, after an older child she had known in the quarters. Those nights in Québec City when she lay in her bed, after the candle stub had spent itself, the darkness became vast. Her loneliness was wide as an ocean and keen as a sword. She would pull Claudine out from under the pillow and tuck the doll in the space between her chin and shoulder, and whisper to her that she had cut her thumb with the paring knife that day, or seen a bird's nest from the upstairs window, or that she'd forgotten to buy apples at the market, and had to go back a second time.

Every time Hetty returned to that ocean of loneliness she groped for something solid. Slowly, as one year turned to two, and then three, she finally felt something beneath her, holding her up. She had seen a boat, long ago on the beach of her island, Martinique. Left by some visitor, it was small and beautiful, with polished wood carved into long curves. The little boat shone in the sun, a rich mahogany, at the edge of the brilliant blue sea, with two long oars laid carefully inside, waiting for its owner's return. Hetty began to imagine herself in such a boat. She might be adrift, but there was something to keep her afloat.

Hetty had a talent for music, something the Belcourt girls did not possess. Once they had taught her the basics, she studied their music books, and was allowed to practice after she had finished her chores. As the family noticed her growing abilities, Hetty was often called upon to play for guests. This led to paid offers to play at parties in the homes of some of those guests, as well as to requests that she give lessons to children. It was at one of these households, where she taught weekly piano lessons to two little boys, that she chanced to meet a young light-skinned, hazel-eyed *mulatre*. He was an apprentice saddler who came to the house one day to deliver a set of new harnesses, arriving just as Hetty was leaving, and they crossed paths on the carriage driveway. They greeted each other with a polite exchange, "*Bonjour Mademoiselle*," and "*Bonjour Monsieur*," he touching his hat brim and she nodding in return. So taken was he by this momentary encounter that he made it his business to ask one of the housemaids who she was, and after that found a way to return to the house the next week at the same time.

As she came around the corner of the house, Hetty spotted him on the walk that led from the back door to the carriage way, knocking something from the top of his boot with his hat. He held his hat to his chest and waited for her to pass. When she stopped to greet him, he bowed.

"Has the Mademoiselle enjoyed her lesson?"

"Oui Monsieur," said Hetty, curious at this special attention. In fact she had not enjoyed the lesson, as these particular pupils whined and fought a great deal, but the pleasure of the moment was quickly overriding it.

His name was Dax Rougeaux, and he was eighteen years old, one year her senior. He asked her name, and after exchanging a remark or two about the weather they prepared to take their leave. This was all that decorum would allow in a first conversation.

"Bonjour, Mademoiselle Hetty," Dax said, bowing again. He mounted his horse, a fine bay Morgan, and went away, leaving her alive with questions.

The next week he waited for her at the bottom of the carriage way. The day was bright but a chill hung in the air, announcing the beginning of autumn. After greeting each other Hetty asked Dax if this were his horse. She had a special love of horses and this one was especially pretty. She reached up to stroke the soft nose.

"He's mine alright," said Dax with evident pride. "His name is Casimir and he's a rascal."

Hetty laughed, saying that every rascal was surely intelligent.

Dax drew a little oval-shaped tin from his coat pocket and presented it to Hetty. A pink rose printed on the lid beckoned her to open it, revealing the sweet-rose smell of the hard candies inside.

She accepted the gift, at once so flustered she had trouble putting it away in the covered basket she carried. She thanked him very much, and thought she saw him blush.

That night, when Hetty went to bed, she spent the candle stub turning the tin box over in her hands. Had it really happened that this young man had thought of her, was perhaps thinking of her now? She recalled Monsieur Rougeaux's smile, the charming gap between his front teeth, the lovely timbre of his voice. Would he come again the next week?

He did, this time with a little bag of candied orange peel. He asked if he might walk with her toward town. This time he pointed out the street of the saddlery where he worked, not so far from where Hetty lived with the Belcourts, but each on the opposite side of a thoroughfare. More importantly he asked about her station. Hetty had already guessed Dax was a freedman, because he owned his horse, had money for candy and was able to come see her when he chose. In answer to his question Hetty just shook her head.

"There's no shame in it," he said, "it's a circumstance of birth, no more than that." She looked up and met his eyes, the hazel color burning with a kind of incandescence. "But God gave us free will," he went on, "and happenstance. I don't believe in accidents."

Hetty learned that Dax Rougeaux was the product of an alliance between a Frenchman and an enslaved African woman. Because of the *Code Noir*, wherein the child followed the condition of the mother, he was born enslaved, but he was manumitted by his father when he turned thirteen. His father had arranged for his apprenticeship with a saddler. But his parents were both gone now, taken by pneumonia during one bitter winter, and Dax was quite alone. He longed for a family of his own, something that Hetty had not yet dared to consider for herself.

Four months later, on their walk back to the Belcourt house, Dax was unusually quiet. When they arrived at the door he asked Hetty if she would mind taking another turn around the block, as he had something important to say to her. They walked slowly and Dax was thoughtful all the while. When they again neared the house, and Dax still had not spoken, Hetty stopped walking and put her hand on his arm.

"Dax," she said, "if you don't hurry up and tell me I'm going to faint from nerves."

"Let's go around once more," he said. They continued walking. "I may have a chance to open my own shop," he said, "in Montreal."

Hetty felt a stab in her heart. "You are going away?"

"If I had my own shop, I could take care of you." Now he looked into her eyes.

"Take care of me?" she whispered.

"Hetty, do you love me?" He gripped her hands. She did. Of course she did. "Will you be my wife?"

She wanted nothing more, but on one condition: her freedom. If there was one thing Hetty knew it was her own heart. She loved Dax, but she would not bring children into the world that could be owned by someone else.

"I will purchase your freedom," Dax declared. "I will work without stopping."

"I have some money too," Hetty said, feeling as though she were floating in mid-air, as if the two of them were rising in a sudden summery updraft. "The lessons!"

"We shall do it together," he said.

"Yes, together."

Thérèse and Nicola Belcourt were at once in support. They had spied Hetty and Dax, curiously passing three times in front of the parlor windows, and plied her with questions. Marriage and all things related were foremost on their minds, as both had come out into society. And as their time in the North had acquainted them with abolitionist views, they did not consider the matter of Hetty's sale an obstacle.

"We'll write to Papa straight away," said Thérèse.

"To be sure you'll be married before I am," pouted Nicola.

Hetty smiled, thinking that just for a moment she could finally have something that the Belcourt girls wanted.

The next year, 1833, brought, as Dax put it, *Divine happenstance*, when the King of England abolished slavery in the Canadas. Dax and Hetty were married, and went away to Montreal.

When Hetty said goodbye to Thérèse and Nicola, they all three wept. The Belcourt girls gave Hetty a set of four storybooks for children.

"Take care, Hetty," said Thérèse.

"And write to us," said Nicola.

Hetty promised she would.

In Montreal, Hetty and Dax learned a new city, in a vital climate of changing times. Beginning her life as a freed person, and as a wife, was a stark and continual wonder. As their children arrived, one by one, Hetty witnessed first-hand the exacting nature of life unfettered by the bitter dangers and constraints of enslavement. Whereas as a child Hetty had been made to stay quiet and follow directions at all costs, her own children wailed like wild animals when they were hungry, clung passionately to her legs when they needed comfort, and shouted out their desires or displeasure for all the world to hear.

Even as she and Dax guided them into civility, she could not help but love their ferocity, their greed for existence. Nor could she forget, as she watched them play and tussle, that countless children elsewhere in the world did not enjoy the same freedom and protection. As such, Hetty and Dax became involved in all manner of abolitionist activities, innovating ways to raise funds for organized efforts in Boston and New York. Time and again they received fugitives that had made it across the border, and needed a safe place to sleep, warm food to eat, and words of encouragement. Hetty and Dax taught the children that though their first duty was to the family, it was a necessity to extend their aid beyond.

Hetty named her children for her forebears. First there was Phoebe, then Olivie, then Abigail (after her aunt, Abeje), then Guillaume, named for her father, and then a child lost at birth. Lastly there was Josephine. In this way she could keep the names with her, even if the people they now represented were entirely different. Her children were miraculous to her. Even now, after almost twenty years of motherhood, of seeing them grow from babies into vibrant young adults, she still wondered where they had come from. She wondered the same about her husband, who was as sweet to her as he had been during their courtship. She wondered if she might one day wake up and find it all a dream.

Josephine was ten this year and regularly said unsettling things. This concerned Hetty, who tried to help her daughter understand what she could and couldn't say to those outside the family. She implored her older children to help with Josie. Hetty told them what she had learned from her aunt, the great healer, from so long ago. Abeje had said that some people are *marked by Spirit*. Perhaps Josie was this sort of person. Hetty said *perhaps*, but she herself had no doubt, not since one day when Josie was but five or six years old. Hetty was combing out and plaiting the child's hair, when she said, "Maman, did you know I used to be an angel?"

"Is that so?" Hetty answered, distracted by a stubborn tangle.

"Yes, I was," said the child. "I came and I stayed with you, but then I wasn't ready to come out, and I went back to Heaven." All at once, in a mad rush, Hetty knew exactly what she meant. She saw again the tiny lifeless body of her fifth child, dead the day she was born, and buried the next. That old grief whipped through her with a punishing force, but was followed by a greater knowledge, a release, that nearly knocked her over. She dropped the comb and scooped up Josie in her arms.

"Why are you crying, Maman?" said the child. "Aren't you going to finish my hair?"

Hetty remembered Tata Abeje as a different kind of person. She was a mountain, yet not actually large. She was fire, yet not actually hot. Rooted as a tree, yet moved easily over the land. Hetty had a distinct memory of the two of them walking along a wagon road together, in a place where the grasses grew tall and wildflowers of all colors bloomed. Ten-year-old Hetty had run barefoot, light and joyous, from one flower to another, laughing. Each was more beautiful than the next. After Tata departed to the sugar estate where she was bound, Hetty was never again able to locate this place. There was no such road at Mont Belcourt. No such grasses or flowers. This was the place Josephine reminded her of, because it was both real and impossible at the same time.

The family had to be careful directing the unusual things Josie said, but they also had to protect her from what she seemed to absorb from the world around her. More than once Hetty found her weeping, inconsolable over a dead pigeon or afraid because there were too many dogs barking outside. She spoke of a *whirlpool* that terrified her. It did no good to tell her that there wasn't any whirlpool, and that nothing bad could happen to her. These fearful moments increased as Hetty began to notice Josephine's body changing—a bit of hair appearing under her arms, her breast buds beginning to form—there were times when Josephine could not be made to get out of bed, or eat her supper, or put on her coat in cold weather. How Hetty wished she could bring her to Tata Abeje. If a healing was needed she would know what to do. And if *marked by Spirit* also meant one came into the world with certain unusual gifts, then Tata would know how to make those grow. But all that was a world away, and a lifetime ago.

The rag doll Claudine sat in repose atop a shelf beside the bed, next to a few other cherished items, such as the oval tin candy box with the rose on its lid.

The first night they spent in that room, in the apartment above the saddlery shop, Dax embraced Hetty. He couldn't help but look at the doll, illuminated by the tallow candle he had placed on the shelf.

"A married woman and still has a doll," he teased.

"She knows all my secrets," Hetty smiled.

"Does she know things your husband does not?" He drew her to him, frowning in mock offense.

She wrapped her arms around his waist, and murmured, "Perhaps." A moment later Claudine was forgotten entirely.

The first doll Hetty made herself was for Phoebe. Hetty was pregnant for the first time and she and Dax were terribly excited. Dax built a cradle, spending hours sanding every inch of its surfaces, and then rubbing beeswax into the wood with a cloth until it shone like gold. Hetty busied herself with preparing miniature clothes and wrappings, and with the leftover fabrics fashioned a doll that was both soft and sturdy. By the time Phoebe had outgrown the cradle and Olivie was on the way, the doll, called Suzette, was a dear friend. Phoebe slept with her each night, and carried her around each day, so that Hetty found her momentarily discarded in all manner of places. Despite having her own doll, however, Phoebe dearly wanted to play with Claudine. Hetty gently explained to Phoebe that Claudine was old and fragile and must stay in her place upon the shelf. Phoebe had a doll, and Maman had a doll, and this was part of the natural order of things.

But Hetty's admonitions, for Phoebe, only served to make Claudine all the more alluring. One day Hetty opened the bedroom door to find Phoebe in the middle of the bed with Claudine clutched in her little hands. Phoebe froze, her big eyes wide with fear. She burst into tears before Hetty even had the chance to scold her. This scene repeated itself so many times that finally Hetty surrendered. Phoebe could have Claudine, it was alright, Hetty told her. Claudine and Suzette could be sisters, just as Phoebe would soon have a sister or brother. Then Hetty found both dolls left hither and thither when Phoebe became interested in the yarn box, or the empty flour sacks, or went after the cat.

The cat was a fine specimen, pure grey with amber eyes, an excellent mouser and patient with the children. It held a special fascination for Guillaume. With four small children in the house Hetty had little time for extra sewing, but she made a special cat doll for Guillaume. The dolls Hetty had made for Olivie and Abigail were fancier affairs than Suzette, as Hetty experimented with more sophisticated constructions and new details as the years passed. The cat doll was yet another step in elaboration, and though Guillaume liked the cat doll well enough, he still much preferred the real thing.

Then finally there was Josephine, who assumed all the dolls in the family were hers, which by then nobody minded, except Hetty when Josie's conversations with them took on a certain tone. Josie sometimes arranged the dolls in a circle and asked them questions. She would stare fixedly at one or another of them, the cat doll say, or Claudine, murmuring small words like, "She did?" and "I don't think so," and "I will." Once when Hetty asked her what Claudine had told her that day Josephine answered, "Oh, she said she's hungry for *afu*, but I told her we never eat that." Hetty was struck dumb at this. *Afu* was a word from her childhood, what her mother called mashed yams, and something she, as a girl, would have pretended to feed her doll. Had she heard Josie right?

"What did you say she wanted, *chérie*?" Hetty asked. But Josie was already prattling on about something else and would not say.

As the years passed, visitors to the house began to take notice of Hetty's dolls, so much so that Hetty began making them as part of her fundraising efforts for the local chapter of the Anti-Slavery Society. They were a popular item at silent auctions and fetched good prices for their charm and quality. Two years prior, in 1851, the funds committee had asked her for a set of dolls for an auction that would accompany an upcoming benefit concert at the Theatre Royal, performed by a group called the Ethiopian Serenaders. Phoebe, Olivie and Abigail were now married, and the growing independence of the other children afforded Hetty the time. The concert was held for the benefit of five new fugitives that had landed in their city.

The night of the concert Hetty and Dax made the acquaintance of one of the fugitives, Mr. Shadrach Minkins, who had already achieved a bit of fame. After escaping from bondage in Virginia, Minkins had made a life for himself in Boston until a year later he was arrested under the Fugitive Slave Act. When he stood trial, however, a group of freedmen broke into the courtroom and spirited him away, and with their support he made it to Montreal. Mr. Minkins went around the room introducing himself during intermission, shaking hands with every single person in attendance, and thanking them for coming. He complimented Hetty on her dolls, and apologized for sitting down with her and Dax uninvited. His health had not been good and he was visibly winded. Dax told him to please rest himself, and Hetty assured him he was among friends. She went off to fetch him some tea.

In a short time Mr. Minkins' health improved and he soon found work as a waiter at a hotel, Montreal House, where he began saving the capital he needed toward his own business ambitions. Dax and Hetty sought him out now and then to see how he was getting on, and to offer their support in what ways they could, and were always glad to find him in good spirits.

One June evening, two years later, Dax and Hetty dressed in their Sunday clothes and took Guillaume and Josephine to the eatery, *Chez Shadrach*, Mr. Minkins had opened with his new wife Mary. The Rougeaux family were invited to a special dinner, along with others in the community who had supported Mr. Minkins, that promised an impressive menu: a whole roast pig, a variety of spring vegetables, and desserts to *delight and amaze*. Hetty smiled at this last part. Mr. Minkins had nothing if not panache.

The Rougeauxes arrived curious to see what Mr. Minkins had done with himself. Guillaume, at fourteen, was now taller than his father, and walked the whole way from the shop holding Josephine's hand. Besides the cat and the other boys on their street, Josie had always been his favorite playmate, even if the games she preferred were not exactly to his liking. He suffered admirably through endless pretend cups of tea and nibbled cakes made of dandelions, and he held up his end of many a conversation among the dolls. Anything to make Josie smile.

Mr. Minkins met the Rougeauxes at the door of the restaurant. He grasped their hands in a warm welcome and led them to a table topped with a little vase of violets and a glowing candle in a glass jar. The room was already filling up with familiar faces. A serving table in the center was laden with covered dishes and the promised desserts. A white woman emerged from the kitchen carrying a tray of earthen mugs and Mr. Minkins waved her over.

"Please meet my wife, Mary," he said.

Hetty took in the sight of the young woman. Flushed pink cheeks sprinkled over with freckles, wheat-colored plaits coiled about her head, the large pregnant belly under layers of muslin.

She said *How do you do* in an accent that belied her origins. Irish to be sure.

"He calls me Mary," she said to Hetty. "I don't mind. I suppose he thinks it's holy. Or else," she patted her belly, "he thinks this is the Baby Jesus." Hetty laughed. She always liked people who didn't bother too much with niceties. "But you can call me Margaret."

"And you must call me Hetty."

The next time the Rougeauxes visited Chez Shadrach, Mr. Minkins refused to take their money. Only when Dax threatened never to return did he accept payment. All that season and into the autumn they went back many times, especially Tuesdays when there were fewer customers and the place closed earlier. The Minkins invited them to stay after hours, and soon there were regular late nights together before the fireplace, the men with their pipes, the women with their tea, and all with many tales to tell. Mr. Minkins had a certain way of turning many a harrowing event into sheer hilarity, which left everyone laughing, though no one more than his wife.

Indeed, Margaret's laugh was free as a child's. When something struck her as funny, and it often did, she lost herself entirely. Pitching forward at the waist, clutching her side with one hand while reaching out for the nearest shoulder or piece of furniture for support, she was helpless until the moment passed. When it did she straightened without apology and got back to work. And she liked to sing. At the end of the summer the Minkinses acquired an old piano and Hetty revived her playing skills. Soon no Tuesday night was complete without a round, or two or three, of song.

Like many, Margaret had come to the Canadas as an indentured servant, fleeing the famine brought on by the potato blight that had starved out her family and everyone else she knew. When the five years of her indenture had passed, having learned the rudiments of letters and figuring from her merchant employer, she found work at the Montreal House where Shadrach was working as a waiter. She soon found he could make her laugh like no one else, but she liked him more for his ambition and ingenuity, and the wistful way he told her she was pretty. Margaret knew of a number of marriages in town between people of different races, immigrants like herself, usually, who had no family to dissuade them. For herself she didn't care a whit about Shadrach's color, this was the New World after all, and it was not long before she threw in her lot with his.

Each time the Rougeauxes visited the restaurant, Margaret had questions for Hetty.

"Hetty," she might say, "what do you think of these curtains?" or "Hetty, how should I mend this broom?" and "Hetty, taste this pie. What is it lacking?"

These bits of conversation endeared the younger woman to her. Margaret listened thoughtfully, turning Hetty's answers over and then coming out with another question on the same thread.

"Tell me about your island," she said to Hetty, those evenings before the fireplace.

"Tell me about your aunt."

"Tell me about Québec City."

In fact, she reminded Hetty of herself as a child. Hetty had wanted to know everything. *Where did the ocean end? Why was sugar cane sweet? Why did roosters crow? Having one's own children turned the mind to immediate concerns. How will I take care of this fever? How will I explain this rule? How will I keep him safe? And now the most pressing question of all: what must I do about Josephine?*

One evening as they were peeling a basket of garlic cloves, Margaret asked after Josie. Hetty stopped peeling for a moment. Earlier that day Guillaume had taken Josie out in the wagon, on an errand for the saddlery, and stopped at a stream to water the horse. Josie, as Guillaume told her later, seemed to envisage one of her fearful whirlpools in the current and became distraught, begging her brother to let them leave at once, before it could *take them away.* How could a mother protect a child from her own imagination?

"I wish I had some idea," said Margaret.

"I too," Hetty said.

The two were quiet some minutes, getting at the garlic heads with their paring knives.

"I never know what to do when Shad is in a bad humor," Margaret said, "though it's different, as he's a grown man." Hetty waited for her to say more.

"You'd not know it, seeing him here at the restaurant," Margaret said, "but at home I sometimes lose him for days. Weeks even. He's sitting way, way down at the bottom of a well. Can't hear me for anything."

"I suppose that's a distance you can never reach," Hetty said. "You'll never know what got laid down in his heart, and you just have to bear it. Be patient with him. He's fighting a battle inside that silence."

Margaret nodded, a grave sadness shaping her expression. "I'm sure it's as you say, Hetty. I'll do my best, though I wish I could do more than that."

That night as Hetty and Dax readied themselves for bed, Hetty said, "Josie had one of her spells today."

"Yes," he said, drawing back the quilts with a heavy sigh, "Guille told me."

Hetty blew out the candle on the shelf that had once been Claudine the rag doll's place. Claudine, together with the other dolls, now kept Josephine company.

Hetty and Dax lay in silence a while, until Dax spoke again. "My mother used to talk of afflicted people sometimes, people who acted strangely, as having *drunk a bad draught.*"

"Did she?" Hetty wished all over again there were someone who could advise her about Josie. Hetty had always gotten the impression that Dax's mother would have been such a person, were she still living. "Did she ever speak of a cure?"

"No," said Dax, "but she was forever bathing me in hot salt water. And bay leaves, when she had them. Father used to say she was making soup of me."

"Weren't you healthy?" Hetty had never heard of Dax being ill as a child.

"Strong as a little ox," he said.

"Well, it can't hurt to try it," said Hetty, already calculating how much salt they had in the pantry and where she could buy bay leaves.

Dax wrapped an arm around her middle. "I have faith," he said.

"In salt baths?"

"In you."

Once Margaret asked Hetty, "Where is the most beautiful place you've ever been?"

Hetty thought back to the beaches of her childhood. How she and her mother sometimes went at dawn to watch the last of the stars fade and the sun fill the world with fire. She thought of the orchards in the springtime, where she and Dax rode out just to look at the blossoms. The trees, bedecked like magnificent brides, full of bees buzzing like tiny grooms. These were among her most beautiful memories, to be sure, but perhaps not the most beautiful of all. Hetty told Margaret about the wagon road she remembered walking with Tata. The tall grass, green and gold, waving in the wind, the many colors of the flowers, and the way the clouds sailed above in the bright blue sky like great white boats.

"What about you?" she asked. "What is your most beautiful place?"

"There was one my Ma used to take us to," Margaret said, rubbing her hand over the apron that strained over her great belly. She described an ancient footpath that led into the hills, the craggy rocks that reared up from sloping meadows, and a small, unlikely pool carved into the stone by a spring. There were markings here and there worked into the stone surrounding the pool. Her mother said it was writing made by their people from ages ago. She called the spot a *thin place*. A type of place where the distance between people and the spirits was so thin that the two could touch.

Margaret never forgot the green of that grass. The sunshine on her mother's hair. Holding the hands of her two brothers and her sister while her Ma told them fairy stories and taught them her special songs. Margaret used to close her eyes to feel just how near to the spirits she might get.

When Margaret's time came she was tended to first by the midwife and then by Hetty and her daughters. Hetty directed them all in her quiet way, sending her older daughters in rotating shifts to help in the home and in the Minkins' restaurant. Phoebe, Olivie and Abigail all had young ones and they imparted their care and advice to Margaret like sisters. Mr. Minkins joked that he was going to have to buy a ticket to see his own wife and son, so often was he shooed away during that first week. Dax consoled him, putting an arm around his shoulder and inviting him to come see the fine saddle he was making for the minister of their church. Peace in the home was made, Dax told him, if the men knew when to keep out of the way.

On the second day after the birth, after Hetty brought a bowl of warm oatmeal porridge in to Margaret, who was resting with the baby, Margaret broke down.

"You are the finest people I've ever known," she sobbed. "I can't tell you what all this means to me." Hetty put down the bundle of washing she had gathered and sat on the edge of the bed.

"We help each other," Hetty said. "We're intended to."

"You have been so kind to me, Hetty, I do thank you." Margaret swabbed at her nose with the corner of the baby's blanket.

"It's not needed," said Hetty. She wondered for the sixth or seventh time at how different a sort of white woman was Margaret Minkins. Margaret hadn't been taught from birth, as had Thérèse and Nicola Belcourt, that people of darker color existed solely for her service. There were no darker people where Margaret was from. A person's worth was determined by what he owned, and since

185

Margaret had owned nothing when she fled the famine in Ireland, she'd had to decide for herself that her life was worth saving.

As it was, Hetty and Margaret occupied the same station, and if any difference existed it was Hetty who ranked higher, as she was older and respected, and much more established in their community. How things sometimes turned upside down, Hetty thought, as if one could turn over a chair or table and find it just as useful.

The Minkinses' scrawny little newborn fattened and grew into a fine baby boy with dark curls and long lashes. Josie was very fond of him and carried him around on her small hip, delighting in every new thing he learned. On one of the Tuesday nights at the Minkins' restaurant, Margaret watched as Joah struggled to crawl over Josie's outstretched legs.

"Do you think he's simple?" Margaret said to no one in particular.

Hetty laughed. Wasn't it their lot to fret over their children? Thankfully, things usually turned out alright.

On one of these nights Margaret asked Hetty, in a low voice, how Josephine was doing lately. She had seen herself how Josie sometimes worried her hands together and grew sad for no apparent reason. Joah was asleep in his wicker bassinet and Josie was just then absorbed in a book.

Of all the considerable knowledge Hetty had accumulated, from experience and reading, and from a lifetime of listening to others, none of it was applicable here. The moods and such that sometimes overcame Josie might be called *spells*, might even be called *possessions*, but what to do about them? She certainly had no wish to seek out doctors with their bitter powders and violent bloodlettings, nor priests who claimed to perform exorcisms with beatings and holy water.

"She reminds me of a fairy," Margaret said, "or like someone caught between the worlds, like the stories my Ma used to tell."

"How was that?" asked Hetty.

"There are all manner of those old tales," Margaret said. "A girl falls in love with a fairy boy, or the other way round, babies snatched away. Someone's always getting stuck in a world they don't belong to."

"What then?" said Hetty, "What happens in the end?"

"Sometimes magic sets them free, sometimes it's a sad end," Margaret said." More often than not, though it falls upon them to make a choice. Hetty looked over at Josie, still quietly reading, chewing on the end of one of her plaits, just as usual as could be. Phoebe, Hetty's oldest, often tried to reassure her that all the children had outgrown troublesome phases. Didn't she remember when Abigail insisted on eating pieces of chalk? The year that Olivie scratched her legs so much she sometimes drew blood, even though there was never any sign of a rash or an insect bite?

"Perhaps I shouldn't worry so," Hetty would say, and Phoebe would smile and kiss her cheek, saying that now Maman was being more sensible.

On a Saturday in midsummer Mr. Minkins asked Dax to come with him to see about a horse he was thinking of buying, and Dax wanted to bring along Guillaume. Few people could appraise a horse better than Dax and he was determined to teach his son what he knew. Every man should know about horses, Dax always said, but that went double for saddlers. So while the men went off in the buggy, Hetty and Margaret took Josie and baby Joah to pick blackberries by the river.

A fresh breeze swept in from over the St. Lawrence, where boats made their lazy way over the water. Neither Hetty nor Margaret said much as they made their way through the greenery to find a good place to begin picking.

The women filled their baskets and Joah rode along tied to his mother's back, while Josie fed him the ripest berries with her fingers.

"Not too many now," said Hetty, "you know what can happen."

"What?" asked Josie, greatly enjoying feeding the baby.

"Far too much laundry," said Margaret, letting loose with her famous laugh and grasping Josie's shoulder to steady herself.

Joah began to grow fussy.

"You two go along," Margaret said. "I'll just feed him and catch up with you."

Hetty and Josie rounded a bend in search of another patch, and Hetty took Josie's small hand in hers. Josie hugged her arm, bringing her face to rest against Hetty's shoulder as they walked. Josie was eleven now and the top of her head grazed Hetty's ear. Josie would likely be almost as tall as she was by this time next year, Hetty thought, and probably all through playing with dolls. She planted a kiss on Josie's soft hair.

"I'm counting the different kinds of plants, Maman," said the girl.

"That so?" said Hetty.

"I think seventeen or eighteen, now."

"What a lot!"

"Six kinds of grass, at least."

Hetty and Josephine found their way closer to the river's edge, and into another tangle of berry vines, just beyond a little eddy of water where a few leaves floated in a slow circle. Hetty glanced anxiously at Josephine, worried the swirl in the water might bring on one of the child's frights. But she was as calm as could be, pulling at the stems of some low weeds to see what could be added to her list. Hetty let out her breath and resumed filling her basket.

But then the wind kicked up off the river, rushing past her ears, and when the sound subsided she heard Josie's voice.

"Maman," she said, her face wrinkling with worry, "will we see any snakes? I don't want to see a snake. Will we see one?"

"Surely we won't," said Hetty. "If there were any our voices would scare them away."

"Then there *are* snakes?" Josie's shoulders hunched up and her hands fluttered at her throat.

"No, no *chérie*, I only meant…."

"I don't like snakes," Josie sobbed.

Hetty crouched before her and stroked her arms, promising again and again there would be no snakes, until Josie finally calmed down and could be persuaded to continue her game of counting plants. Hetty resumed her berry picking, imagining what Dax would say about false promises, and praying that no snake would show itself that morning.

Soon Margaret appeared with the baby in her arms, sound asleep, and the muslin carrying cloth draped around her neck. Hetty suggested they take a rest, and they climbed up the embankment to find a dry spot in the grass to sit down. The sun was shining and the air was warm, but it had rained the day before and the earth was still damp in places.

Margaret spread out the muslin in the shade of a white birch tree and laid Joah down on it. Then she took off her shoes and stockings and let her toes wiggle in the air, which made Josie laugh and ask Hetty if she could take her shoes off too. There was no one else around and so no harm in it, except that suddenly a little garter snake emerged from behind the tree and caught Josie's eye. She shot up with a scream, and ran.

Hetty made to follow her, but Margaret was quicker.

"Stay with Joah!" Margaret called back, running after Josie.

Hetty looked on helplessly as Josie and Margaret raced further away. Joah had flinched in his sleep, but hadn't woken.

Some minutes later, just as Hetty had resolved to pick up the baby and follow them, she saw them returning, Margaret with her arm wrapped around Josie's shoulders. Her hair had come loose.

"I've promised her a special song," Margaret said, when they arrived back at the birch tree. "Haven't I, Josie?"

"I'm sorry I ran off," Josie said, looking at Hetty with tired, sorrowful eyes.

Margaret sat down on the grass. "Will you sit with me, Josie?"

Josie looked up at Hetty, who smiled. "Go on," Hetty said. "I'll lie down next to Joah."

Margaret's lilting voice painted pictures in the air.

Long long ago in this ancient land
A battle took place where two hills now stand
And on the plain there lay the slain
For neither the battle was won

So the bard did sing of these fairy hills
Where bloom the white flowers and daffodils
One big one small Si Bheag Si Mhor
And never the battle is won

Josie relaxed against Margaret's shoulder, and soon closed her eyes. A few minutes later she was asleep, and Margaret left off singing. Hetty felt quite drowsy herself.

"Hetty," Margaret whispered, "do you remember the place I used to go with my Ma, the spring pool back in Ireland? The *thin place?*"

Hetty nodded, waiting for Margaret to say more.

"When I am near to Josie, I feel as though I'm there. Hetty, I believe Josie herself is like a thin place." Margaret looked up at the sky for a while, then turned her eyes back to her friend. "My Ma used to sing a certain song, one she sang only at the spring pool."

"Would you sing it for us?" Hetty whispered back.

Margaret cleared her throat and began to sing in Irish, not English. The strange sound of the words blended with the melody, and seemed to carve the air, like water rushing over the hard edges of stones.

In her mind's eye, Hetty saw a pool rippling in a wide stone basin. The words Margaret sang pointed to markings scattered here and there on large rocks, alighting on one and then on another like dragonflies, and then flying away down a path between two green hills.

As Hetty followed the path the earth grew drier until a red dust covered her bare feet. She felt a warm weight on her back, and the tight muslin carrying cloth tied across her chest. It did not seem

191

strange to her that Josie was a baby, or that the path beneath her feet widened into a road made for wagons, with tall grass growing on both sides.

The road rolled up and down with the hills. The sky above was blue, with white clouds sailing like boats, and the fields around were rich with flowers. Hetty thought it must be well past midday, as the sun was not high. She must think about what to make for supper. The others would be waiting, and hungry.

She couldn't see too far ahead, as the sun was in her eyes, but she could make out a single tree on a rise, and thought perhaps she saw a figure standing beneath it.

"Who could that be, Josie?" she said. "Whoever it is, I know they won't mind if we stop there for a rest."

Hetty walked further and then knelt to untie the carrying cloth, so Josie could step to the ground. Not a baby now, but her tall, long-legged self again. Josie ran lightly down the road and into the grass.

"So many flowers, Maman! Look how pretty! I want to make a bouquet for Papa." Every time Josie bent to pick a stem Hetty lost sight of her. Gradually they approached the rise, Josie skipping ahead of Hetty, with bunches of flowers in each hand.

The tree was full of shadows.

There was a figure, a woman, Hetty could see her now, holding out her arms. The voice was deep, raspy with age, but unmistakeable.

"Ayo, my dear."

Hetty had not heard that name, her other name, in what seemed like centuries. She faltered and stumbled forward.

"Come, child."

Strong arms kept Hetty from falling. She clung to the long blue skirts. Leathery hands lifted her face. Hetty saw the eyes like black fire, the high round cheekbones, the face of her aunt, her Tata Abeje.

Flowers fell at their feet. Josie stood by with empty hands and Tata turned her gaze on her, reaching out to lay her long fingers over the back of Josie's head.

The setting sun burned red, bathing the fields in amber light and putting a glow through the branches of the tree. Tata was singing, a low, rhythmic song, and she drew lines in the air over Josie.

Hetty could feel her own heart beating in time with the song. She felt the rush of blood through her body like a river.

The sky darkened, turning the fields blue, then black, as night fell and the first stars appeared.

A baby was crying.

Hetty opened her eyes.

Margaret bounced Joah in her arms. He flailed his little fists, protesting the injustice of waking up after sleep, and then rubbed at his eyes.

Josie was a little ways off, crouching in the grass, and seeing Hetty ran to her, smiling.

"Maman, look, three kinds." She held a clump of tiny flowers in her cupped hands, red clovers, daisies and miniature violets.

"Will you bring them home to show Papa?" Hetty asked, not quite fully awake yet.

Josie picked out a daisy and tickled Joah's leg with it, making him laugh despite his tears.

"There now, that's better," Margaret said. The baby squirmed and she set him down. He sat on his fat knees, reaching for Josie's flowers. "Josie," Margaret said, "can you put a braid in my hair? I can't go back to town looking so wild. Shad will scold me." She smiled at Hetty and then looked out toward the river. "Isn't this a beautiful place?"

"Very," said Hetty, picking up one of Josie's daisies.

Josie stood behind Margaret, her clever fingers at work weaving Margaret's hair into a thick plait, her brow furrowed in concentration.

Hetty looked down at her own hands, twirling Josie's flower in her fingers. They were Josephine's hands. They were Tata Abeje's. They were the earth, baked by the sun. As if the earth had risen up and shaped itself into a living, breathing woman. As if such a thing could be.

Guillaume

Montreal

1883 - 1889

Guillaume Rougeaux was just past his forty years the first time he saw himself in a photograph, a daguerreotype of him and his wife Elizabeth, called Bess, and their six children. It was the year 1883. Their oldest son, Albert, stood to Guillaume's left, tall and stern, a serious young man of nineteen, working for the railroad and engaged to be married. Dax, the baby, set on Elizabeth's knee, and the others, beside their mother on a velvet-draped bench.

The taking of the photograph was a happy, if curious, occasion. They had two pictures made, one to hang in their own house, and one for Maman, even though she lived just next door and saw them each and every day, and even though she was not alone, since Papa had passed. Guillaume's youngest sister, Josephine, was still at home. Bess put the daguerreotype in a varnished wooden frame and hung it in the bedroom beside the large oval mirror on the dresser. In this way Guillaume studied it every Sunday when he fixed up his tie for church. What he saw when he looked at himself in the photograph were his broad shoulders and wide-set stance that gave the surprising impression of a sawhorse. Which is what he said to Bess. "I look just like a sawhorse!" And to which she replied, her attention mostly on the linen she was folding, "I did always think that same thing myself."

Guillaume's sister Josephine was tall for a woman and built like an iron rail. While her brother took after their father physically, and their sisters after Maman, she took after neither parent. How did such different fruits fall from the same tree? Maman always said she resembled her old aunt, back on the Caribbean island of her birth. Josie had had a few admirers as a girl, but no serious suitors. She was fine to look at, she was kind, intelligent and capable in the important things, but she was different, and the older people gently discouraged any of their sons who took an interest. Josie herself was not concerned, said often enough that she was not the marrying kind. Maman worried over her, just as she had when Josephine was young, but Josie told her she had long ago considered herself in a kind of solitary marriage with the *Holy One*. This was the kind of strange thing she said. And in truth she did seem as happy as any of the rest. Unusual as she was, she was at home in the bosom of her large family, a strange dark bird among a barnyard full of handsome cockerels and hens and broods of fluffy chicks.

Now that Maman had grown frail, it was a great comfort to all that Josephine took care of her. Josie often took her nieces and nephews on walks along the riverbanks in fine weather, acquainting them with the names and natures of most every kind of plant they saw; she had gleaned much from local almanacs, and more by her own forays. She regarded the plants as friends, and had the children press so many flowers in the family Bibles that any reading produced a rain of dried petals. The children loved their Auntie, all accepted her difference, if they even noticed it. Josie and Maman never lacked for anything, as they were kept well supplied by the family with all the goods necessary for living. If Josephine appeared different from her peers and Guillaume did not, it was only by chance. His difference remained on the inside.

When Guillaume was eighteen two things happened: he fell in love for the first time, and was engaged to be married, though this concerned two different people rather than one.

He was engaged to Bess, who was his best friend, not counting his sisters. They knew each other from school and from church and just about every criss-crossing of the community. Elizabeth was buxom, always laughing; she spoke English and possessed a smooth, ebony complexion, unlike Guillaume, who, because of his French grandfather he never knew, was brown like a cake of raw sugar. One day in summer she asked him to help her tote a load of cedar shingles from a neighbor's home to her house. They took a shortcut through a patch of forest near a canal, sharing the load of a large wicker basket, until they stopped to rest a few moments on a grassy embankment. They spoke easily together and then fell silent, watching the water.

Elizabeth cleared her throat.

"What about marrying me?" she said, laughing at his shocked expression. "Why not?" she said. "We know everything about one another, and we're the best of friends." The openness in her face bent his heart.

Guillaume's brow knitted up like the cinch on a gunny sack, his throat squeezed so that his words barely escaped.

"You'd want me?" he asked.

"Of course I would," she said, her voice descending from bold to soft. "I mean, I do." He took her hand. The thought of them marrying, of making a family together, was enormously comforting. If it had to be done, and it did, Bess was the one.

"You sure?" he asked.

"I've given it a lot of thought."

"Let's talk to our parents then," he said. He helped her up, an arm around her waist. She put her arms around his neck and laid her head on his shoulder, but he trembled inside.

Their parents were naturally delighted, gave their permission and their blessing, and set the wedding date for one year later. Now, as Guillaume and Papa worked together in the saddlery, Papa began to thread their dialogue with all the wisdom he had gleaned from married life as to what made a good husband and a good marriage.

"You've got to lead, but follow too," he might say. Or, "Take care of her. She will be your rock and your refuge."

Guillaume took his father's words to heart, even if he didn't yet know what they could mean. Papa was everything honorable in a man, and Guillaume's dearest wish was to live up to his example.

That autumn they had an unusual visitor. He was a young itinerant preacher, an American from a family of freedmen, the Clarksons, in New Haven. He was making a pilgrimage around the region, to spread the word of God, and, as he said, to educate himself by seeing more of the world. Emmet Clarkson appeared in church, seated with the Minkinses, the Rougeauxes' closest friends. He wore a well-fitting, if slightly worn, black suit with a dark blue cravat, and held his black brimmed hat in his hands. During the service Guillaume, seated nearby with his family, found his gaze drawn repeatedly to the stranger's striking profile.

Later, during introductions between the Rougeauxes and the Minkinses, Guillaume took in Emmet Clarkson's erect posture, his smiling eyes, his charming how-do-you-dos, his resonant voice. He was twenty-three or twenty-four. He stayed a fortnight, lodging with the Minkinses, then with another family, and then with the Rougeauxes. He led two prayer meetings in each home, conducted in a different style than the community was used to, but all were well received. He spoke of character, of duty, of the sacredness of man, and also of humility. He quoted scripture with well-versed alacrity, and when he punctuated his orations with a reverent *Let us pray* Guillaume felt faint.

Guillaume was as intoxicated by Clarkson's presence as he was mortified. Clarkson noticed Guillaume's rapt attention during the prayer meetings and interpreted his interest as a true connection with his message. He clasped a warm, firm hand on Guillaume's shoulder and remarked to Papa on the beautiful nature of his son's evident piety. Guillaume's face burned like fire. Then, worse, or better, when he lodged with them he shared sleeping quarters with Guillaume. Maman fixed up a pallet and they insisted the young preacher take the bed, which he refused. Those four nights Guillaume looked askance as the other man undressed and replaced his suit with his nightshirt. The lamplight shone on his wide, bare shoulders and the long dipping line of his spine. They lay but a few feet apart, sharing some revelation of the day, and each time Clarkson said, "Shall we pray, Brother Guillaume?" Guillaume prayed for the impossible; that Emmet Clarkson would remove his nightshirt and that Guillaume would remove his own, and that they would lie together the whole of the long night.

It was awful when he left. The family saw him off as he disappeared down the road, having hitched a ride out of town in a neighbor's wagon. The last glimpse of him, waving his black hat in the air, left a crushing ache in Guillaume. But aside from imagining

201

the young preacher's hands when he touched himself, there was nothing to be done. Surely this pain was punishment for the sin of desiring a man in the first place. Perhaps, thought Guillaume, he should take God's side against himself. He would easily have done so, if it weren't for Josephine.

Josie, as with all her peculiar ways, had her own relationship with God. She attended church with the family, but never seemed to pay attention to the sermons or Scriptures. Instead she sat with her eyes closed and her lips moving, visiting her own interior temple where she communed in her own way. She didn't even say the word *God*, but rather used Maman's term, the one brought with her from her island. The *Holy One*. Maman herself rarely said it anymore, preferring to say *Dieu* or *God*, in harmony with the vernacular of the community. And now Josephine knew, with her piercing and infallible insight, the full extent of her brother's affliction.

"At least don't torment yourself," she said to him one evening as they fetched water from the pump outside. The twilight air was crisp. Soon enough they would cover the pump for winter and melt great pans of snow by the stove. Guillaume rubbed his hands together and glanced at the back door just to be sure they were alone. "And don't imagine the Holy One made a mistake in making you. We are all made on purpose, just as we are."

After a long moment he said, "What do I do, then?"

"You just love, however you can. That's what we all must do." She was awfully young to be so sure, not more than sixteen, but he knew she was right.

On his wedding night, in bed in the dark with Elizabeth at his side, he said a silent prayer and thought of Emmet Clarkson. Afterward he prayed for Bess' forgiveness. The years rolled forward and the children came. Guillaume took for granted that everyone had dear things that they lived without. His parents had suffered terrible losses in their young lives. The Minkinses had too. They lost the first two of their four children, a little boy and girl Guillaume had known and loved in his youth. No one was spared hardship.

Once when Guillaume was a boy, he was in the stable grooming the old chestnut quarter horse they called Nantucket, when one of the short brown hairs flew into his left eye and became lodged high up inside. No amount of flushing by Maman was able to remove it, nor could she see it and pluck it out. The eye became red and inflamed, and for days it stung and watered. The lid swelled and oozed pus, half blinding him. With only one eye to see through the world suddenly appeared flat. He reached for things that were too far away to grasp, and he stumbled over curbs and uneven ground. At last though, the hidden hair worked its way out. The infection cleared and was quickly forgotten, as just another in a thick catalogue of childhood injuries and ailments that passed through the ranks of the children. Yet, now and again, Guillaume thought he could still feel the hair, when he was tired, or angry, or, years later, if a man chanced to remind him of Emmet Clarkson.

For years Guillaume made an annual trip in late June to Québec City to purchase his hardware for the saddlery. Papa had done the same all his years in Montreal, as loyal in his business relationships as with family, and now Guillaume did business with the hardware man's son. In years past it was a week-long journey by horse and wagon. Now, just a day on the train. He would stay one night at a guesthouse that was quiet and clean, and served simple but hearty meals. With his transactions complete by mid-morning the next day he returned home, arriving late, though at that time of year always before dark. It was a pleasant trip when the weather was fine, and he welcomed those rare hours of solitude.

Time had a way of speeding up or slowing down, it seemed, depending on circumstances. Soon after the taking of the photograph, the daguerreotype that hung on the bedroom wall, baby Dax took his first steps, and soon after that it was time once again for the journey to Québec City. Guillaume was unsettled at the thought of leaving just now, even for one night. Elizabeth, strong and healthy all her life, had still not fully recovered from Dax's birth. She grew winded climbing stairs or hefting laundry or even straightening too quickly when lifting the baby from the floor. She waved off Guillaume's concern. It was nothing she was worried about, and the older children helped her with everything. Albert would be home that week from the railroad anyhow, and with Josephine just next door....When she kissed him goodbye early the next morning he felt sufficiently reassured.

Guillaume arrived at the guesthouse later that evening, having walked the distance from the station. There were six rooms in the place, and by now he had stayed in each, every time a year older. Five guests besides himself were served supper by the proprietress, Madame LeBlanc. All were seated around the familiar long oak table: a young couple, two French Canadians and an Englishman from Toronto. The Englishman was in textiles, he said, also in the city on business. His name was Hathaway. His salt and pepper hair was cropped rather short. Guillaume noticed the black brows that hovered over his blue eyes. Guillaume's left eye began to sting and he rubbed at it with a knuckle. He concentrated on his chops.

After supper the young couple and the proprietress retired

early, leaving the four men to linger with tobacco and stories made more amusing by the company of strangers. After some time two more went off to bed, leaving Guillaume and the Englishman.

They got on very well, a mutual energy animated the conversation, despite the late hour. They got onto the subject of fruit trees as both men, it turned out, cultivated a few of their own in their back gardens. Hathaway knew of nothing better than a ripe freestone peach in summer, so full of juice one had to lean forward to eat it.

"No, Sir," Guillaume argued. The best fruit of all was the Van cherry, in his opinion, and he went on to describe its texture and flavor, and the loveliness of the tree itself, which he pruned in his own yard late each winter with the utmost care. As he spoke his gaze was lost in the lace curtains that hung in the window, and when he turned back to his companion he realized the Englishman had fixed him with a stare, eyes cobalt under the coal-black brows.

Guillaume flushed with a violent heat. He reached for his teacup.

"It's a pity there's no billiard table," Guillaume said, having choked down the last of the cold tea. In fact he was a great lover of the game, and often took his older sons, Albert and Ross, to play at a local tavern. Guillaume had an instinctive understanding of speed and spin and angle, and won so easily his sons preferred to play each other. In that case Guillaume would circle the table while the boys played, calculating the best shots and offering advice on the better way to grip the cue.

"Ha!" Hathaway laughed, "I'm glad there isn't one. Abominable game."

"Don't you play?" Guillaume smiled at the Englishman's irreverence.

"When forced," Hathaway said. "But it's not bad for business, I will say that. Given that I always lose. Makes the clients jolly and likely to buy more of my wares."

"What do you prefer, then?"

The conversation rolled on, from games and sport, back to fruit trees and onward to rail travel. The clock struck midnight and still neither of them took their leave. Finally, after the clock struck one, Hathaway rose.

"I'm certain we'll need our rest," he said.

Guillaume nodded and stood also.

He followed Hathaway up the stairs. The Englishman opened the door to his room, opposite Guillaume's.

"Would you care to come in," Hathaway said quietly.

Guillaume stood petrified, wavering on the threshold.

"My wife," he said at last.

Hathaway nodded, a wistful smile. "Of course," he said. "Goodnight, then."

Guillaume lay awake the whole rest of the night. Many times he thought of rising, approaching the other door, and softly knocking. He knew that if such a knock came to his door he would be powerless to resist. But no such knock came, and when the dawn greeted him he was exhausted, utterly torn between relief and regret.

The Englishman was not present when breakfast was served. The French Canadians asked after him and the proprietress said he'd had to leave at first light. Guillaume ate his eggs and porridge in silence, but suddenly Madame LeBlanc was at his side. She brought out a gilt-edged card from her apron pocket and held it out to him. A calling card.

"Monsieur Hathaway asked me to give this to you," she said.

"Ah," said Guillaume, surprised, "thank you."

He turned it over in his hands, feeling the thickness of the paper, and the subtle indentation of the ink-pressed letters. *Francis R. Hathaway*, read the card. *Textiles.* A Toronto address. Nodding, he tucked the card away in his coat pocket.

Guillaume returned from his journey to find all in good health and spirits. Preparations were under way for Albert's wedding. There would be a church ceremony followed by a party in the meeting hall. Albert was a man now, and his bride, Genevieve, a thoughtful, sturdy young lady. The morning of the wedding Guillaume and Bess stood at the altar having a brief word with the pastor as Albert escorted Maman to the pew where all of her daughters were waiting. How tall and fine he looked, with Maman so small and aged, yet elegant, smiling and hanging on his elbow. It seemed so short a time ago that Maman sat with little Albert on the piano bench teaching him his scales and melodies, and all of the songs they could sing together. His seriousness was apparent even then, his brow furrowed as his tiny fingers reached for the keys. She was such a patient teacher, and told him many stories of the island of her birth, of all the happy things, and Albert sat enraptured, imagining Martinique to be the most beautiful place on earth. Life was so very rich and full, thought Guillaume, surely any ache could be forgotten, at least for the moment.

Less than one week later Maman, as it is said in the Old Testament, was gathered to her people. That night Maman and

Josephine had spent a quiet evening. Josie read aloud from Psalms and Maman listened with her eyes closed and a trace of a smile, but then said she had a touch of a headache. Josephine urged her to go to bed early, and said she would bring in a cup of tea. Standing at the stove before the heating water, Josephine felt a tremor in her spine that in an instant became so great she stumbled back. A brilliant wind, she told Guillaume later, rushed through the house, passing clear through her body and out through the window.

When Guillaume found Josephine at his door, brought there by a frenzied rapping, her face shone with tears. She reached for him.

"Maman has gone to be with Papa."

But the greatest shock came another night, three months later. All the rest of the household were asleep, but Guillaume had stayed late in the shop, finishing a pair of saddles to be delivered the next day. At last he climbed the stairs, holding a candle aloft, and made his way to the bedroom. Quietly he set the candle on the nightstand and began to undress. He looked at Bess' curled form under the quilts. She was still. He went forward and listened for her breathing.

Guillaume hurried to wake Ross, and sent him running to fetch Dr. Laurent, who lived only a few streets away. Jonty he told to go next door for Aunt Josephine. The girls, Eleanor and Melody, woke from the commotion and met Guillaume in the hall, clinging to his sides. Mercifully, little Dax still slept.

Dr. Laurent arrived with Ross and Guillaume led him to the bedroom to examine Bess. Josie had gathered the children in the girls' room to wait, until at last Guillaume came for them. The doctor explained that Elizabeth's heart had stopped, and that she was gone. The girls flung themselves at their mother's feet, sobbing, the boys knelt by the bed, and Guillaume gathered all of them in his arms, all of Bess' children, except for Dax, who was downstairs with Josephine, until things quieted down.

Guillaume was overcome with a dreadful, hollow weightlessness, as if the earth had stopped turning and he had nothing but his two arms to keep his family from flying away. A long, long river of tears cut a path through the night, until the sky paled, and the bleak dawn broke, unwanted, outside the window.

Whereas Maman's passing brought a deep but quiet grief, the sudden loss of Elizabeth ruptured the fabric of their lives. The web of the family drew closer together during this dark season. Josephine moved into Guillaume's home to take charge of Dax, now just two years old, and to help support the other children who, though much older, were still in need of care. Josephine and Guillaume's three older sisters visited daily, and Albert and Genevieve took over the apartment next door, above the saddlery.

Guillaume went through the tasks of each day crushed with the weight of Bess' absence. When he dressed each morning it confused him greatly that she wasn't behind him doing the same. When he went downstairs and she wasn't in the kitchen he had the impulse to look for her in the backyard. He was two people, the one that knew Bess was gone and grieved for her, and the one that couldn't yet make sense of it. But at the end of each day, when he said goodnight to the children, he did what he knew she would have wanted. He told them that she loved them, and that she was watching over, and because he believed it they did too. Thus they survived the longest and coldest winter of their lives.

When summer rolled around again, the pain of loss had become a small measure less immediate. Guillaume tended to his work and his children, and to Bess' memory. Dax, now three, learned he had the power to make the family laugh, and enlivened the household with his antics, and Josephine provided the anchor needed by all. Soon it was time for the journey to Québec City and Guillaume brought along Ross, who was fifteen now and most likely to take over the saddlery one day. Albert was a railroad man, and Jonty would surely follow him there. Eleanor and Melody, children just yesterday, were already becoming young women in their own right. It was almost with surprise that Guillaume remembered the Englishman. Their meeting only one year ago seemed as distant as a foreign shore.

Close to another year passed, and then it was April. The snow gave way rapidly to green budding things. The handful of fruit trees in the garden began to bring forth their delicate blossoms. Guillaume still deeply missed Bess, and Maman, but there were rare days when his remembrance of them came briefly and gently.

One late night he woke, restless, but not from grief. He rose from bed and opened the window, letting in the spring air that struck his bare skin, making him shiver. He thought of the Englishman, and, filled with an unexpected sense of possibility, lit a candle and drew a cedar box out from beneath the bed. Under a pile of odd receipts and papers the calling card was still there, edged in gold ink, bearing the name and address.

Carrying the candlestick, he stepped over to his writing desk.

He sat with his steel pen and inkwell, staring at the paper for some time not knowing what to write. At last he began.

> *Dear Sir,*
>
> *Perhaps you may remember me, a saddler from Montréal, as we met nearly two years ago at the guesthouse LeBlanc in Québec City. Sadly, my dear wife Elizabeth passed away not long thereafter. In any case, I enjoyed making your acquaintance. This coming July 19th I will again be in Québec City on business, staying at the same lodgings.*
>
> > *Sincerely,*
> >
> > *G. Rougeaux*

Guillaume had written letters only rarely, but even had he a lifetime of experience with correspondence, this would have been awkward. He blotted the ink and folded the letter carefully, then he addressed an envelope. He felt as if he were stepping off a precipice, and his heart beat wildly. Francis Hathaway might have moved away, might have died, might not remember him or wish to. It was beyond ridiculous. When morning came he hurried to the post office, before he could change his mind.

Days became weeks, became one month, then two, and still no reply. Guillaume chided himself for the vanity of sending the letter at all. He was a father, a *grand*father now, no less, with all manner of responsibility for his family and community. What had he hoped to gain? It was folly. He saw that now.

And so he put the matter away, just as he had so long ago with Emmet Clarkson. The end of June approached and Guillaume made his preparations for Québec City just as he always did. Ross would not accompany him this time. Josephine had all the children engaged in renewing the interior whitewash of the entire house, and so when the day arrived Guillaume was again alone.

Guillaume sighed and smiled as he gazed through the window of the train car at the passing landscape. How time marched on. Dax was four years old, a little man who thought himself very big indeed now that he was an uncle. Albert and Genevieve had had their first child, a robust creature they called Elodie. Dax was allowed to hold the baby in Elizabeth's old rocking chair, provided he did not squirm out from under her. If he rocked a little too fast the baby let out her funny laugh that surprised them all by sounding like an old man's. How Bess would have liked to see all that.

The gentle jostling over the tracks made him sleepy. He dozed more easily now than he ever used to. Perhaps this would be his last trip to Québec City. What with the goods available these days in Montreal, the expense of the trip was really no longer justified. Quality studs and buckles and the like could be found for lesser prices right at home.

Guillaume arrived at the guesthouse and rang the bell at the street door. He knew from his last visit that the place was under new ownership, and that the new owners honored Madame LeBlanc's custom regarding colored guests. Madame LeBlanc, aging too, had gone to live elsewhere with a son and daughter-in-law. Madame Fournier, the new proprietress, ushered Guillaume into the small foyer and up the old stairs. Her brisk step rustled the indigo skirts of her dress, as they followed the stairs up to the second floor where the kitchen, dining room and proprietor's quarters were located. The proprietress produced his room key from a desk drawer, and Guillaume went up another flight of stairs to room number four.

He unlocked the door and set his old leather valise on the floor beside the bed. The valise, which he used on every trip, was a wedding gift, crafted by his father. It sported a set of brass buckles purchased long ago right in this very city. Québec was the city of his father's birth and his mother's youth. Guillaume kept the leather of the valise oiled and wrapped in paper between uses, and it was still in excellent condition.

Guillaume looked about the room. The furniture was all still the same, the bedstead, chair and small bureau, but a new enamel pitcher and basin had replaced the old. The Fourniers had also invested in new linens, heavier scrubbing, and curtains more in line with the current fashion, giving the place an air of refreshment. It was just past five o'clock in the afternoon. Madame Fournier said that supper would be served at seven, and that she hoped he liked mutton stew. After washing up he removed his shoes and lay down on the bed. He rested an arm across his eyes, and let out a long breath.

Madame Fournier, it turned out, was a good cook. The stew was fragrant and satisfying and served with a rich black bread. The handful of guests were polite and the conversation was pleasant, though Guillaume did not feel particularly here nor there. He let his thoughts drift as if they were children, leading him away from the adults' table. An hour or so later, the supper dishes cleared, Madame Fournier returned to the dining room with a teapot and tray of cups.

Voices of the guests and the clatter of the tea things on the table muffled the sound of the doorbell from downstairs. Madame Fournier straightened.

"Was that the bell?" she asked, looking toward the stairs. All fell silent a moment and the second ring came through clearly. "Ah!" she said, wiping her hands over her apron and heading out. "That will be Monsieur Hathaway."

Guillaume snapped awake. Had he heard right?

Already there were two sets of footsteps on the creaking stairs. Guillaume stood.

The dining room door pushed open, Madame Fournier followed by another figure, both foreign and familiar. It was Hathaway, after all.

Guillaume was speechless.

Madame Fournier introduced the Englishman around the room, and he nodded politely. And then the blue eyes under their heavy black brows, turned toward him. Hathaway held out his hand.

"Monsieur Rougeaux," he said, "I'm glad to see you."

Guillaume knew not whether his feet still touched the floor. He reached out, and the two men shook hands.

"Mr. Hathaway," he said.

Francis Hathaway settled into a chair opposite Guillaume. The guests took their tea. Guillaume looked upon the Englishman when he dared. He had the same lean features, the salt and pepper hair was a bit longer and perhaps had a touch more of the salt. Now and then their eyes met and Hathaway smiled.

Another hour or two passed, and the other guests retired, and then Guillaume and Hathaway were alone. It was dark outside now, and rain ticked lightly against the window pane. The Englishman spoke.

"I was very pleased to get your letter," he said, explaining he had been away in Ottawa until just last week. Given the rate at which letters traveled, there was no time to reply. He had only been able to reserve his place at the guesthouse by chance, since an associate of his was journeying just then from Toronto to Québec City, and carried the message for him.

"And I am terribly sorry about your wife," he added gently. "You must miss her very much."

"I and the children," said Guillaume.

Hathaway nodded.

"Have you a family?" asked Guillaume. They had spoken of many things in their first meeting, but not this. No, Hathaway did not. He had a married brother near to him in Toronto, but the rest were back in England.

"We are so different then," said Guillaume. He could not imagine existing outside of his large family, living so untethered.

"Are we?" Hathaway ventured. Guillaume didn't know. He smiled.

"Why did you come?" he asked.

"Why did you?"

An unbearable longing welled up in Guillaume's chest.

"I wanted to meet you again," he said simply.

"And here we are," the Englishman said.

Their first kiss broke his heart. In a capsule of darkness and silence, they stood together inside the Englishman's locked door. Hathaway gripped the edges of Guillaume's vest, near the collar, pulling him close. Countless times Guillaume had invoked the image of Emmet Clarkson, or some other man, when he had been with Bess, and now the sheer reality of it was almost too much to bear.

Hathaway led him to the bed and drew him down so they sat side by side. He discerned Guillaume's shaking hands, held them gently, and then brought them to the buttons at the front of his waistcoat.

"Help me with these, won't you?" he whispered.

Guillaume obliged, grateful to have some direction, especially when his brain seemed to be on fire, and his only prayer was that he would live until morning, and not expire before this thing, this extraordinary thing, could be done.

When the line of sky beyond the curtains went from black to deep blue Guillaume pulled away and found his clothing. Listening to Hathaway's light, even snoring, he crept from the room to his own down the hallway.

He awoke in his own bed to the sound of the breakfast bell. Eight o'clock, so much later than he ever slept. Down in the dining room some of the guests from the previous night were present, some had left early to continue their journeys in different directions. Francis Hathaway was among those not present, and Guillaume was relieved. He was a stranger to himself. It took all of his concentration to eat, nearly forgetting in which hand he was used to holding the knife and in which the fork.

When Guillaume emerged from the guesthouse, the bright sky dazzled his eyes. The rain-washed streets, thick with life, lay decorated in blue mirrors. Somehow Guillaume managed to attend to his purchases and return to the station, where he boarded his train, and finally sank into a dreamless sleep.

Josephine sensed the change in him at once, but left him alone. The activities of the household carried on as usual. It was a peaceful summer, business was good, and the children were growing up. Ross took over the deliveries from the saddlery and little Dax spent hours in the shop, hammering at scraps of leather and chattering to his father about what kind of saddles he was making. A lightness buoyed Guillaume, even at the weary end of the day. The colors of the roses that grew at the front of the house, the ones Elizabeth had planted before Albert was born, seemed richer than before.

One month later, in August, a letter came from Toronto.

It read,

> *My Dear Monsieur Rougeaux,*
>
> *I wish to inform you that I shall be in Ottawa on business the first half of October, staying at the Sherbourne Inn. I believe there are some opportunities in saddlery in this city that may interest you, should you like to discuss them in person.*
>
> *Yours sincerely,*
>
> *F. Hathaway*

Guillaume read it several times over and then tucked it into the pocket of his vest, overwhelmed with a sudden turmoil. Certainly he had thought they might possibly meet again, but every time the thought arose he pushed it aside. It was one thing to allow himself one night, a night outside of his real life, that would never be repeated. It would be quite another thing to pursue knowing this man.

He kept the letter with him all the next week, taking it out to read again here and there, as if this time he would discover an answer in its short lines. At times he imagined going to Ottawa, the touch of Hathaway's hands, the sound of his voice. But then reason would come and throw a heavy curtain down over the visions, covering them with the old sadness and resignation.

One evening Guillaume sat in the parlor after supper with Josephine. The girls had taken Dax out to play in the street and the other boys had gone to visit a neighbor. Josephine sat by the open window in Elizabeth's rocking chair, leaning forward to use the last of the evening sunlight for her sewing. There was never a lack of hems and breeches to mend.

"What's troubling you, Guille?" Josephine never wasted time on preamble. Guillaume shook his head, rubbed his tired eyes, and then took Hathaway's letter from his pocket and handed it to her. She traced her fingers over the ink and around the edges of the paper. "F. Hathaway," she said, musing. "A friend?"

"Could be," he said.

"If you wish it?"

Guillaume cleared his throat and shifted in his chair. Josie laid her mending aside and looked at him a long time.

"What's stopping you?"

"It's not for a man to do," he said at last. "Not what an honorable man does."

"Why do you say so?" Josephine's voice was low and steady.

"Papa," he said, "was the best kind of man. Can you say he wasn't the best kind of man?"

"And you must be like him?"

"Of course."

"Oh, Guille," she said, "yes, Papa was of the best kind, but there isn't only one kind of good man."

"I know that."

"No, I don't think you do."

Guillaume coughed. He swallowed. He rubbed his eyes again and his fingers came away wet. "Maybe I don't know anything," he allowed. He covered his face with his hands. Josie came and put her arms around him.

"My brave brother," she said, "let your heart live. Let it be as the Holy One made it."

They sat in silence awhile, and then Guillaume said that if he could no longer justify his annual journey east to Québec City, neither did it make sense to be going away again so soon, this time west to Ottawa.

"It need not make sense," Josie smiled. She took his face in her hands and kissed his forehead, just as she did with the children.

Guillaume penned a new letter:

Dear Mr. Hathaway,

I should be glad to discuss the opportunities you mention, and shall make my travel

*plans for early in the month of October. I
thank you for your invitation.*

Sincerely,

G. Rougeaux

The long days of August came and went, and then September opened with a chill. The children readied their books for school, the roses in front faded, dropping brown petals, and Guillaume wore his woolen shirt in the shop, buttoned to the neck. Each night he snuffed out the candle thinking he was one more day closer to October. And then, all at once it was the 3rd, and Guillaume, leather valise in hand, found himself boarding a train for Ottawa.

The inn was not far from the station, somewhat grander than the guesthouse in Québec City, but still a modest place; it was near to a park on the Ottawa River. He asked for Mr. Hathaway at the reception desk. The clerk replied in a chilly tone that Mr. Hathaway had gone out that morning and did not say when he was expected back. It was however nearing the supper hour and the clerk stated, "You may wait for him here." Two upright chairs stood against the wall opposite the desk, on either side of a tin umbrella stand.

He glimpsed a number of passersby outside, horse carts taking their wares to wherever it was their business lay. Guillaume caught the clerk watching him once or twice. Indeed, Guillaume wondered himself just what he was doing there. A cup of tea would have been very welcome, something to settle the nerves. But then, out the window Guillaume saw him, Hathaway, drawing nearer up the walk in the company of another man. Guillaume stood as the two came through the door, engaged in an animated conversation.

Surprise flashed across Hathaway's face and Guillaume thought he saw a flush rise at his white throat. He strode toward Guillaume and clasped his hand in greeting.

"You've made it," he said, smiling.

Guillaume glanced at the other man. Hathaway read his look and quickly introduced his companion. His name was Hurst, another textile merchant, and they'd just finished a meeting.

Hathaway addressed Hurst. "Will you be dining with us here?"

"No," the other man sighed, consulting a pocket watch, "Mrs. Hurst is expecting me. We'll draw up the papers at my office tomorrow."

"Very well," Hathaway said. When the other man departed he said to Guillaume, "Let's get you settled in here, you must be tired." He turned to the clerk. "Monsieur Rougeaux will share my lodgings tonight. He is my associate and we have much business to discuss." Indeed, it was not unusual for two men to share a room, provided there were two beds, which there were.

The clerk eyed Guillaume.

"I'm sorry sir," he said, "it's not permitted."

"What's not permitted?" he asked.

"The Inn does not serve *Ethiopians*."

Hathaway shot a glance at Guillaume. Unruffled, he spoke again.

"Monsieur Rougeaux is not from Ethiopia," Hathaway began slowly, as if addressing someone stupid. "He is a master saddler from Montreal. We have a joint venture in *upholstery*, and if you will not serve him then we shall take our business elsewhere. Please cancel my fortnight's reservation, and tell the management I am most disappointed."

The clerk looked shaken. It was the offseason and a sudden two-week vacancy would not please his superior. "Perhaps we might make an exception for one night," he said. "I shall go ask upstairs."

"Good idea," Hathaway said. He was not a man of great wealth, but his comportment spoke of his belief in his right to be in the place he chose, and with whomever he chose.

When the clerk returned they knew they had won.

"One night only," he said.

Hathaway wasn't finished. He addressed Guillaume. "How long were you planning to stay?"

"Two nights," Guillaume said.

They didn't wait for the clerk's answer. Hathaway snatched up Guillaume's valise from the floor at his feet and headed for the stairs.

The room was on the top floor and when they had entered Hathaway bolted the door behind them. They each let out a long breath.

"*Upholstery*," said Guillaume. They burst into muffled laughter, and fell into each other's arms.

A tallow candle burned on the bedside table. Hathaway held Guillaume's hand, gazing at the contrasting hues of their intertwined fingers.

"In school, back in Sussex, they told us Africans were primitives," he said, "and that slavery was invented for their own good."

"To civilize us," Guillaume said.

"Right."

"Did you believe it?"

"When I was little. I believed everything."

"As we do."

Hathaway shifted his body and tucked a hand under his cheek. "So Africans were primitive, the red Indian a savage, Jews were dirty and the Chinese were thieves and liars."

"The natural order."

"But they hated me too, you know, the other boys in school. They called me *dainty*, a *girl*, *Little Lord Hathaway*. And then they'd try to bash my head in."

Guillaume watched Hathaway's face as he spoke, imagining this beautiful man as a once vulnerable child. "Was there no help for you?"

"My brother Edward, yes. If he was near he'd fight them off. I was a weakling and couldn't defend myself. But Edward stood by me. He knew what people said about me and he told me to forget them. He always said, *You're fine as you are, Frankie. You're fine as you are.* I had to make a choice on who to believe."

"Your brother reminds me of my sister Josephine."

"Does he?"

"Very much so."

"Then we are both blessed."

Francis told Guillaume about a certain incident, a day back in Sussex when he was twelve and Edward was away. There was a cousin, James, of the same age, with whom he'd always been close, and a wrestling match in the cellar turned suddenly into something more exciting. That is, until Francis' father appeared and nearly killed them both. James he banished from the house and Francis he whipped within an inch of his life. Indeed he might have murdered his son, had his wife not intervened.

"Later when Edward came home and saw what our father had done he was furious. That was the night he started talking about going to America. He said one day we'd go, the two of us." Hathaway stretched and turned over. "There was a globe in the school library. I used to look at the mass of America, at Africa and the size of it, and China too. And the tiny dot that was England. Was most of the world thieves and savages, then? I dared to think it was all a lie. I made up my mind to find out the truth for myself."

There were scars, Guillaume could see them now, several white lines across Francis' lower back where his father's belt buckle had scored the skin. Guillaume moved closer and pressed his lips there, again and again, as if he could draw out the pain and replace it with tenderness.

All that winter they exchanged letters. Guillaume wrote how he and Ross were studying the making of some other leather goods now, after Ross had become curious about how his grandfather had made the valise. Jonty was still intent on following Albert into the railroad industry. Melody and Eleanor, both especially musical, played a piano duet at the church's Christmas service. Josephine was teaching Dax his numbers and letters. Guillaume wrote, *Please tell me something about England*, by which he meant, *Tell me more about you, in your younger years. I want to know everything.*

Hathaway did write of England, things he hadn't yet told, of his voyage to Canada with his brother as young men, and how Edward still dragged him out rowing when the weather was good enough. He wrote of the day-to-day in Toronto, of the price of silks from India, of friends, and of the theater and opera, which he considered his own private church. Hathaway wrote, *Please tell me something of Montréal, in the old days, before the expansion*, by which he meant, *Tell me about you in your younger years. I want to know everything.*

They met again in Ottawa in the spring. Guillaume told his family, one night at supper, that he would be away for five or six days this time. Melody asked, "What will you do there, Papa?" Guillaume answered truthfully that he would be visiting a workshop where craftsmen made leather satchels, to observe some of their techniques and purchase some new tools.

"And," he said, "I will visit a friend."

A look of apprehension passed through the faces of the children, the girls especially. They cherished their mother's memory and feared their father might someday marry again.

"My friend Mr. Hathaway," he said, remaining, with great effort, casually composed. The children relaxed and smiled.

"You met him last fall, didn't you, Papa?" said Eleanor. Guillaume said he did, and that this time Ross would be in charge of the saddlery in his stead. Ross shone with pride and straightened in his chair.

"And I hope to find another book for Auntie."

"Books for Auntie!" little Dax cried out, clapping his hands.

Since childhood, Josephine had had a great interest in all things botanical, and over time had acquired a small number of books on plants and their properties. She kept dozens of things growing in pots indoors, and outdoors in the warmer seasons. Dax was fascinated by the illustrations in her botanical books, particularly the ones that showed both the interiors and exteriors of seeds and blossoms. Adding another volume to Josie's treasured collection was the least Guillaume could do. He was so grateful to her, for everything.

The days in Ottawa with Hathaway were glorious. They took every measure of discretion and thus created every possible shelter for their intimacy. On the last night, as they lay among the bedclothes, Guillaume asked Hathaway the question that had been nagging at his heart. He did not assume any claim on this man, but he wanted to know. He shifted and took a breath.

"Francis."

"What is it," Hathaway murmured, rolling over to face him.

"Are there others?"

Hathaway remained quiet a moment or two.

"There have been," he said.

"Many?"

"Not too very many."

"What about now?"

"Would it matter very much to you?"

Guillaume considered this. Perhaps yes. Perhaps no. Perhaps both at once. Before he could answer Hathaway spoke again.

"Anyway, I seem only to be capable of loving one man at a time."

Guillaume reached for him, still amazed at how dear Francis had become to him.

"I too," he said.

The seasons passed and there were more visits, more letters. In the next year Hathaway occasionally had business in Montreal and

Josephine suggested to Guillaume that he be invited to suppers, though they dared no other meetings. Hathaway brought gifts for the children, and for Josephine. His quiet charm won them all over. Two years later she insisted he be invited to Ross' wedding.

"Sometimes the best hiding place is in plain sight," she said, and Guillaume could not argue.

Another year later he traveled to Toronto.

Francis had his housekeeper fix up the spare room for his guest and prepare a special meal, and then he sent her home to her family. He met Guillaume at the station, and asked him if he wouldn't mind dining the next night with Edward and his wife.

The guest room went unused and Guillaume discovered his friend anew in his private quarters. There were things he had chosen with care, there were photographs, the small garden with the famous peach trees. There was a cat.

"Do you like it?" Francis asked.

"Very much."

"I wanted you to see it," he said, "for I may be leaving."

Guillaume, who was looking out at the garden, turned to face him.

"I was thinking," Francis went on, "that with my new contacts, my business could do just as well in Montreal."

Just when Guillaume thought nothing more could surprise him, the floor dropped away.

Francis took both his hands and looked into his eyes.

"You would do this?" asked Guillaume.

"Yes." Francis' voice was gentle.

"Are you sure?"

"We are not young," Francis said. "Whatever days I have left I wish to spend as many of them as possible with you."

What was possible, indeed in all the world there was no place for them, and yet, there they were. Perhaps there was a new country, one not found on a globe that had been traced all over with such darkness—a new country where there were fruit trees and quiet Saturdays together, where Francis would come often to dinner, but never agree to a game of billiards. After dinners with the Rougeauxes, Francis might even develop the habit of leaving without his gloves, and Guillaume might sigh, and say to Josephine and the children that he had better just take the gloves over to Mr. Hathaway, and that he would be back directly. But if he got back home late once in a while it would be alright, because they would understand that Papa and Mr. Hathaway always got to talking, and always forgot about the time.

Eleanor

Montreal & New York

Late 1800s

Eleanor's earliest memory was of sitting beside her grandmother Hetty, called Mémé, on a piano bench. On the other side of big, sweet-smelling Mémé was her oldest brother Albert, with both hands on the white keys, following Mémé's gentle instructions and plunking out a nursery song. Eleanor was only two or three, and she would have to wait another year or more for her chance at lessons with Mémé. An eternity. Mémé allowed her to sit beside them as long as she remained quiet, which she did, absorbing with her ears and eyes, and whole heart, everything that was happening before her.

When Eleanor's turn to learn finally came, Mémé was taken aback. "My, oh my," she remarked to Papa after the first lesson. "I don't believe that piano will stand a chance against her." Eleanor's younger sister Melody eventually enjoyed the lessons too, and though she played like an angel, as folks later said, it was with a distracted air that sometimes led to careless mistakes. Only Eleanor seemed to mind Melody's carelessness, since she took her own playing so seriously, attacking the instrument with quiet ferocity. When they practiced a duet as older girls, Melody giggled lightheartedly when her fingers fumbled, which frustrated Eleanor so much that she sometimes left the room in tears. Melody always followed her, hugging her around the waist and murmuring apologies and promises to do better, but in the end her nature won out and Eleanor would be upset anew. Finally, Auntie Josephine stepped in and declared no more duets, allowing harmony to return between the sisters. But this was later, when Eleanor was sixteen.

Mémé passed on when Eleanor was only twelve years old. The children clung to Mama and sobbed, never dreaming they would also lose her too only a few months later. When their mother died, Eleanor's world all but ended. Auntie Josephine came and held things together at home, and Papa bore up the family like a ship in a storm. A year passed, and another, and though the storm abated, none were left unscathed. Mama's death affected each of her children differently. Melody, for one, became more protective of little Dax, so much so that sometimes the adults had to step in so that he might play without her constant admonitions. Ross and Jonty pulled together tighter. For Eleanor it was as if there were a hole in her heart, once Mama was gone, leaving her unnaturally exposed. It was strange to Eleanor how other children she knew who had lost parents seemed to carry on much the same as before. Grief looked so very different from the inside.

There was only one thing that still touched her as it had before Mama died, and that was music. As for the piano, Mrs. Allison, the choir director from church, brought Eleanor and Melody under her tutelage, determined to pick up musically where their grandmother had left off. Mrs. Allison was skilled with choir arrangements and directing soloists, but nothing was dearer to her heart than a duet on piano, especially as the centerpiece of a holiday service. When Auntie came to speak with her about Eleanor and Melody, Mrs. Allison agreed to arrange for the girls to play separate pieces.

With the change in the program, Mrs. Allison had a chance to see Eleanor play disentangled from Melody, and was taken aback. Eleanor Rougeaux had real potential.

Mrs. Allison, a white woman, was aware that scant opportunities existed for a colored girl to pursue her music, and wondered if there were any schools in the region that might accept Eleanor. She wrote letters to Toronto, Quebec City, Boston, and New Haven. At last she learned of a school in New York City, The National Conservatory of Music of America. It was open to musicians of all colors, women, and even some students who were blind or crippled by polio. Auditions were held every spring. That very evening she paid a visit to the Rougeauxes.

It was February and still bitterly cold. Auntie answered the door, and it was several minutes of unwrapping mufflers and woolens before she could identify the visitor. By then Eleanor and Melody had come into the foyer, along with Papa and Dax, the youngest. Mrs. Allison was ushered into the parlor to sit and soon held a steaming cup of tea in her hands.

"Mr. Rougeaux," began Mrs. Allison, "as you know, I believe Eleanor has an exceptional talent." Eleanor's face grew hot, and she stared hard at the floorboards. Mrs. Allison told them of the Conservatory and the auditions, that the school was supported by numerous sponsors and that from the auditions two hundred students would be selected for their summer program. Of these two hundred, up to half would be invited to continue at the Conservatory for four years. There were scholarships sufficient to provide tuition and basic living expenses for those in need. At this Eleanor could no longer decipher the words exchanged. Her ears filled with a roaring noise, and she thought her heart would fly from her chest.

Papa was dubious. He thanked Mrs. Allison most sincerely for her interest and time, and for her faith in Eleanor. The family was indebted to her. But he was not eager to send his child away to a foreign place. She was only eighteen and anything could happen to a colored girl all alone in a big city.

Mrs. Allison understood this and was prepared. She handed Papa the letter she had received from the school. There were a number of reputable boarding houses for young ladies where the out-of-town female students stayed, and the conduct of all the students was strictly chaperoned. The good standing of the Conservatory depended not only upon the musicianship it produced, but also on the behavior of the students, both in and outside of the classroom. The letter made very clear that for the students fortunate enough to be selected, their personal responsibility was as great as the opportunity. Anything less was grounds for dismissal.

"All that is needed," Mrs. Allison concluded, "is train fare to New York and back."

Papa folded the letter carefully and handed it back to Mrs. Allison. He thanked her again, promising to give the matter his thorough consideration.

When Mrs. Allison had gone he sat down again by the fire and looked at Eleanor.

"Well, *chère*," he said, "what do you think of all this?"

Eleanor was speechless. Never had she dreamed that something like this was possible. When she found words she said, "I want to go." After which her heart echoed, *I must go.*

Papa turned to Auntie. "What do you say?" he said.

Auntie, who was uncharacteristically silent during the meeting, did not alter her position in her rocking chair. "I say that was Fate knocking at the door," she said, "dressed up like Mrs. Allison."

Eleanor watched Papa's face. It shone with pride and glowered with concern. She loved him very much, and if she did go it would be hard to say goodbye. She watched him as he looked into the hearth. She was already imagining herself on a train.

Papa would consider permission, but there was still the question of the various expenses. Eleanor's older brothers were working now, but Papa was still the sole support of Auntie and three children, as well as aiding Eleanor's Aunt Phoebe who was recently widowed. Funds were already stretched to their limit.

But then Mrs. Allison let it slip to the church choir that Eleanor Rougeaux had before her an opportunity, and almost overnight a purse heavy with silver coins materialized. For Eleanor it was one wonder after another. Two months later she boarded the train for New York. She carried Papa's valise packed with necessities and a headful of his and Auntie's advice. Papa especially had warned her that she would soon be in the regular company of men they didn't know, and that she must not let anyone *take liberties*. Eleanor was not known to be a great beauty, but she had a sweet face and an attractive figure, and Papa knew a thing or two about men. Still, he trusted his child. She had never been too interested in the boys she knew, tending to regard them as cousins, if she noticed them at all. She was very unlike Melody, whose open innocence and warm admiration of a series of boys gave a father cause for concern.

Eleanor had only a vague notion of what exactly these liberties were that a young man might take, and those thoughts certainly weren't foremost in her mind. She was leaving home with the dream of studying music at a conservatory. Papa and Auntie both told her that her Mama would have been proud, and to Eleanor that meant the world.

The whole family accompanied her to the station, to board the train, a second-class car, that would be departing at 5:00 in the afternoon and arriving in New York City the next morning. Papa took pains to find another colored family traveling south, that Eleanor could sit with, and he came aboard to help her stow her valise and dinner basket, and fold her coat over the hard wooden seat. He stood with her as long as he could while those passengers of darker colors like their own, or native, or sunburned Chinese, crowded into the car. Eleanor clung to his hand, and then he had to go. She leaned out the window and waved to him, and to Auntie and her brothers and sisters, her heart brimming with goodbyes and more hope than she had ever imagined it could contain.

All newcomers to the great city of New York are awed upon their arrival, and Eleanor was no exception. Haggard from the long, hot, rattling hours of travel, she was swept up into the crowd the moment she stepped off the train at Grand Central Station. Eleanor felt the same kind of electricity that she felt in the piano when she played, but now it was all around her, in the air.

It was just about ten in the morning. The family she had traveled with had taken their leave at a station an hour or two north of the city, and now she was alone. She tugged her valise along and sought out, again, the safety of other colored folks, such as at a small grocery with a lunch counter that served hot drinks and buttered rolls. From there she had directions to a boarding house called the Vance where she had arranged for a shared room. Auditions at the Conservatory were to begin that very afternoon.

The National Conservatory of Music of America was housed in a grand five-story building sandwiched between two slightly taller ones, with a stairway on either side leading up to arched entryways. Throngs of young people with instruments filled the stairs and the sidewalk outside. Eleanor soon found herself seated and clutching her sheet music, on a bench in a large classroom on the first floor, having registered at a long table of Conservatory secretaries taking names. Prospective students were to have prepared a piece to play, and were to expect sight-reading and ear tests. Eleanor was relieved to see numerous dark faces in the crowd, including a pretty young girl around her own age hugging a violin case.

"Hey," said the girl, dropping down beside her on the bench, "mind if I sit here? I'm so nervous I could faint."

"That's alright," said Eleanor. The girl's eyes darted around the room and she chewed a fingernail. Eleanor asked, "Violin?"

"And voice," the girl said. "You?"

Her name was Alma. Alma Cole, just up from Kansas City and with nowhere yet to stay. The girls were soon ushered in different directions, but promised to meet later outside and see if there was room for Alma at the Vance.

Eleanor waited for more than an hour in another classroom that was packed on one side with young people waiting their turn. Three judging professors sat at a large table near a piano on the other side of the room. While Eleanor waited she heard music played both clumsily and beautifully, and she found herself assaulted by waves of hope and despair accordingly. When her name was called she stood and walked to the piano as if facing her executioner. She placed her sheet music, a sonatina by Clementi that Mrs. Allison had given her, on the music stand of the piano and began to play.

It was over before she knew it.

The panel thanked her and called another name. How she had done, she couldn't say. She had made one or two small mistakes, but thought perhaps it hadn't gone too badly overall. Eleanor and Alma found each other later amid the thinning crowds leaving the Conservatory.

"I'm so glad to see you," Alma said, seizing Eleanor's arm. "How'd it go?"

"Okay, I guess," said Eleanor. "How was yours?"

"Just awful," Alma said. "Let's go get something to eat. Are you hungry?"

First they went back to the Vance and found that another shared room was available.

"Oh, thank Goodness," Alma said, dancing Eleanor in a quick hug. "Someone is watching over me, I know it."

"Me too," said Eleanor. "Let's take it as a good sign."

Around the corner they found a small eatery that served great plates of potato salad and beans with pork, a place that would become their regular haunt. Eleanor was amazed at how much Alma could eat. Elbows on the table and cutlery waving she swallowed slice after slice of bread with her meal, guzzling it all down with glasses of milk. Where it all went in that thin frame Eleanor couldn't guess, though she did learn that Alma had arrived from Kansas City that very day, and hadn't had a bite since the day before. So Alma had come to the city alone, just as Eleanor had, and from even farther away. She also had been encouraged by her church, the pastor's wife in her case. Alma's greatest fear was not making it in and letting her mentor down. Eleanor was not so much afraid of disappointing another as she was of having to return to where she started. Now that she'd taken flight, the plain old ground looked awfully dry and bare.

After their meal the girls walked to a nearby park. The sun hung low in the sky. Eleanor had watched the sunrise that morning through the dusty windows of the train. It seemed ages ago.

"Do you know *Home, Sweet Home?*" Alma asked.

Eleanor did not. "Let me hear you sing it," she said.

Alma looked up and then down, as if gathering her voice, a gesture Eleanor would quickly come to know.

"*Mid pleasures and palaces though we may roam,*" Alma sang, her voice soft but so clear it seemed to arc in the air.

> *...A charm from the skies seems to hallow us there*
> *Which seek thro' the world, is ne'er met elsewhere*
> *Home, home*
> *Sweet, sweet home*
> *There's no place like home...*
> *And exile from home splendor dazzles in vain*
> *Oh give me my lowly thatched cottage again*
> *The birds singing gaily that came at my call*
> *And gave me the peace of mind dearer than all*

"That was beautiful!" said Eleanor with feeling. "Oh, you are sure to get a place."

"Do you really think so?"

"Oh, yes."

A pang struck Eleanor as she imagined all her family back at home, so far away. But just as quickly the shadowed, white halls of the Conservatory rose up and she was filled with a terrified longing. Music played her heart, a powerful instrument to be sure.

Early the next morning the girls dressed and readied themselves to return to the Conservatory. The list of names for the second auditions would be posted on the doors. Folks were lined up again on both staircases when they arrived, huddled together in front of the lists. There were cries of joy and indignation and sorrow as people found their names, or didn't. Eleanor now had a friend to hope for, and was elated to see both her and Alma's names on the list.

When the heavy oak doors opened a group of some two hundred prospective students were allowed inside and divided into six large classrooms. Cole and Rougeaux being near opposite ends of the alphabet, the girls went in different directions, but not before gripping hands and whispering "Good luck."

The panel of judges behind the table introduced to Eleanor's group were four black professors—three men in long coats and a woman in a charcoal dress—and a beautiful, young-looking white woman of regal bearing who turned out to be the founder of the institution, Mrs. Jeannette Meyers Thurber. One by one the auditioners took their turns, playing their prepared pieces and performing sight and ear tests. There was no clumsy playing this time, with more than a few auditioners playing brilliantly. When it was Eleanor's turn she began the piece with her customary quiet attack, and found the sight and ear tests not too difficult. When she stepped up to the table to return the sheet music to the leading professor, she saw that Mrs. Thurber smiled at her approach, gave a little clap of her hands and murmured, "*Un diamant brut!*" Eleanor's hope rose a notch. She prayed that she had enough of the *diamant* and not too much of the *brut* to make it in.

She found Alma in the hallway looking dejected, certain again her audition was terrible.

"That's what you said last time," said Eleanor, "and it wasn't true."

And indeed it was not, as they learned the next morning when both their names appeared on the short list of the one hundred new students accepted.

Eleanor sat, disbelieving, in the Conservatory's auditorium, together with Alma and the other lucky young musicians, as they listened to words of welcome and instruction from Mrs. Jeannette Thurber, two of the senior professors, and the somber, gray-haired Conservatory Director. When the new students were dismissed, the group milled about making acquaintances. Among the new students, Eleanor counted some twenty other colored folks, besides herself and Alma. One of these, a young man with large, kind eyes approached and introduced himself as "Sam Higgins, clarinet and oboe." He was from Baltimore, and just like that their duo became a trio. They found a place nearby to celebrate with dishes of ice cream, swapping stories about their audition moments, in order to relive the magic of the day.

Soon enough their days were packed with all things music: theory, technique, harmony, history, repertoire. Eleanor lay down in her bed each night feeling as if her mind could not contain one more thing. Her body and her hands ached in a whole new way. She felt exhausted, but so alive, and aware that it was a rare gift to be immersed in one's own element. The new students, and Eleanor among them, looked upon the senior students with great admiration, and toward the professors with reverence. The latter held the keys to a vast kingdom that, despite all her natural talent, Eleanor was just beginning to know.

Gerard Batiste was one such ambassador, a young assistant professor, light-skinned with a devilish smile. Originally from New Orleans, he was known not only for his skill and good looks but as a composer, which at the Conservatory had earned him a particular respect. He had twice won a prize in their yearly competition of new composers, which led to his appointment to the faculty. He taught the introductory class in piano theory and technique to the new summer students, as well as leading their individual lessons. As an instructor he was exacting. He strode around the classroom emphasizing points in a sonorous voice, while his hands flew in large gestures, painting the air with the great concepts of music.

Among the Conservatory's colored students, Professor Batiste held a special kind of status. Though they earned the support and esteem of a number of the Conservatory's white faculty, they counted on Batiste to understand the added challenges they faced in the music world, to defend them in the face of insult or condescension, and to champion their right to be there. They flocked around him outside of class, eager to ask questions and hear anything he had to say.

A week into individual lessons, Professor Batiste was impressed with Eleanor's facility on the piano, noting her near-instantaneous incorporation of new information, and her razor-like focus. He began calling on her to demonstrate various techniques for the other students, and gave special attention to correcting any bad habits he spotted in her playing. Eleanor was deeply flattered, drawn by the intensity in him she recognized so well. At last someone understood the fire that lived within her. And this, together with his voice, his eyes, his beauty when playing, and of course the music, set over her like a spell. When the third week of May concluded he asked if she would help him with one of his compositions the next Saturday morning. The Conservatory was closed on weekends, except for recitals and children's lessons on Sunday afternoons, but as an assistant professor, Batiste had keys and access. The school encouraged its teachers to work on their own projects after hours.

That Saturday he asked her to meet him at nine and she was there by eight, clutching her handbag and the sheaf of sheet music he'd given her days before. He was working on a *scherzo* he called *La Flor de Mai* and she already knew it by heart. In the first hour they sat side by side on the bench, with Batiste demonstrating and Eleanor echoing while he either nodded or shook his head. She was conscious of the warmth of his arm when it grazed her shoulder. Then he had her play alone while he paced behind her, intent on listening, and leaning over her intermittently to make notes with a pencil on the sheet music. "Let's try it this way," he said now and again, as if his project had become mutually theirs.

There was a central problem to be solved in the piece, the resolution of which remained frustratingly elusive. Four hours flew by, and then he thanked her. She returned to her room at the Vance, heart aflutter. Eleanor had told Alma that she had an extra lesson that morning, and when they met later that day and Alma asked about it, she said only that it went well. She didn't say she was *working together* with Professor Batiste. Or that she was aflame with something for which she did not yet have words. She wasn't sure why she was suddenly keeping secrets from Alma, but maybe it was because she didn't want to appear boastful. Or foolish.

The second Saturday, addressing the same problem in the music, Batiste asked her to listen while he played a slight variation. Considering the variation, Eleanor thought the piece was a little flat, perhaps if there were more contrast in the middle? Batiste stared at her a moment and then gave something a try. He played it over again, changing a few notes here and there, and then jumped up. "That's it!" he cried, laughing out loud. "Damn it, that's it!"

And then he was embracing her. The warmth of his body pressed against hers, flooding her senses with the heady smell of sweat and aftershave lotion. His lips grazed her ear. Never had anyone held her so close. She was moved, touched in that empty place in her heart that had been with her ever since her mother had died and left her, despite all her family, so very alone. Perhaps he felt it too.

But then, flashing over this tenderness came a wave of alarm. She felt his lips, his breath on her cheeks and at her throat, his hands running over her breasts, and then down under the hem of her dress and underskirts, traveling up her legs. She did not have a clear idea of what a man and a woman might do together, only something that occurred in secret after marriage, and that preceded the birth of babies. She didn't know what could happen in a music room, but whatever was happening now was surely a liberty not to be taken. And yet she didn't want it to stop.

Somehow Batiste knew just how to maneuver around

Eleanor's elaborate corset and underlayers. Her arms moved as if by their own accord to circle his strong neck. She clung to him as he fumbled with his belt. He leaned her against the wall of the studio, then lifted and entered her, thrusting desperately, then moaning, "Oh, God," before going still.

They remained like that for some minutes, catching their breath. He drew away and they rearranged their clothing. Eleanor was not entirely sure what had just happened and was momentarily overwhelmed by the throbbing, stinging sensations between her legs. Batiste picked up the sheet music from the piano and closed the fallboard over the keys.

"That's enough for today," he said. "I'll see you home."

Monday in class, and all that week, he did not single her out as he normally did. He did not ask her to work with him the coming Saturday. His addresses to her were cordial, even kind, but gave no hint of the intimacy that had transpired. Eleanor did her best to focus on the lesson. What had she expected? She didn't know, but, whatever it was, the lack of it left her crushed and confused. During the lunch break Alma noticed her downcast state and asked her if something was the matter. What could Eleanor possibly say? Only a concealing half-truth, that she wasn't feeling quite well. Alma asked her if she was homesick, and she said yes, because perhaps that was also somewhat true.

As the weeks went on Eleanor learned to set the incident with Batiste aside; certainly there was so much more to occupy her mind. When not immersed in learning at the Conservatory, Alma and Eleanor, and Sam Higgins, took advantage of their weekends to traverse the city. Sam, who always had his nose in the papers, found countless free events at Madison Square Garden, just blocks away, and in Central Park. They saved carfare by walking everywhere, wearing out their shoes, but learning the city block by block. When they befriended senior students they were invited to parties that often turned into the fiercest of impromptu battles between harps, banjos, guitars, violins, and of course piano. The new students were sometimes dared to show what they could do, and once Eleanor accompanied Alma, whose pure mezzo soprano was already gaining attention, in a new rendition of *There is a Balm in Gilead*, which earned them whoops and hearty applause.

She might have forgotten that day with Batiste entirely if not for the fact that in mid-July, her menses weeks late, she began to experience a telltale nausea, and, worse, fatigue. She recalled her mother, early in her pregnancy with Dax, when Eleanor was just a girl, and seeing her run out back from the kitchen when sickness overcame her. Mama had explained that she was alright, soothing Eleanor's worried brow with her cool hand—it was just the new baby getting comfortable. Now, however much Eleanor still didn't understand about baby-making, the pieces came together in her mind, leaving her to face the unthinkable.

Alma again noticed her change in mood.

"Nora," she said, "it's the heat that's getting to you, is that so?"

"That must be it," said Eleanor, trying to smile, "and maybe a bad frankfurter at the Park."

"Poor Northern Chickadee," crooned Alma, wanting to cheer up her friend. "You aren't used to it, like we are." By *we* she meant anyone from the southern states. "And the recital, of course. There's a whole lot of pressure on us now."

Excitement and anxiety surrounded the upcoming Summer Recital, the 15th of August, wherein the new students would be vetted and separated into those accepted for further study and those turned away. But Eleanor felt herself slipping away from this hopeful group. If what was happening to her was indeed the thing she dreaded, her future as a serious pianist was about to be snuffed out like a candle. And what would become of the rest of her life? She would be a fallen woman, disgraced and ruined.

She went to see Batiste. He kept hours at his small office on the top floor after classes on Wednesdays. She waited in the hall, seated on a chair while other students filed in and out, conferring with him on one thing or another, until the last one went and she could hear him gathering his things to leave. She stepped into the office and stood opposite his writing desk.

"Miss Rougeaux," he said, looking up, a placid smile drawn on his face.

"Mr. Batiste," she began, not knowing how she would reach the end of her sentence, "the day that you and I worked on your composition...."

"Yes?" he said, seeing her falter.

"When we, when you and I..." she bit nervously at her lips. "It's that I am with child now."

He stared at her blankly. She felt a wave of nausea and swallowed hard.

"That's regrettable," he said, standing up. He placed a leather briefcase on the desk, pulled a pocket watch from his vest and consulted the hour. "But it's really no concern of mine."

Whatever blood she had left seemed to drain away.

"No concern," she wavered.

"Where you have been, or what you have done with yourself, or what you are *going* to do, Miss Rougeaux," his voice was chilling through the smile, "is your business. Do us both the great favor of not bringing it up again." A touch of menace lingered in his words. Indeed, she had nothing on him. Any complaint she made he could easily deny, and would only bring worse upon herself. He moved past her into the hallway and held the door until she followed. Then he locked the door and strode away.

She missed classes the next day. It scarcely mattered now. She stayed in her room and Alma worried over her, but she couldn't speak. The worst had become all too real. Early the next morning, while the other girls still slept, Eleanor found her thoughts pulled to *Nocturne in C-sharp minor*, by Chopin, the piece she was to play at the recital. Her fingers itched. She badly wanted to play. She rose soundlessly and made her way to the Conservatory. Practice rooms were open before the start of morning classes and she found an empty one. She sat at the bench of her favorite piano, all gleaming black wood and a gorgeous sound. No sheet music sat on the music stand; she didn't need it. Instead she saw the traces of her reflection in the piano's lacquer finish, as if she were a ghost contained inside. *Maybe that's just what I am*, she thought, *a ghost.*

Eleanor warmed her fingers, her wrists, her shoulders, flew through her scales and arpeggios and dove into the *Nocturne*. If playing this piece at the recital was to be her farewell performance, then she would play it for all she was worth.

August the 15th arrived and Eleanor passed the day as if in a trance. She did not participate in the nervous chatter, in the murmurs of encouragement amongst her peers. When her turn came she stepped up onto the stage and nodded to Mrs. Jeannette Thurber and the Board, stationed at a long table on the side opposite a baby grand.

Eleanor began to play. Her fingers stretched and ran over the keys. There was no audience, no Board, she was conscious only of the music flowing between herself and the piano. Every note danced in her heart, and she rose and fell together with the melody.

When she finished there was a silence, deep and eternal. She closed her eyes.

And then applause, like ocean waves crashing.

Jeannette Thurber stood clapping, with a white handkerchief clutched in one hand, and then crossed the stage, dabbing at her eyes. She gripped Eleanor by the shoulders.

"How far you've come, my dear, and in such a short time," she said, in a voice only Eleanor could hear. "Players like you are the reason for all my work. You are my reward. It will be an honor to see where you go from here." She leaned forward and planted a kiss on Eleanor's cheek.

The next day the newly selected students received their official letters of invitation to the Conservatory. Alma Cole and Sam Higgins were among them. A celebratory gathering was planned for the evening at a nearby restaurant. Eleanor didn't go. She tucked her official letter into her valise with her other things, left a note for Alma at the Vance, and made her way to Grand Central Station. She didn't say goodbye.

Eleanor's train arrived late in Montreal. It was getting dark, but the street lamps were lit and there were a few last traces of light in the sky. She was tired and had to sit down several times to catch her breath. At last she arrived at her own street. She passed the saddlery shop and stepped up to her front door, where all the windows were dark. Eleanor bit her lip and rapped with the brass knocker, shaking with mortal fear at what might come next. There was nothing at first, then the faint sound of stirrings from upstairs. There was a glow in the foyer, as someone was carrying a candle, then she heard the door unlatch, and Papa's face appeared.

"*Chère*," he whispered, "my Heavens, it's you. Come in!" He took up her valise and set it inside. Auntie came down the stairs in her nightdress and embraced her. She took Eleanor's face in her hands and looked at her intently. There was no hiding anything from Auntie. She'd have to come out with it right then and there.

"Come sit down," Auntie said. They all went into the parlor and Auntie lit one of the lamps. There were more footsteps on the stairs. Melody appeared with sleepy eyes that leapt wide awake when she saw Eleanor, and threw her arms around her. Auntie asked Melody to please warm a mug of milk.

"What have you to say, child?" Auntie said gently.

Eleanor's voice shook. "I did a terrible thing," she managed, "and I'm sorry for it, but it's too late now."

Papa was alarmed, but kept his voice low. "Are you hurt?" he asked. "Is anyone hurt?"

She couldn't look at him as she said the awful words, "I believe I'm having a baby."

Papa stood up and crossed the room. Eleanor was suddenly terrified he would walk out the door, that he would leave and never speak to her again, but he only went to the window. The women waited in silence. Melody returned with the milk and sat silently beside Eleanor on the sofa. Finally, Papa turned and sat back down in the chair. He rested his elbows on his knees and gripped his hands together. He would not press her for any more details than necessary.

"Will the father take responsibility?"

Eleanor shook her head. "I wouldn't want him to anyway," she said.

"What about the child? Do you want the child?"

The truth was she did not. All she had now was the truth.

"No," she said.

Melody put her hands over her face and hunched forward. Eleanor could hear her stifled sobs. They were all quiet a good while, and then Auntie spoke.

"Ross and Mathilde will keep the baby," she said, as if she had just come from conferring with Eleanor's older brother and his wife. "He'll be an orphan and no one will know from where." She looked at Eleanor. "Child, you will have to go away." Now Melody's sobs were audible.

"Now, now," Papa said, "Josie, please. Nothing needs deciding now."

But Eleanor had decided already. And what Auntie said was true. This would be the only way for the baby to both stay in the family and avoid the stain of illegitimacy. Ross and Tilly were the most likely choice, if they were indeed willing, as they had only one child, nearly weaning age, while the others in the family either had more or were unmarried. And Eleanor could not go away and then reappear at the same time as the baby.

Eleanor looked down at the floor. "I'm sorry," she said again. What inadequate words for what she had done, for what would be required to go forward. The child would have to be provided for.

If Eleanor went away to live somewhere else that would also cost. And then there were the untruths her whole family would have to support. That in itself was inexcusable.

Papa and Auntie looked at each other, and Papa ran his hands over his head. He always did so when he wished to clear his mind. "Every family has its secrets," he said.

"And that's our business only," said Auntie. She stood and beckoned the rest to do the same, declaring with the gesture that their meeting was finished. "You are tired," she said to Eleanor. "You need your rest." And then she added, "The Holy One doesn't make mistakes."

Eleanor and her sister and brothers had heard this refrain from Auntie countless times, but now it struck her ears with some thunder. *Even this?* Auntie read her face. "Yes, *chère*," she said, "even this."

Ross and Tilly came to the house the next evening, and sat drinking coffee with Papa in the kitchen. Auntie thought it best to let them discuss it alone, and kept the girls busy upstairs sorting scrap cloth to make baby clothes. Dax she sent out to do some chores in the stables. They heard Papa at the foot of the stairs.

"Josie, bring Eleanor down, would you?"

Eleanor rose and Melody squeezed her hand.

Down in the kitchen Ross and Tilly's little girl Sarai toddled over to her and Auntie, clutching at their skirts. Eleanor reached down to hold her tiny hands. She couldn't look at her brother or sister-in-law.

"We'll take the baby in, El," Ross said. She glanced up at Tilly, but her sister-in-law had turned her face away. She and Mathilde had never been close.

"Thank you Ross," she managed, "thank you Tilly."

Mathilde looked at her with a face composed but edged in anger. She was not pleased at all.

"I'll do whatever I can to help," Eleanor promised desperately.

Ross looked from his wife to his sister.

"Take Sarai," he said to his wife. When she had left with the child he turned to Eleanor. "She'll come around," he said. "Sarai had a bad croup when you were away, it was hard on Tilly." He looked at their father. "Deliveries in the morning, I'll be there early." He meant the shop next door, and that he would take everything in stride, two things that made Papa proud.

Eleanor had inherited something of her father's broad frame, and her mother's curves, features that readily hid some extra weight. As October deepened into November, heavy coats concealed her growing belly that now strained at the buttons of her dresses. Auntie Josephine, with Eleanor and Melody's help, widened her coats, saying they could be taken in again later. Eleanor wrote to the Conservatory to say that she would gratefully accept their invitation, but that she must wait until after the winter holidays. When the letter came from the Conservatory to say they would expect her at classes March 1st, Eleanor sensed that she had been granted a reprieve straight from Heaven. She had the equal sense that she must never take it lightly or make such a grave error again. Any sign of frivolity on her part would send down a judgment both swift and harsh. A second chance was in her hands, a third chance would never come.

Papa engaged in a discreet search for a place where Eleanor could go, a place with someone who was known well enough but who could also provide her an anonymous existence. Mr. Hathaway, Papa's English friend whom the children had come to regard as an uncle, knew such a person. Mrs. Isabelle Delaney had been his housekeeper years ago in Toronto. He sent a letter to her and she wrote back to say she could receive Eleanor, and that she knew a midwife in the area who could assist when the time came. And so it was arranged. At such times as anyone inquired, Eleanor had returned to the Conservatory to continue her studies. There had been an opening and to secure it she'd had to leave without saying goodbye to anyone but the immediate family.

The day of her leaving Ross came again, and Albert with his family. Eleanor's other brother Jonty had work and had said goodbye the night before. Dax was a big chap of eleven years old now, but still he hugged her as he always had, and Melody kept close, helping her with everything, even when she didn't need it. Mr. Hathaway came too, bearing a rectangular parcel under his arm, wrapped in paper and about the size of one of Papa's ledgers. He gave the parcel to Eleanor, saying it was an early Christmas present. Papa gave her a fine new valise from the shop and Auntie oversaw all preparations. She asked Papa if he would take her alone to the station. When night began to fall it was time to go.

It had snowed two days before but the roads were clear enough and the buggy rolled smoothly behind their horse. They were quiet most of the way. The wheels of the buggy crunched softly over bits of snow, and the horse blew out through his lips now and again, resigned or satisfied or hungry, or whatever it was that made horses do that. A horse's life was simple at least. Eleanor kept a hand on the valise, feeling as if the weight of it lay heavily on her chest. She didn't deserve presents, she knew that. A question burned in her throat.

"Papa," she said, feeling terror steal over her again, "would Mama have been ashamed of me?"

He thought a long moment.

"No, *chère*," he said at last. "I don't believe so." He recalled to her when Jonty once hit his head on the pump, jumping down off the fence. Mama was furious. She heard Jonty, all of eight or nine years old, howling in the yard, and shouted *Damn you!* She marched him inside to bandage him up, then she sent him to bed. Once the floor and clothing were cleaned up and supper was ready she left everyone downstairs and took a bowl of soup up for him. He could have fed himself, he wasn't so bad off, but she gave him the soup spoonful by spoonful. Then she made him lie down and lay right beside him, singing his favorite lullabies until he went off to sleep. That was Mama whatever the case. She forgave her children everything.

Papa helped Eleanor find a seat on the train, near to another family should something be needed. He tucked the valise against the wall and gave her the woolen blanket from the buggy. Having been on trains and in New York gave Eleanor a piece of confidence in her ability to travel alone, and this, despite everything, laced the sorrow of parting with a thread of adventure. She hugged Papa as she had when she was little.

"Write as soon as you can," he said.

The train sped into the night and she was alone. The woolen buggy blanket, familiar in its blue and green plaid, kept her warm.

She thought of Mama, and hummed all the lullabies she would have wanted to hear her sing, until she fell asleep.

She arrived in Toronto at first light, bleary-eyed from a fitful sleep, and feeling as though she were emerging from a long, dark tunnel. The hours-long stops in Ottawa and Kingston had seemed like cold, silent places underground, threaded through with strange dreams. Stumbling down onto the platform with her valise she searched among the loose crowds of people. Mrs. Delaney's daughter, called by the strange name of Maxis, was meant to meet her. Some distance away she spotted a tall, black-clad figure who stood alone and carried no luggage. As she approached she saw it was a woman with an impassive, and somewhat mannish looking, middle-aged face. The eyes lit upon Eleanor with recognition.

"Miss Rougeaux?" she spoke in a throaty voice.

"Miss Delaney, hello." Eleanor put out her gloved hand. Maxis Delaney did not return the gesture. The older woman's eyes lingered over Eleanor.

"This way," she said finally, and turned to walk in the direction of the grand entrance.

Downtown Toronto at a first glance, was not wholly unlike New York. They caught a streetcar and then had several blocks to walk to the Delaney residence. Maxis trudged forward, leading with her shoulders, unconcerned when Eleanor, struggling with the valise and the weight of the pregnancy, lagged behind. At last Maxis stopped at a small, street-level door and brought out a key. They entered an equally narrow hallway and went up a flight of stairs to another door, where Maxis rang a bell by pulling a cord. Eleanor heard movements and shuffling footsteps and then the door opened upon the elderly Mrs. Delaney, who was small with white hair, and dressed in gray woolens that matched her eyes. Her face crinkled in a timid smile, a relief to Eleanor after the initial Maxis encounter. Mrs. Delaney brought them into the kitchen, gave them tea and asked Eleanor about her journey, and how Mr. Hathaway was getting on.

The house was small and dim and cramped, and though the tea warmed her, Eleanor shrunk at the thought that she would spend the whole winter in this place. She was used to her own house, with its constant bustle and activity and ringing of voices. And she had been in New York, surely the most thrilling place on Earth, studying music. Now she was to be shut away with these two strange white women. But if this was her punishment then she would swallow it.

The small kitchen occupied the whole of the first floor, underneath which was a root cellar, accessed by a trap door. After the tea, and some toast with a funny-tasting jam, Maxis left for her job caring for an invalid in a wealthy neighborhood across town. Mrs. Delaney showed Eleanor upstairs. On the second floor two tiny bedrooms squeezed either side of a short hallway with a water closet at one end and a cramped set of stairs at the other. Eleanor's room contained a bed, a wardrobe and a small window that looked out onto the back garden, where three adjacent buildings made it a bare well of fallen snow. Eleanor unpacked her things and placed them in the wardrobe. She laid the buggy blanket on the bed, which brought a measure of comfort, and then withdrew Mr. Hathaway's package from the bottom of the valise. She would wait to open it, so as to have something to look forward to.

Mrs. Delaney entered the room, knocking lightly on the

half-open door. She carried a stack of linens. "You'll need these," she said.

"Thank you," Eleanor said, and then rummaged in her coat pockets for the envelope of banknotes Papa had given her for her board. This she handed to Mrs. Delaney.

"Papa said this would be enough," Eleanor faltered, "for my stay."

Mrs. Delaney's pale cheeks colored. She took the envelope and tucked it away in her apron. Then she surprised Eleanor by saying, "I'm sorry to take this from you. A girl in need...."

Neither said more.

"I'll just be off to my marketing," said Mrs. Delaney. "I expect you are tired."

Eleanor didn't know if she was tired or not, but she didn't want to be left alone right then.

"Can I come with you?" she said. "I can carry things."

"Yes, alright," said the elder woman. She gave a little smile. "That will be very nice."

When they went out again, each with a large basket on her arm, it was beginning to snow. Eleanor took in anew the unfamiliar street, the buildings, the passing carts. They stopped at a vegetable seller and a butcher. Mrs. Delaney inquired in a grocery about having a sack of flour delivered and a wheel of cheese, large items she paid for with banknotes from the envelope Eleanor had brought. Past noon they returned to the house, where Mrs. Delaney served a soup that she'd had simmering on the stove. They ate mostly in silence and Eleanor offered to do the washing up. Mrs. Delaney assented, and then apologized that it was time for her *wee rest*. She made her way up the stairs and Eleanor soon heard her snoring.

Dishes washed and dried, Eleanor crept up the stairs thinking she would have one of the ginger cookies Melody had made for her. There were two or three dozen in the tin she had stashed in the wardrobe, and she meant to ration them out for herself. But then, in the hallway, the second set of stairs caught her eye. It must be an attic, she thought. She padded down the length of the hall and then slipped into the narrow passage. The stairs creaked mightily. She stopped at each one, checking for the sound of snoring, until she stood before a tiny brown door with a brass knob. Mrs. Delaney slept on.

It was indeed an attic, with dust-covered shapes just barely illuminated by the daylight that filtered in through the dirty glass of a miniature window, set in bare brick. The ceiling was so low Eleanor had to stoop even when standing directly in the center. There were a few trunks and crates tucked into the edges where the ceiling met the floor, and something larger covered in a tarpaulin at the farther end. The size and shape were familiar, but it couldn't be. Her steps disturbed so much dust she had to cover her mouth and nose with her sleeve, and her eyes watered. She lifted a corner of the tarpaulin, catching the faintest gleam of polished wood, and then a bit of scrollwork encrusted with more dust, and then hinges of a fallboard.

A piano.

The tarpaulin hit the floor, sending up a thick cloud. Eleanor gingerly lifted the fallboard and ran her fingers over the keys. Two or three were missing or broken, and it was in poor tune, but a real piano nonetheless.

She heard a rustling, and the sudden sight of Mrs. Delaney at the attic door nearly caused her to jump out of her skin.

"Oh," she said. "You've found Mr. Delaney's piano." She stepped into the attic. "A rare thing, isn't it? He had to take it almost completely apart to bring it up here. He was in cabinetry, thank goodness." She wrung her hands in a kind of friendly nervousness. "Do you play?"

The next morning Maxis left early to look after her invalid and Mrs. Delaney departed to where she cleaned the offices of a small law firm two mornings a week. Eleanor, having already eaten more than her ration of Melody's cookies, returned to the attic. She had found a broom and dustpan in the kitchen and also brought up a bucket of suds and some rags. The attic was nearly as cold as outdoors, but her efforts at dust removal and rearranging, plus the natural added heat of pregnancy, quickly had her perspiring. The piano now stood ready; one of the trunks, with the tarpaulin clean and folded on top, made a decent bench.

Eleanor sat and ran through her scales. Quickly she learned which keys struck notes in or out of tune, and which few were missing their hammers, because they gave out no sound at all. Poor as the instrument was, touching it was an immense relief. As her hands moved, her imagination rushed in to replace the absent notes, and because she heard this internal music so clearly, the notes that were off bent to their proper form. The heaviness that weighed on her neck and shoulders lightened, and the old electricity shot through her fingers. Like a feral beast, the instrument became tame, charmed into producing a melody, and then another and another. She played the nocturne she learned at the Conservatory, and then the *études*. She even played the *scherzo* of Gerard Batiste, which became an ode to the twists of her own life, and to the unmapped horizon toward which her young vessel sailed, recklessly, cautiously, and with no other choice.

That night before bed she opened Mr. Hathaway's package. A moment after tearing the paper four books of sheet music lay spread out on the blue and green plaid blanket. *The Complete 32 Piano Sonatas of Ludwig van Beethoven*, with an envelope of banknotes pressed between the pages of the first volume.

"My word," she breathed. Whether or not she deserved it, there was hope after all.

All that winter she studied the sonatas, played Mr. Delaney's feral piano in the frozen attic, and did her best to help the Delaney women with the running of their modest household. Her belly grew with the unknown baby inside, and she sometimes dreamt at night of a child laughing, playing a game of hide-and-seek where what was hidden was never found.

Her time came in early February. The labor came on quickly, beginning in the afternoon. The hours did not pass easily for Eleanor. As the waves of pain increased, so did her fear. Fear that she would die, that the baby would die, that either or both would be her punishment, but that first she would be crushed in the Devil's grip. She lay, gasping between contractions, wondering how soon death would come, and then the pain came on again, obliterating any thought at all.

Just before midnight the baby's head emerged, and then the rest of him, the fluid, and finally the afterbirth. The midwife wrapped the baby, saying he looked fine and that she wished all her births went as well. Eleanor lay in a daze as the midwife placed the baby in her arms and helped him to feed. She studied his tiny form with wonder and trepidation: the thin dark curls that clung to his damp head, the little flared nose, the dark eyes that gazed at her a moment and then shut again.

Eleanor asked Mrs. Delaney to write a note to her brother and sister-in-law for her. She wanted them to call the child Gerard, as it suddenly seemed urgent he have something of his father. Eleanor would not, could not, care for the baby herself. She felt acutely the lack of space in which to hold him, and yet at once she cared immensely for his welfare.

There was Gerard Batiste, and now there was a Gerard Rougeaux. He would be Ross' son, and Mathilde's, if he survived. Relief that she was free was at once overwhelmed by the shame that she should want that freedom, and that she should have it at all.

Maxis came and took the child away. She would journey with him, a bottle of milk and an eyedropper, to Montreal and then return alone. Eleanor lay sunken in the bed, bruised and torn. When her milk came in, her breasts swelled and hardened, and then a fever came upon her so strong she dreamed someone was throwing pot after pot of boiling water over her. For days she lay delirious, demons and angels clashing above her, scattering over the ceiling and singing strange versions of songs she thought she knew. Only Isabelle Delaney interrupted the cacophony, feeding her broth with a spoon, and taking away sheets that were soaked with sweat.

At last the fever broke. Eleanor woke in the dark and lay awake some time, until she heard the great clock in the hall strike five and she knew it was near morning. She got unsteadily to her feet and made her way to the bureau where she found there was still some water in the pitcher, which she drank greedily, and then lay down to sleep again. When she woke next it was daylight and she heard Mrs. Delaney in the kitchen. A little while later, Mrs. Delaney pushed open the door and caught Eleanor's expression.

"Oh," she gasped, "thank Heavens, you are looking better. I was just about to call a doctor."

"I'll live, I guess." Eleanor tried a smile.

Mrs. Delaney leaned over her and put a cool hand on her forehead.

"Think you can eat something?"

Eleanor felt a lurch in her stomach. It was coming back to life.

"Porridge sounds good," she said, but then began to cry. Mrs. Delaney sat on the edge of the bed.

"Don't cry now," she said. "Things will turn out alright." She didn't seem sure.

Eleanor wished with all her might it was her own mother sitting there instead of Isabelle Delaney, but she couldn't say so. The older woman stood again.

"Porridge," she said. "You need your strength."

Another week passed and in body Eleanor was much recovered, the elasticity of youth being on her side. Mrs. Delaney took her to the Dominion Bank to exchange Mr. Hathaway's banknotes for American money, and sewed her a special wallet to keep it all safe. They took in Eleanor's two dresses, returning them to close to their previous width, and even Maxis helped with that. She was surprisingly handy with a needle.

"I do thank you both," Eleanor said to them, the night before her leaving, "for all your help, and all your kindness."

They were seated at the kitchen table with their after-supper tea.

"Oh," said Mrs. Delaney, a blush rising in her cheeks, "we shall miss you. Won't we, Maxis?"

Maxis fixed her stare on Eleanor. It wasn't so unnerving now.

"And so shall Da's piano," she said. The trace of a smile spread across her face and she emitted a low hiccuping sound. Maxis was laughing.

"I will send it a card next Christmas," said Eleanor, and she and Mrs. Delaney burst into giggles, as Maxis hiccupped louder.

Eleanor returned to New York a wiser woman, with a new sense of determination and purpose. She knew she would see Gerard Batiste at the Conservatory but felt her business with him was finished. For her mistakes she could blame no one but herself. If there were any repairs to be made now it was with Alma. The Vance was full, but Eleanor got a room at another boarding house on the same block. She left a message for Alma at the concierge desk and the two of them met the next evening at a café.

It was dusk and a late winter snowfall glowed around the streetlights. Alma sat across from Eleanor, stirring her cup of coffee with milk and cinnamon that was a specialty of the café. She wouldn't meet Eleanor's eye for the longest time.

"I'm sorry I left without saying goodbye. Without telling you why."

Alma heaved a sigh and looked out the window before speaking.

"Why didn't you?" Her delicate eyebrows knit together, the hurt was plain to see.

"I just couldn't," Eleanor said.

"You couldn't tell me?"

"No."

"You were in trouble."

"Did you know all along?"

"I thought maybe."

The girls were quiet a while, then Alma spoke again.

"Nora, where's the baby?"

"In Montreal, with my brother's family."

"Mercy," Alma breathed.

Eleanor was grateful to see that by the time their coffee was finished her friend had forgiven her and their intimacy was renewed. More than half a year had passed and they had much catching up to do. When they left the café they strolled arm in arm, not caring that snow piled up on their shoulders.

There were no more secrets between the two, as their years as students continued and saw them grow steadily toward womanhood. Sam Higgins remained a close friend, and Eleanor found mentors in a number of the faculty, and even in Jeannette Thurber herself, who invited Eleanor to tea in her drawing room many times.

Ever interested in "polishing her diamonds," Jeannette Thurber frequently made these invitations to the Conservatory's most promising students, particularly the young ladies. She had taken an early interest in Eleanor. They always began and ended their talks discussing music, but visited other subjects of life as much as Eleanor allowed. Mrs. Thurber observed the younger woman grow quiet when asked about her family in Montreal. She guessed the reticence could have something to do with Eleanor's delayed entry into her studies, but never pressed her for details. Instead, Mrs. Thurber offered encouragements and suggestions on Eleanor's playing. She spoke philosophically about finding hidden doors and seeing whether or not they could be coaxed open. Eleanor drank in the advice, along with her tea, gathering Mrs. Thurber's words like jewels scattered on the ground, even if their meaning sometimes eluded her.

Gerard Batiste left the Conservatory for another appointment after Eleanor's first year was complete. He nodded to her in the halls, but that was all. She avoided his classes, assuming that would be to their mutual relief. If he ever had his way with other students she never heard about it. By the end of her studies Eleanor had received numerous recognitions, and upon graduation was offered an assistant professorship.

In the next few years, as the century raced toward its end, she spent her days with her young pupils at the Conservatory, and her evenings in private lessons, anything to get together a few more dollars to send home to her brother Ross. Despite the opportunities afforded to her by the Conservatory, there were few avenues indeed where a musician who was a woman, and colored too, could make her living. The private lessons had to be sought among colored folks, where funds were generally scarce; teaching children, often reluctant ones, was uninteresting at best. Eleanor understood how fortunate she was to have her work at the Conservatory, but even there she wasn't truly herself. Her art was playing music, not teaching.

Eleanor enjoyed the annual Conservatory Faculty Recital, as she was always one of the few invited to play more than one piece. In those first years after graduation she traveled the city to various auditions. Mrs. Thurber encouraged her to go, and gave her personal letters of introduction and endorsement to give to each company and orchestra director, yet no one ever hired her. Again and again Eleanor saw her former classmates and colleagues, always men, almost invariably white men whose talents did not come close to matching hers, succeed. While Eleanor walked to the homes of her pupils in the worst weather to save a few cents, and endured the humiliation of each failed audition, her musical counterparts secured positions and acclaim and professional ascension of every kind.

Still and all, life in New York City had a lot to offer. Friday and Saturday nights, Eleanor went with Alma and other friends to parties, and dance halls on occasions when she could spare the money, where a new music called Ragtime had exploded onto the scene. And music was not the only thing in the air. Folks talked, debated the essays of W.E.B. Du Bois and Booker T. Washington, and articles in Negro papers like the *New York Age*. They discussed what must be done against the violence and poverty that afflicted them all, especially, almost unspeakably, those in the Southern States. A great deal was said about the *advancement of the race*, advancement in opportunity, in achievement, in equality. Over and again Eleanor felt as if she were waking up to the world, and to her own place in it, however lost or found that might turn out to be.

In her daily life Eleanor flew from one place to another. She could almost always keep ahead of the loneliness that trailed her like a shadow. She missed her family, her home, and her mother. Jeannette Thurber once said to her at tea that loneliness was like malaria. *Once infected you are never entirely free of it. You have your spells.* But back to her home was where she could not go, because now there was another. A little boy to whom she had given life and a name, but not given herself. She had violated a sacred contract that she had never meant to sign, and could never undo, slashed a wound that nature couldn't heal.

When she stopped long enough she wrote letters to Papa, to Auntie, to Melody and the others. She asked after Gerard. Tilly had another child now and so he was one of three. Eleanor was relieved to hear from Melody that Tilly cared for him, that Melody herself often helped with the children and that Gerard was a fine little fellow. And that Jonty and Dax took him out riding whenever Jonty was home off duty from the railroad. The first year after Eleanor had graduated from the Conservatory, Melody wrote letter after letter asking when she would return to Montreal. "There is no talk whatsoever," she assured her sister. Orphans were a dime a dozen, really; it was the rare family that didn't at some point take in a parentless child. Eleanor sometimes replied "next year" to Melody's queries. It was a decision she deferred, especially while life continued to unfold in New York. But any time she saw a little boy Gerard's age, one of her private pupils perhaps, the sight stabbed at her heart with steady insistence.

Alma was doing well for herself, performing in clubs and private concerts. Singing was a razor-thin avenue where a woman might succeed in music. No club would hire a woman to play any instrument, least of all a piano. Eleanor was happy for Alma, to be sure, but with a measure of envy. Alma, having met many new friends in her work, was going with a young man called Jack Zebulon who was a brilliant musician. Though Jack had no formal training, he played anything and everything with strings—guitar, banjo, mandolin—and could burn up a piano without even trying.

Jack had a friend, Sam Jupiter, who was a big talker. He aimed at putting together an all-Negro orchestra that would tour Europe as representatives of Dr. W.E.B. Du Bois' "Talented Tenth." It all seemed terribly far-fetched to Eleanor, but times were changing. Who knew what was possible?

"Frangipani," Sam Jupiter said one night. He, Jack and Alma sat with Eleanor and Sam Higgins, clustered around a tiny table at the crowded club where Alma was between sets. Alma always put Eleanor on her guest list, and gave her dresses now and then, saying she couldn't wear them anymore, but Alma never lorded it over her.

"Frangipani," said Alma, "what's that?"

"A tropical flower," said Joop. Now that there were two Sams everyone took to calling Jupiter "Joop" and Higgins "Hig."

"A beautiful, exotic flower," Jack said, making eyes at Alma. Alma always said Jack only ever thought about two things, and music was one.

"What about it?" said Alma.

"The Frangipani Orchestra," said Joop, "that's going to be the name of it."

"Funny name," said Eleanor.

Jack looked at Sam Higgins. "When are you going to get yourself a girl, Hig?"

Sam laughed. "Soon as Eleanor will have me." He winked at her, and Eleanor smiled at the joke. Though Eleanor enjoyed the friendship of the young men in their circle, she scrupulously avoided all things romantic. She would have no more Gerards, Batiste or otherwise. Eleanor had witnessed traditional courtships in her family and community while growing up. Most everything that took place between young people happened under the watchful eye of elders, with serious courtships ending in either marriage or the occasional carefully guided separation. Nowadays, in modern New York City at least, a whole class of unmarried youth sought their fortunes alone, far from family ties, doing their best to create alliances with no one to advise them. This was the case with Alma and Jack, who were drawn together by a mutual passion for both their art and a pretty face. They made a striking pair to be sure, but what mattered was that underneath all that their affection for one another grew.

Alma confessed to Eleanor that she was in love with Jack and that she hoped he would ask her to marry him, though not right away, since babies would put an end to her career. Jack was good to her, though susceptible to the lavish attentions he regularly received from other women, and his flirtations were often the subject of their lovers' quarrels. If once in a while Alma was sufficiently distressed and weeping in despair over their future, Jack would show up with flowers and sweet words, and those kisses that she could never resist. Eleanor was glad to share her friend's confidences, whatever they consisted of. She worried sometimes, but had no reason to foresee for her friend the disaster that had befallen her what seemed like a lifetime ago.

Joop seemed all talk for the longest time, but then he did it. He found two investors—white businessmen with a love for music and contacts in Europe—a rehearsal space and a group of twenty-five musicians and singers under the direction of a respected conductor, one Lemuel Harris. Joop drew up contracts for Alma and Jack, Eleanor and Hig, without even asking them, and all readily accepted. For Eleanor it was nothing less than a revelation. A career as a performer, even if only for a few months, was suddenly coming into view. She felt exactly as she had the night, when she was just a girl, that Mrs. Allison had come to the house to tell them about the Conservatory.

The orchestra's repertoire would include an ambitious range of classical and popular pieces, and spirituals with both new and traditional arrangements. The famous Antonin Dvorak served as Director at the Conservatory during Eleanor's years there (one of Jeannette Thurber's many coups), where he became enamored of, and influenced by, American Negro music. Joop secured his endorsement of the Frangipani project, and this opened additional European doors.

In his role as conductor Lemuel Harris had to contend with personalities as well as the music. Some members who were used to being the stars of the show now were to be collaborators. Jack, who was as opinionated as he was charismatic, was one of them. "Play along for now, Jack, please," Lemuel would say, wearily. "Let's talk after." And then the two would debate for hours, over glasses of Hell Gate beer, usually ending with Lemuel taking Jack's ideas into account, and Jack stepping back in respect of Lemuel's position.

The Frangipani Orchestra booked a seven-month European tour for the better part of the year 1900, the turn of the century itself. They would be ambassadors to a whole new age, voyaging to Hamburg, then overland to Berlin, Prague, Brussels, Amsterdam, on to Paris, the British Isles, and down to the French Riviera when the weather turned cold. The salaries were hardly extravagant, but there was enough to send something off to Ross and Tilly after covering modest expenses for food and lodging.

Eleanor made a special arrangement for the transfer of funds home to Montreal, and then gave her notice at the Conservatory together with a long, heartfelt letter of thanks to Mrs. Jeannette Thurber. Mrs. Thurber had her to tea in her sumptuous drawing room where they could have one of their intimate talks, about life and music, Paris where Jeannette had studied, and the changing times. Eleanor was twenty-seven years old and about to embark on an unimaginable journey. She would have so much to write home about.

Thus, in early April of 1900, the Frangipani Orchestra left its port in New York City aboard the *RMS Umbria* to voyage across the Atlantic. Once landed in Hamburg, Joop blossomed into a master organizer, pulling together arrangements for hotels, venues, train travel and publicity as if he'd done it all his life. Their first performance, in a small concert hall with extensive gold scrollwork on every architectural edge, brought a standing ovation that would prove to be the first of many.

Every concert included one or two of Eleanor's piano solos, usually Beethoven, Bach or Haydn, as she was first among the orchestra's classical specialists. She accepted the audience's enthusiastic applause each time with a modest bow, and with a measure of relief that for now her moment in the spotlight was over. For her, the glory was in the music itself. She was at last living the life of an artist, and that flame in herself she'd had to guard so carefully burned brilliantly as never before. If she played for anyone in particular it was Jeannette Thurber, who hovered in her mind's eye, nodding in approval whenever Eleanor was able to locate and unlock one of those mysterious hidden doors. If there was one that stayed set stubbornly on its hinges, or remained hidden altogether, Eleanor heard Mrs. Thurber's voice inviting her anew. *Further, my dear, take it beyond.*

As the weeks became months, the company became a true family, a band of nomads with a single mission. When tensions arose among the company members, as they sometimes did, it was Lemuel Harris who put out the fires. He had a great capacity to soothe and bring out understanding in even the hottest tempers. Just as New York had thrilled Eleanor in her younger years, the European cities they visited were a marvel. She found she enjoyed German wurst and sauerkraut as much as anything she had ever tasted in New York. Hearing other languages on the streets and seeing the endless stream of new sights were yet another kind of music.

Eleanor bought stacks of picture postcards to send home, filling their backs with her tiniest script in an attempt to mail away as much of herself as would fit there. On the rare occasion that she received a letter back, having given her family an address in a city they would reach in two or three months' time, she pored over it first with anxiety that it would bear any bad news. When there was none, to her relief, she would re-read the letter carefully, always hoping to discover something about little Gerard. Sometimes there was a mention of Ross and Tilly and *the children*, from which Eleanor could extract, if not any particular details, a report of his general well-being.

In every city the Frangipani Orchestra received invitations to parties, to visit the occasional large estate or historical site with local dignitaries. In Paris, they attended the *Exposition Universelle*, where they viewed wonders of the world and fantastical innovations of the future. It was astounding to Eleanor that the company rode in any train car, and stayed at any hotel. The white passengers, or other hotel guests, regarded them with curiosity, for the most part, and not much else. If once in a while a set of eyes fell coldly upon them, or an insult was hurled on the street, it was still far less than what they were used to at home.

People from the audiences, time and again, waited on the street for the company to leave the theater. They wanted to shake hands or flirt, and offer flowers and gifts. They wanted to tell the muscians what the performance had meant to them. One young man in Berlin gripped Eleanor's hand and shook his head with feeling. He hadn't much English, but kept repeating the word "Beautiful."

All those auditions in New York that had come to nothing, even with Mrs. Thurber's glowing letter of endorsement, had left a bitter taste in her mouth. At her last appearance in an audition hall, the director had refused to let her play. He claimed that they had already filled the position, even though a man was playing while several more were waiting their turn. He pinched her elbow so hard while steering her out the door, she dropped Mrs. Thurber's letter and he stepped on it. Eleanor retrieved the battered paper and tucked it into her bag. On the streetcar home, she took it out and read it over and over. The words affirmed her talent, her training, her devotion to her art—those rare and hard-won treasures that should ensure a real career. She read the letter another time, then tore it to shreds.

Eleanor had taught her classes, given her private lessons, and contributed pieces at occasional benefit concerts. She made her living with music, but not in the way she was born to. Now, in Europe, she had a place such as she had never had before, not as a single star, but as one of a constellation. She felt she could occupy the whole sky.

As the summer wore on the company all looked forward to their visit to London in July. Joop had arranged a performance at Westminster Hall for none other than the delegates and participants in the First Pan-African Conference. The delegates included leaders from Africa and the West Indies, as well as Great Britain and the United States. Among them would be the eminent Dr. W. E. B. Du Bois, and it would be the great honor of the Frangipani Orchestra to perform for these visionary leaders, whose object was nothing less than to *"...secure throughout the world the same facilities and privileges for the black man as the white man enjoys."*

The concert was held at the end of the last day of the Conference and was relatively brief, with little time to mingle afterwards as the delegates were soon to be whisked away to a tea on the Terrace of Parliament. Nevertheless, the company threw themselves into the performance heart and soul, as this was a rare moment and a very special audience. The Orchestra performed a shortened adaptation of the last movement of Dvorak's *Symphony No. 9*, for which Jeannette Thurber had suggested the subtitle *From the New World*, and a rendition of *Old Zion's Children Marching Along*, with Alma's solo that soared as never before, and arrested all who listened. Mr. Henry Sylvester Williams, a barrister from Trinidad and one of the conference leaders, declared the Frangipani Orchestra a "jewel in Africa's crown," and expressed the heartfelt thanks of the delegates, and apologies in equal measure, for their hasty departure. There was a flurry of handshaking and then the delegates went on their way, leaving the Orchestra alone to pack up their instruments. Conductor Lemuel Harris told the company they had made him proud, and Joop strode around nodding, hands in his pockets, saying nothing because he was all choked up.

Later in the evening, after their supper at the hotel, the celebratory mood persisted and many of the company went out to, as Hig always said, "see what they could see." Jack and Alma wanted to find a music hall where they could see some entertainment and have a few drinks, and Eleanor, though feeling tired, went along with them. Just as they were leaving the hotel Hig showed up with Della Saunders, another of the company's singers, on his arm. Della it seemed had designs on Hig, and it looked to Eleanor that he was being a good sport about it. Kind as ever, if not exactly eager prey. They found a place several blocks from the hotel, drawn by the lively music and voices of carousers that issued through an open door.

It wasn't too large a place, maybe a hundred patrons seated at tables around a small stage, with a bar on one side, and low-slung wooden beams across the ceiling. Once they were seated at a table, Jack asked the barmaid what was good to drink, and she said the ale they made in-house was very nice.

"Are you Yanks, then?" she asked. Jack said they were and that they were musicians on a European tour. "Well I never," she said, smiling so that her cheeks bunched up under her eyes in such a way that Eleanor wondered if she could still see. She was still smiling when she returned with a pitcher of ale and a tray of glasses. "Mr. Davies says the first one's on the House if you'll play us something a little later," she said.

"I don't see why not," said Jack, flashing one of his famous grins. "Della," he said, leaning toward her, "why don't we do *Ride In, Kind Savior?*"

"Alright," said Della, "I'd be glad to."

The barmaid went back to the bar to speak with the man who was evidently Mr. Davies. He waved a hand at them and they all waved back. Eleanor sipped her ale and let her eyes wander to the stage where a young man batted out a tune on a piano and a woman both danced and sang. Soon enough they settled in and ordered another pitcher. Another singer took the stage, accompanied by the same young man at the piano, and after a few more numbers went to take a break. The barmaid came back, accompanied now by Mr. Davies. They shook hands all around.

"Would you do us the honor now?" asked Mr. Davies, addressing Jack. Jack said they would, and Mr. Davies called out, "Ladies and gentlemen, we have some visitors from America!" There were cries of approval from the crowd and Jack and Della made their way to the stage, where Della belted out the song while Jack worked his magic on the piano. Tremendous applause and demands for another got a few more songs out of them, ending with Jack spinning out a generous dose of Ragtime. Several in the crowd rose to shake Jack's hand and slap him on the back, and give polite little bows to Della. Laughter and smiles abounded. But then Eleanor caught the young piano player glaring from the corner, with a look in his eye that made her terribly uneasy.

"Let's go," she whispered to Alma when they were all sitting together again. "I don't think everyone here is friendly." But Jack was having a grand time and wasn't ready to leave.

"Della and I will see you back," Hig said to Eleanor. "I think we're all dog-tired."

"We'll be along soon," Alma said to her. "Don't you worry."

With that the three of them left, bidding the locals goodbye and stepping out onto the street. Eleanor could still hear Jack's laugh ringing out from inside.

It was still dark when she heard knocking. She sat up in bed, confused. She heard knocking again, and her name being called, along with Della's. She and Della had gotten to bed some hours before in their shared room at the hotel, and now there was someone knocking at the door.

"What is it?" said Della, alarmed but still not quite awake. Eleanor hurried to the door. It was Hig, with Lemuel and Joop. Their breathing was ragged. Joop's hands shook as he wiped at the sweat on his forehead.

"Eleanor, it's Jack," said Lemuel, his voice breaking.

"At the hospital," Joop said.

"Alma needs you," said Hig.

The vapors of sleep scattered from Eleanor's consciousness just as the floor seemed to disappear. Three men had attacked Jack near the music hall, dragged him into an alley just as he and Alma were walking past. They had done him some serious damage before help came, drawn by Alma's screams. He'd been taken to the hospital at Westminster Abbey, and Hig and Lemuel went with Eleanor in a hansom cab. Joop stayed behind to talk with the rest of the company and to make sure everyone stayed cool.

Eleanor, Hig, and Lemuel rode the whole way to the hospital without speaking. Eleanor was hardly aware of much other than the sound of the horses' hooves on the cobblestones, and the sight of breath steaming from their nostrils when the cab passed beneath the street lamps.

Upon their arrival Hig and Lemuel found a supervising doctor while Eleanor hurried to the ward where Jack was. She made her way through the stone corridors as if in a terrible dream, and found the smaller hall where a figure wove unsteadily on her feet.

Alma lifted her stricken face and Eleanor feared the worst. Alma stumbled forward and clutched at her, her awful wail filling the air around them.

"What's happened, tell me, please," Eleanor begged.

"He's alive," Alma managed at last. She was shaking so badly her teeth chattered. "They beat him bad." His face was a mess, broken ribs. "And they…" here the keening sobs overtook her again. "They, they stomped his hands. Oh Lord!" The cry tore itself raw from her throat. "They broke up his hands."

Jack was discharged in two days' time and they took him to the hotel, where Alma stayed by his side, administering ice and iodine, and begging him to accept the bone broth that Eleanor asked for in the kitchen. The police said there was nothing they could do, as the attackers had run off so fast. The doctor said Jack would recover the use of his hands, but never again would he have the dexterity that made his art possible.

Boisterous Jack lay in bed, silent as death, staring at the plasters covering his hands. Only when he slept did he make a sound, and these were the low moans that belied his pain. On the third day he said something.

Eleanor had come with Lemuel. She had made Alma go up to the room Eleanor shared with Della to get some rest herself.

279

Eleanor held a bowl of broth with some bread soaking in it, and Lemuel stood with his gloves in one hand, nattering on about a new arrangement they would try with the strings. Jack cut him off.

"I wish they hadda killed me," he said softly.

"Jack, no," Eleanor whispered.

Lemuel brought a hand to his eyes and pinched the bridge of his nose, turning away.

Jack shifted and turned his face toward the wall.

"Sister, let me be now, please."

Eleanor rose, terrified. She looked over at Lemuel, who had sunk into a chair.

She returned that evening to see what could be done. Alma met her at the door. Her face was drawn with exhaustion and there was a new light of fear in her eyes.

"He won't take anything. Not even water." she said.

Jack lay motionless in the bed, turned still toward the wall. Whether he slept or not Eleanor couldn't tell. The curtains were drawn but the window was open a crack, letting in a little air and noise from the street, and enough light to see. She stepped past Alma and began to gather the used linens and discarded bandages from beside the bed and heaped them in the corner.

There came a knock at the door. Alma went to see. Eleanor expected her to send whomever it was away, but instead she stood back and several figures filed into the room. First Joop, and Lemuel, and then a handful of men and women Eleanor recognized as some of the esteemed lecturers and West Indian leaders, delegates from the Pan-African Conference, and then, to her greater shock, the refined, angular features of Dr. William Edward Burghardt Du Bois himself.

Hearing all of this Jack roused and took in the unexpected sight. He struggled to sit up and Alma went to help him. Mr. Henry Sylvester Williams, the barrister from Trinidad, spoke first.

"Brother," he said, "we have heard of the attack, and we have come to speak with you, if you are willing."

They all waited, and Jack nodded.

"The crime you have suffered," Williams went on, "is nothing less than what our people have suffered for hundreds of years, and make no mistake, we grieve with you. This is precisely why we all are here in this city, and we are here to offer you any support that we may."

Sam Jupiter spoke next.

"Jack, we want you to continue the tour with us. As conductor."

"You have a conductor," Jack said, his voice hoarse from three days of silence, and all he had endured. He looked over at Lemuel.

"I'm stepping down," Lemuel said. "I'm going back to the States. Already packed."

Jack was quiet, and then said with a bitter finality, "I don't want no pity."

"Pity." A voice of great clarity came from the group, and Dr. Du Bois stepped forward. He sat in the chair alongside the bed and locked eyes with Jack. "Pity is not what we are about."

A hush filled the room, much different than before, a silence heavy with expectation.

"How many of us have been maimed, brutalized, murdered?" Du Bois said, echoing Williams' sentiments. "Countless numbers.

You know that as well as I do. Every one of us here knows it, far too well."

Jack stared at him. Tears welled up and spilled over.

"All I ever wanted to do was play," he said. "My whole life. That's all I ever wanted."

"Music is your great gift," said the Doctor, unblinking. "It's your soul. And that doesn't depend on the body. Other bodies will play for you, if need be." He leaned forward. "Mr. Zebulon, we need you," he said, "your colleagues, your friends, your people. We need you. We can't afford to lose you."

"It would be a great honor to have your company play in my country," Barrister Williams said. "If you come we will show you the spirit of the Trinidadian people. And you will show us yours. And we will all be uplifted."

When the unofficial delegation took its leave, Eleanor and Hig slipped out after them and he went with her to her own door. There was nothing but nothing left to say. Hig wrapped his arms around her and she leaned into him, letting herself be held for the first time in so very long.

Joop held a meeting of the company the next day in the large, empty theater they would play in that night. Jack was present, bandages and all, with Alma on one side and Eleanor on the other.

"You all know as well as I do that there ain't nothing I can say that will make this any better." He looked at the ceiling, as if some kind of useful words might show up anyway.

"Those dogs that pass for men can rot in Hell for what they did," Della said, and many in the company called out their agreement.

"We all feel like that, Della," Hig said, "but we've got to look ahead to what happens next. Let's hear what Joop has to say."

Joop paced back and forth in front of them. He worried his hand over his forehead. "For all that things are going good over here, we can't get too comfortable. Everyone should be on their guard. We can't let this happen again."

Eleanor put her handkerchief to her face, but there were too many tears for it. The ugliest truth was that Jack would most likely never play the way he did before. In an instant, those men had stripped him of everything most dear. It could have happened to any one of them.

"But I will tell you one thing." Joop's voice wavered but his words rang like a clock striking the hour. "I have never been so proud of anything as I am of all of you. You have made me proud and you have made Dr. Du Bois proud. What we're doing is important, and nothing's going to stop us."

The company voiced their support and Lemuel went to Joop's side, putting an arm around his shoulders.

Joop held his hands up to quiet things down.

"Now I need to tell you that our conductor will be leaving us. He'll be sorely missed." Gasps and murmurs filled the room. "Lemuel, why don't you say your piece."

Lemuel stayed quiet a moment before speaking. "Look," he said, "I've got to go." He shook his head back and forth. "I could tell you that I got a better offer, but there's no way there's a better offer anywhere. Most of you know I'm a believer. My Creator tells me to go home now, and I'll abide by that. I feel the same as Joop. My work with you all is the proudest I've ever done. I do thank you."

"In light of things," Joop said to the group, "I hope you will join us in supporting our new conductor." He lifted a hand toward Jack, and Jack, leaning heavily on a cane, stood up. It would take him months to fully recover, but he stood there on his feet.

One by one each member of the Frangipani Orchestra stood up too, and gathered close around Jack in a circle, arms laid over shoulders. Someone started to sing and everyone joined in.

Stand still Jordan
Stand still Jordan
Stand still Jordan
Lord I can't stand still

Together they would do the impossible.

In the coming months Eleanor witnessed Jack grow into the role of conductor with dignity and determination. If before he was a touch vain, thriving on glory, now he moved with an inner strength. If he didn't laugh as much as he used to, now when he spoke he always meant what he said. The group became his instrument, the place he applied his art. He demanded the best in them, and found ways to challenge them so that the company reached new heights. And when there was praise he refused the credit. Eleanor saw changes in Alma too, and in Alma and Jack as a couple. She saw true devotion. These rivers ran deep.

And there was another thing that was new. Hig had a talk with Della and told her that while he cherished her friendship, his heart was set on another. He asked Eleanor if she wouldn't mind his company at supper, on walks, during their evenings off. They sat together on the long train rides, and she slept with her head on his shoulder.

Near the end of the tour, as the year 1900 drew toward its end, the Frangipani Orchestra received its official invitation to Trinidad. The journey would include passage and accommodations, eight public concerts, tours of the island, exchanges with native musicians and meetings with schoolchildren and teachers. And even though the Orchestra was not a democratic outfit, as Joop always said, the company voted unanimously to accept the offer. They would return to New York briefly, reunite with their families as they were able, and then sail again—this time to the Caribbean, and a whole new adventure.

In March of 1901, the company sailed from New York to Florida and then on to Trinidad, landing at Port of Spain. Amid the crowds on the busy pier Eleanor happened to see a notice board with listings of steamboats that took passengers to the islands to the north. There was one the next day to the island of Martinique, where her grandmother was born. Mémé Hetty, to whom she owed her life in music, who came from a place farther away than anything she could have imagined when she was just a baby watching her brother Albert at his lessons.

She knew at once she would go.

The company had several days before their first Trinidadian engagements so it would cause no trouble to take a short side trip.

"I'll go with you," Hig said, when she told him.

"No, Hig, I think I'll go alone," she said. They were both surprised when she said it. In truth there had been very few times she had made any journey by herself, though each of those had marked a moment of great change in her life.

Hig frowned. Eleanor guessed what he was thinking. "I'll be safe," she said, giving his hand a squeeze.

"I shouldn't let you," he said, but not with anger.

Only twice had she ever seen him angry. When Jack suffered the attack, and later when she confessed to him her secret, about Gerard, the child. He was furious that Professor Batiste had taken advantage of her—that was his view—a defenseless young girl. Both of these things broke his heart, he said, but what made it alright in the end was that both she and Jack lived on and thrived.

"Hell, Nora," he'd said. They were walking at the time, on a terrace of the basilica in Marseille, one of the last cities on the company's tour. He took a deep breath, blew it out slowly and then turned toward her. "I'm glad you told me. I don't want there to be secrets between us." He held both her hands in his and kissed them. "I want to make my life with you," he said. "When you say so, we'll do it."

Eleanor stood on the deck of the steamer, wind whipping at her face and the ends of the scarf she had used to secure her hat. The steamer had left Trinidad behind and now there was no land in sight. Albert used to say that when he was grown he would visit Mémé's island, but he had never had the chance. He married Genevieve and the babies started coming. The closest he ever got was to name one of his children after it, because Mémé had taught him that Martinique was so beautiful.

Eleanor disembarked at the town of Fort-de-France and found her way down the pier, a bit shaky from the journey over the open sea in a smaller vessel than she was used to. She headed toward a cluster of buildings near the beach, flanked by waving palms, where she found what looked like a café. It was mid-morning and the heat was stifling. She wished for nothing more than some shade and a cool drink. Stepping through the doorway she found the place empty, save for a young man busy scrubbing something behind a whitewashed counter.

"*Bonjour*," Eleanor said, slumping into a chair. Really she was feeling dizzy, perhaps she had gotten a little seasick.

"*Bonjour Madame*," said the young man, approaching. She asked for something to drink and he disappeared through a small door out the back. She leaned against the wall and closed her eyes. The young man returned with an earthen pitcher and a glass, but when she tried to speak she was overcome by a swallowing darkness full of tiny dancing lights.

The next thing she knew she was stretched out on a bench in a shady courtyard. The young man was fanning her with a tea towel, and a matronly woman bent over her, patting at Eleanor's cheeks with her hands. When Eleanor roused, the woman helped her to sit up. She told her in a French dialect that she must change clothes. Eleanor gathered that she wasn't the first person in Victorian dress to faint in this woman's presence, and accepted her assistance into a small room off the courtyard, without argument.

The older woman, dressed in the typical Caribbean style Eleanor had glimpsed in Trinidad, rummaged in a trunk and pulled out a white linen gown and a blue shawl. With the authority that a mother holds over a small, misbehaving child, she quickly separated Eleanor from the layers of her clothes and helped her to unlace her corset. The rush of blood freed from its bindings caused her to feel lightheaded again and she sat down on the trunk, naked now except for her chemise and drawers. Then she lifted her arms and allowed the woman to slip the linen dress over her head. A moment later she was back on the bench in the courtyard, with a glass of coconut water.

The matron was called Marbeille; the young man, Abel, was one of her sons. The café belonged to her family and was, as Eleanor would learn in the next few hours, one of their many enterprises. Did Eleanor need a place to stay? They had two rooms they rented to guests.

"So," Marbeille said to her, once Eleanor was installed in a small, comfortable room on the other side of the courtyard and finally much revived, "are you a daughter of the Island?" Eleanor told her that she had come from America, and that her grandmother was born on the island. That she grew up on a sugar estate called Mont Belcourt. She had heard Mémé speak now and then about her childhood, but in truth Eleanor had learned very little. What was it Mémé used to say about her elders? She had an aunt who healed the sick. The name came back to her now, emerging suddenly from some long-forgotten place.

"*Mémé Abeje?*" Eleanor asked aloud. Could that be right? Why would she have referred to her aunt as *Mémé?* As a grandmother?

Marbeille's eyes widened in recognition and surprise. "You are a *p'tit* of *Mémé Abeje?*"

"The granddaughter of her niece," Eleanor said. "Do you know that name?"

"Everyone knows that name, child."

Early in the afternoon the café filled with diners, locals stopping to eat amid the labors of the day, and all manner of people coming in from fishing and passenger boats, or who otherwise did business in the busy port town. Several more of Marbeille's grown children had shown up and were at work with her in the outdoor kitchen that occupied one side of the courtyard. They brought out large plates of cassava cakes, a spicy bean and vegetable stew, and fried fish with plantains. Marbeille greeted patron after patron with the news that, by some miracle, a *p'tit* of Mémé Abeje was here with them from America. Most everyone knew one story or another about the legendary Obeah, the great healer, and they were eager to tell Eleanor what they knew. One man, who alternated pulls on a pipe with spoonfuls of stew, said to Marbeille, "Old Silas still lives. Perhaps she should go to see him."

Eleanor struggled to keep up with the stories. Creole was so very different from the French she knew. It was a revelation that an ancestor of hers was known here, since it was not likely there was anyone who could have remembered Hetty, who had left the island as a girl. Silas was Mémé Abeje's last apprentice, a *quimboiseur*, the man with the pipe had said. He lived in a village not so far from his own, and was known for his healing abilities. He was quite old now, though, and did not work so much anymore.

"My wife has business that way tomorrow," said the man with the pipe. "I know she would not mind the company."

Eleanor spent much of the later afternoon and evening at the beach, in an area of shade afforded by a stretch of dense foliage. She had brought with her a thin sheaf of paper and a fountain pen she had purchased in Paris, intending to write a letter home to her family in Montreal, but these remained tucked away in her handbag. Once she touched the sand, she began to take in the immensity of sea and sky. She let her ears attune to the rush of the surf and her hands stayed still, folded together in repose. The murmur of the waves and distant cry of an occasional gull were very welcome.

She remembered Auntie Josephine's words, said one night when Eleanor was a girl, some time after they had lost Mama. Eleanor and Melody were in the kitchen after supper washing dishes in basins of soapy water, when a plate slipped from Eleanor's grasp and shattered on the floor. It was only a bit of crockery, but at that moment it seemed the most terrible thing in all the world. She crouched on the floor, weeping inconsolably, and Auntie came and put her arms around her.

"Lay it down," Auntie said, of all the burden Eleanor carried in her heart. "Lay it down."

She heard Auntie's voice now, speaking to her of the weight of the past.

Lay it down.

A breeze played over her bare legs and she let her feet dig into the white sand.

When the sun had dropped lower in the sky, knots of children came along and fed themselves into the waves, splashing and laughing. A young man came down the beach wearing a peaked woven hat with a wide brim, a beat-up old guitar over his shoulder. It was Marbeille's son Abel, the one who had caught her when she fainted earlier that day. It surely didn't seem like the same day, but much longer ago. He nodded to her and smiled, took a seat on an overturned rowboat and began to play. Some of the splashing children gravitated toward the music and danced together on the sand. The sunset colors tinted Abel's white shirt and black skin with touches of rose. His hands fluttered like moths over the strings of the guitar, the children danced, and the music floated between the waves.

One of the boys, bare-chested and in short trousers, squatted near Abel, watching him play. A boy perhaps the same age as Gerard. He looked over at her for a curious moment, a strange woman he'd not seen before. She saw his dark eyes briefly, then he turned his face back to the music.

The sun sank into the sea and the sky stretched overhead dark blue. A single star appeared and hung over the black sea. An old lullaby of her mother's came to mind, and she sang to herself, as she had on a dark night years ago, though it was different now. The breeze a light hand on her cheek.

Eleanor woke before dawn and slipped on the linen gown. Her back was stiff from her first night ever sleeping in a hammock, but she felt lighter and refreshed.

Marbeille was up, lighting the stove and throwing out yesterday's coffee grounds. They had arranged that Abel would accompany Eleanor to the village of the man with the pipe, and from there she would go with the man's wife to see the *quimboiseur*, Old Silas, the last living apprentice of Mémé Abeje. Marbeille gave Eleanor a mesh bag to hang across her shoulders, in which she had placed a number of small round fruits and a tattered silk parasol. At Marbeille's instruction Eleanor had gone to a shop near the café the afternoon before to purchase a sachet of tobacco and a bottle of rum, to bring as gifts. The shopkeeper accepted American silver, and used a scale to reckon the pricing. Eleanor placed the rum and the tobacco in the mesh bag, carefully so as not to crush the fruit, and set out with Abel on a narrow road that snaked up into the hills.

In less than an hour they reached a small village and the home of the man with the pipe. His wife looked to be a contemporary of Marbeille, but did not quite have her outgoing manner. The elder lady led a small brown donkey on a rope, laden with two large sacks, and they continued on a smaller road, farther into the mountains. The sun was up now, with a heavy heat rising from the thick greenery on either side of the path, while hidden insects whirred, and birds called. Eleanor was grateful for the parasol and the little fruits that she shared with her companion, who smiled at her now and again, but kept mostly silent.

After perhaps another hour they arrived at a cluster of huts with walls like woven baskets, and approached one that had a pigpen, several chickens strutting around, and a large mango tree with small green fruit that draped over the thatched roof. A woman that looked to be Eleanor's age in a colorful dress and red headscarf stepped through the open doorway and the three women exchanged greetings. Eleanor's companion explained her presence there, and then with a wave continued up the path with the donkey. She would be back later for their return journey.

The woman in the red headscarf introduced herself as Sidonie. "You have come to see Papa Okun?" she asked. Eleanor had learned that Old Silas was also called this way. Sidonie had such a lively, fresh face Eleanor did not think she could be the wife of an old man.

"Is he your father?" she asked.

"My great uncle," said Sidonie. "He is just sleeping now, but we will have a talk with him later. It's lucky you came now. We don't know how much longer we will have him with us." Sidonie told Eleanor that Papa was mostly blind now and had suffered a sudden paralysis in the last rainy season that left him unable to walk or speak clearly. She said Papa's relatives took turns caring for him, and that it was an honor to do so, because in his long life he had cared for a great many people.

Sidonie asked Eleanor to wait a moment and went inside. She came out of the hut with a large basket of dried bean pods and led Eleanor around the back to a stand of shade trees, the smallest of which was covered in white and yellow flowers. Eleanor stepped closer to the tree, recognizing the distinct shape of the blossoms. There were five fleshy white petals, arranged just so, with deep yellow centers. A frangipani. She remembered from the drawings that decorated the publicity materials of the Orchestra. Sidonie knelt down beside her with the basket and commenced to shelling beans. Eleanor sat too, to help.

"What is this tree?" Eleanor asked.

"We call this *arbre de couleuvre*," said Sidonie. Snake tree. "At night it releases its fragrance, though you can still smell it now." After a moment of quiet shelling Sidonie continued. "We make many medicines from this tree, from the leaves, the blossoms, the bark. It cures ailments of the skin and blood, the bowel and fever."

"Papa Okun has taught you this?" Eleanor asked, and the other woman nodded.

"Every plant has its spirit, its guardian," Sidonie said. "The flower of the snake tree also teaches us. It is love long in absence."

"Love long in absence," Eleanor murmured.

"We love our flowers here, you know," said Sidonie. "Our

island is not only called Martinique, but also *Ile aux Fleurs*. And it also is called *Pays des Revenants*."

The country of those who return. Things were known by so many names, Eleanor mused. *Frangipani* or *snake tree*, *Old Silas* or *Papa Okun*. Even she herself had been called in different ways, *Eleanor, El, Nora, chère.*

Coughing was heard from inside the hut.

"I will just check on Papa," Sidonie said, rising. She was gone for some time. Eleanor finished the shelling and then just sat, wondering if she should go in too, but before she could decide Sidonie emerged and said, "He is ready to see you now."

Eleanor followed Sidonie into the hut, where the figure of an old man lay in a hammock. His head, covered in a thin white stubble, appeared large atop his shrunken body. Sidonie knelt down on a mat beside him and motioned for Eleanor to do the same.

"This is Eleanor, Papa," she said. "The granddaughter of Mémé's niece." The old man reached out a wizened hand to Eleanor and she took it in hers. His grip was firm and the fingers long. He must have been much larger in his younger years, and strong. With great effort he spoke a few garbled words.

"He says he doesn't see with his eyes now," said Sidonie, "but he sees with his heart."

There was more of the garbled speech and Sidonie interpreted.

"Papa says the spirits are very pleased you have come to pay your respects. He says your ancestor was a powerful healer. She was a mother to him, and a great teacher."

Eleanor knew nothing of spirits, they were no more real to her than fairy stories, but she felt a presence in that small room, as if the frail old man were a towering giant. Not fearsome, but somehow very big. She felt an electricity in his hand that still gripped hers, akin to the way she sensed the music inside an instrument. Yet he was already tiring. He said something else and then closed his eyes, catching his breath.

"He knows your grandmother," said Sidonie, "because Mémé has told him about her. She was called *Ayo*."

"My grandmother was called Hetty," said Eleanor, wondering if perhaps he was mistaken.

He spoke again, and Sidonie said, "Yes, he remembers from a letter received by Mémé long ago. The child's parents called her Ayo, their word for *joy*." There was a long silence, during which Eleanor wondered if the old man had fallen asleep, but he spoke once more.

"Papa will offer you a blessing now," Sidonie said. She went to retrieve Eleanor's bottle of rum from the chest by the front doorway. After removing the cork with a thin knife she spilled a few drops in each corner of the hut, murmuring something Eleanor couldn't make out. She struck a match and lit a small bundle of dried herbs that smoldered in a clay dish, giving out a fragrant smoke. She fanned at it with her hands and set it on the mat beside Eleanor.

Eleanor closed her eyes a moment. She heard a faint humming sound—the old man was singing. She saw herself riding a train alone in wintertime. She saw the tiny, familiar, wet body of a newborn child. Jack's crushed hands wrapped in plaster, Alma weeping. Now another newborn child, drawn away from the body of its mother, and a man crying out. Strong arms lifted Eleanor, and held her. She heard a voice from ages ago murmuring her name. Her mother, younger than she could remember.

Mama.

The smell of broken earth filled her nostrils, the smell of a grave, of birth blood. The ringing sound of an earthen pot striking stone and shattering rushed her ears, the first cry and the last.

And then the sound of music, a piano, a melody she had never heard but that moved her heart, and she saw that a young man played, a young man with hair combed in minute dark waves. He was dressed in a suit, and held a thin cigarette in his lips, and his fingers moved over the keys so gracefully.

Step by step the melody played on, until the notes reached her, as if knocking on a door.

Eleanor opened her eyes.

She was there in the hut with Sidonie, and the old man, Papa Okun.

She still held his hand, but his grip had relaxed and his breathing had become rhythmic. Sidonie gently took his hand from Eleanor and laid it over his chest. He was asleep. She motioned for Eleanor to follow her outside again, and back to sit under the frangipani. Sidonie picked up the basket, the shiny red beans now separated from their husks.

"I must tend to some chores now," she said. "Why don't you rest awhile."

Eleanor did suddenly feel remarkably sleepy. The grass was soft and welcoming and she lay down, with her arm folded under her head.

She awoke when Sidonie touched her shoulder.

"Sister," she said, "it's time to eat something. Madame will come for you soon." She held out a bowl of yellow porridge and stewed vegetables. Eleanor sat up and took the bowl. The handle of a flat wooden spoon stuck up from the middle.

"How can I thank you?" Eleanor asked. "You and Papa Okun." She still did not know what to make of these events, of the blessing, but she sensed it was terribly important. She felt as though she had been passed from hand to hand, ever since disembarking and fainting into Abel's arms.

Sidonie smiled. "It is a great gift for Papa to offer a blessing to one of Mémé Abeje's bloodline," she said. "The *Island Mother* has brought you here, and this is an honor for us all."

"The *Island Mother?*" asked Eleanor, baffled once more.

Sidonie shook her head and smiled again.

"Have you not felt her?"

Eleanor had one last evening on the beach near Marbeille's café. In the morning she would take a steamboat back to Trinidad, to rejoin her company. Abel did not come with his guitar, he was needed elsewhere. But the children came again to splash and play.

As she watched she felt Mémé's gentleness, and Mama's boldness, very close by. Something inside herself had been ripped away. The feeling was raw, but open. She felt new.

Behind it all there was a great stillness. And out of the stillness arose a new clarity, fully formed, that after Trinidad she would return home, not to New York but to Montreal. She would face her family, and she would see Gerard.

On the heels of that, she thought of Hig. Suddenly she missed him dearly. Of all the people close to her, she knew no finer than he. If it was possible for her to make a life with another, it would be with him. But she would have to make one more journey before she could know for sure.

In the summer of 1901 Eleanor Rougeaux traveled by train to her native city, where she had not set foot in more than ten years. The Hudson River Valley was green and brilliant, Lake Champlain wide and sparkling. Eleanor had now been to so many places on the globe, but never was she more full of anticipation than she was now, about to see her home again.

At last she stepped off the train at Central Station. Two old folks, a man and a woman, thin and with white hair approached her.

Papa.

Auntie.

Accompanied by a tall young man, her baby brother Dax.

Dax carried her trunk, laden with gifts, to the old buggy drawn by a new horse. The old house was smaller than she remembered, even though it was emptier. Only Papa, Auntie and Dax lived there now, three people where eight had once filled the rooms. The wooden furniture was all the same, but the curtains were new and the sofa had been reupholstered. Auntie's many potted plants took up more space than they used to.

Dax brought Eleanor's bags up to the bedroom she and Melody had once shared.

"I better get back downstairs," Dax said. "Auntie will give me a hiding if I don't help her with supper."

"You cook?" Eleanor was still getting over the shock of seeing him so grown.

"Don't laugh," he said, smiling sheepishly. "Auntie doesn't understand about women's work."

"Lots of cooks are men, you know," she said. "Outside the home."

"Yeah, *outside*," he said, ducking out the doorway. "See you in a little."

Eleanor sat down on the bed. It didn't seem real yet, being there, and she couldn't see even one step ahead. Eleanor would be reunited with her sister and other brothers, and all their children, and then with her other aunts and the cousins. Mrs. Allison, her old choir director, was gone now, as were a number of Eleanor's relatives, but she would see firsthand how life was going forward without them.

How changed everyone was, and how much the same. Children had grown into adults, adults had aged, new children had been born. Melody was married, expecting her fourth child already. The family held a picnic in a park by the Canal Lachine her first Sunday afternoon. Eleanor knelt on a blanket with Melody, shoulder to shoulder as they always used to work, uncovering dishes and slicing pie when she heard someone say, "Ross and Tilly are here!" She stood up, her heart pounding.

Her brother and his wife approached. He carried a small child, their youngest, and Sarai, their oldest, now a big girl of twelve, held the hand of a younger girl. Ross approached Eleanor and embraced her. "My, oh my," he said.

"Tilly," Eleanor said, holding out both her hands. Mathilde clasped them in hers and looked into her face.

"You haven't changed," Mathilde said. "But you look so fine I would not have known you." She introduced her children.

Ross looked around. "Gerard!" he called, waving.

One of a cluster of boys at the canal's edge separated himself from the group and ran toward them. "Mama!" he said, skidding to a halt and looking up at Tilly, " Paul has a fishing rod and they think he caught something. Can I go home and get mine?"

"Not now, son," she said, smiling, brushing off his white shirt and short black pants. "Meet your Aunt Eleanor."

The child turned toward her. He had his father's mouth, and his light coloring. And her eyes.

"How do you do?" he said.

"Very well, thank you," Eleanor managed, "it's so very nice to meet you."

Eleanor watched him all that afternoon, sneaking glances so as not to stare.

She saw him tumble with the other boys. Saw him lift up his little sisters when they fell. Saw him put away more pieces of blueberry pie than anyone else.

Not long ago her brother Albert had acquired a spinet piano, something from a junk heap, and Dax had helped him restore it. When Albert could he taught his children, and Dax brought Gerard, who was immediately fascinated. Gerard's older cousin Elodie, Albert's first child, had already taught him everything she knew. Whenever he was over at his Uncle Albert's he played, even little songs of his own creation. Very soon into Eleanor's stay they had a little group assembled of her nieces and nephews to meet at Albert's home for informal piano lessons. Albert's wife Genevieve came into the parlour now and again to tell the smaller children to hush and pay attention. Once in a while she suggested a hymn and they all would sing it.

Gerard, Eleanor quickly noticed, had a remarkable ear, and clever fingers that seemed to do whatever he wanted with hardly any practice. One afternoon they sat together on the piano bench while Eleanor took him through the scales. The other children, grown tired, had gone off in search of other amusements and now it was just the two of them.

"Did you know I'm an orphan?" Gerard said suddenly, keeping his eyes on the keys.

"Yes, I did," said Eleanor.

"Do you know where I came from?"

Eleanor froze. Oh, what could she say? She couldn't lie. Nor could she tell him anything. That was up to his parents. She teetered on the edge of danger, but a moment later he rescued them both.

"I came from Toronto," he said. "Papa told me."

"I see," said Eleanor.

"I want to go there one day and see what it's like," he said.

"That's a fine idea," she said.

"I want to see New York too," he declared. "Mama told me you went there to study music, and that's how come we never met you before."

"That's right," she said. And then she ventured, "Would you like to study music at school? When you're older?"

He frowned, keeping up the scales in excellent time. "That all depends," he said. "Do they make you eat greens in music school? Because I hate greens."

Eleanor laughed. "When I was at music school I ate a lot of potato salad. And beans."

"Okay, then," Gerard said, "yes, I would like to go there."

She watched him play, this boy-child that had come from her. Music filled the room.

That evening Eleanor went out with Papa to sit in the back

garden. A couple of wooden stools and a tin pail stood at the base of one of Papa's cherry trees. By now the fruit had been mostly harvested, either eaten or put up in mason jars by Auntie, but a few cherries still clung to the branches here and there. Papa picked a handful and gave them to Eleanor.

"Did you miss these, *chère?*" The lines around his eyes when he smiled were much deeper now.

"Oh, I did," she said. "Every summer."

He sat down on one of the stools and she sat beside him on the grass.

"How is your friend Alma?" Papa asked. Eleanor had mentioned her so often in her letters.

"She and Jack finally made it official," she said. "Church of City Hall."

Papa laughed. "That's nice."

"How is Mr. Hathaway?" Eleanor hurried to the question before Papa could ask about Hig.

"Just fine," he said. "Terribly interested in your career, as always. He'll be over for supper tomorrow, you can tell him everything that's new."

It would be good to see Mr. Hathaway. It was good to see everyone, so why did she feel as though her heart were breaking?

"And how are *you*, Papa?"

"I'm happy," he said softly. "You are here and I'm very happy."

She laid her head on his knee. He held her hand and stroked her cheek.

"We're all happy you're here."

"I'm sorry I stayed away," she said.

"You couldn't help it, *chère*" he said. "I know that."

Eleanor put aside the letter she was writing to Hig and lay down in her childhood bed. She watched the last of the summer light fade from the window, a breeze playing at the curtain. What was it she had been so afraid of for all these years?

What she could see was that Gerard was a happy and cherished child. Surely that was enough. He wasn't hers, but maybe they could be friends. If Eleanor could give him anything perhaps it would be to help him in his music. She would speak with Ross and Tilly about it, when they next had the chance. She touched the cool cotton of the pillowcase by her cheek, and the edge with Auntie's embroidery of tiny blue flowers.

She drifted into sleep.

Back on the beach on Martinique. The island of her grandmother, the island of flowers, white sand and bending palms, the country of those who return. A child danced at the edge of the water. He splashed and laughed.

His voice echoed as he called, *Mama!*

Eleanor took his hand and they entered the water, warm, vast. They swam.

And then it was not Gerard, but a swimming turtle.

A voice said, *Lay it down now, Child.*

A lone sailboat scuttled over the water, leaving a wake like the undulating veil of a bride.

Lay it all down.

Historical Note

Though *House of Rougeaux* is a work of fiction, there are a few real historical figures in the book. However, the appearances of these people in the story—the Reverend Charles Este of Montreal, Shadrach Minkins and his wife Mary, Dr. W.E.B. Du Bois, the Trinidadian barrister Henry Sylvester Williams, and Jeannette Meyers Thurber, the founder of the National Conservatory of Music—are fictional. In the case of Mary Minkins (called Margaret in this book) nothing is known about her other than that she was Irish, and that the couple's first two children died from illnesses when they were very young.

Acknowledgements

Heartfelt thanks to Colleen Frary, Leah Catwrangleur, Leora Hoshall, Elena Andrade, Damon Orion, Erin Renwick, Grace Duong, Eunice Martel and Miriam Stzybel for their generous feedback on parts or all of this work. Thanks to my mom Jo-ann Rosen for enthusiastic reading, to my dad Louis Jaeckel for eagle-eyed proofreading, to my father-in-law Bill O'Connor for insider information on Philadelphia in the 1960s, to Anna and Natalie Cal for their guidance on writing about music, Shannon Bodie for the wonderful cover design, and to my partner Chris and child Asa, in particular for Asa's help in discovering Guillaume Rougeaux's character, and in general for their ongoing support, skepticism, suggestions, trust and love.

Special thanks to Dr. Tracy Butts, Rebecca Alderson, Vanessa Winn, and Nadine Ijaz, for their invaluable insights and perspectives. Inexpressible thanks to Erika Lunder for making a place in the world for this book and guiding its creation in myriad ways, and to Neesa Sonoquie, my editorial Kung Fu master, who kicked my arse until the book arrived at its true self.

Of the many books and articles I read for this project I am especially indebted to the painstakingly researched and impeccably written *Sugar in the Blood: A Family's Story of Slavery and Empire*, by Andrea Stuart (Random House 2012); and the extremely informative *The Road to Now, A History of Blacks in Montreal 1628 - 1986*, by Dorothy Williams (Véhicule Press 1998).

About the Author

Jenny Jaeckel's previous titles include *For the Love of Meat: Nine Illustrated Stories, Siberiak: My Cold War Adventure on the River Ob*, and the graphic memoir *Spot 12: Five Months in the Neonatal ICU*, which was the winner of the 2017 Next Generation Indie Book Awards.

Originally from California, Jenny Jaeckel lives in Victoria, British Columbia, with her husband and child. Find out more about Jenny Jaeckel at www.jennyjaeckel.com.